The Dream World Series

Dream World

Book 1

S.J. Hitchcock

The right of S.J. Hitchcock to be identified as the author of this work has been asserted by him/her in accordance with the Copyright, Designs and Patents Act 1988.

No part of this publication may be reproduced, stored in a retrieval system, or transmitted in any form or by any means without the prior written permissions of the publisher, nor be otherwise circulated in any form of binding or cover other than that in which it was published and without a similar condition being imposed on the subsequent purchaser.

Copyright© 2013
All rights reserved

S.J Hitchcock

Dedication

I would like to thank my family for their continued support, and to my friends who have read many drafts of this novel, and of course my beta readers and street team. Without them, I would not have achieved my goal.

On this journey, I have met many new friends. Some at a local writing group, which I attended for the past year, and through social media websites.

One lady I would love to personally thank for her help and support has to be Sharon Brock, a colleague and friend, who also created the original cover for Dream World, and character images.

I would also like to thank Nicola Mahood for creating the new book cover for The Dream World Series, she has done an amazing job, thank you.

I have to thank, Lesley Hare for all the hours she has spent reading through the book with me, picking up on any edits I have missed. Thank you.

I would also like to thank Alec Hawkes, for proof reading and for editing. Thank you.

And to one lady, who has kept me on track, when I was feeling down, has to be thanked too, she has been my biggest fan and rock throughout this journey. I cannot thank her enough. Kimmy Jackson, I thank you.

I would also like to thank a few of my other friends who have supported me on this journey, they are –

Julia Cooper, Rachel Penny, Jessica Carolyn Madden, Sandra Martin, Susannah Hutchinson and Adele Symonds.

Table of content

Prologue - The Accident
Chapter 1 – The Funeral
Chapter 2 – In His Arms
Chapter 3 - The Band N & N
Chapter 4 – Memories
Chapter 5 – Rudolf
Chapter 6 – Flashback
Chapter 7 – Another Side Of Karen
Chapter 8 – Happy Families
Chapter 9 – Dream Invader
Chapter 10 – Daydreams
Chapter 11 – Arriving In The UK
Chapter 12 – A Fine Young Man
Chapter 13 – Star In The Making
Chapter 14 – Acting Out
Chapter 15 – Greased Lighting
Chapter 16 – Karen Free Day
Chapter 17 – The Climbing Wall
Chapter 18 – Looking For Joshua
Chapter 19 – New Guy
Chapter 20 – Back To School
Chapter 21 - A Perfect Shade Of Brown
Chapter 22 - I'm Not Nuts
Chapter 23 – Poor Guy
Chapter 24 – Pretend Girlfriend
Chapter 25 – One Bite Is All It Took
Chapter 26 – The Date
Chapter 27 – Dear Diary
Chapter 28 – Rescue Plan
Chapter 29 – Like Mother Like Daughter
Chapter 30 - A Walk In The Park

Chapter 31 – Aliens
Chapter 32 – Craig
Chapter 33 – Stop Living In Your Dream World
Chapter 34 – Mean Girls
Chapter 35 – Double Date
Preview of Book 2
About the author -
Other works –
Glossary -

Prologue
The Accident

~ Debbie ~

Ten minutes, just ten more minutes that was all I would give my mother before ringing home again.

Perched on the edge of the wall, holding on tightly to the strap of my bag I watch the passing traffic. A single droplet of water makes its way down my face, stopping at my chin, before dripping onto my hands, staring briefly at it before turning my attention back to the road. Searching for my mother's green hatchback, wishing I was buckled up in the car.

I sighed, wishing she would hurry up. My hair was dripping and the chill of the air caused me to shudder; regretting not drying it as Wendy suggested. She of course washed and dried her hair after our swimming session.

I had been trying for days to talk to my mother about the changes to my body, or the lack of them. Other girls were sprouting these enormous breasts. Where were mine? It was enough to make me scream.

The road was busy because it was Saturday and the market was on. Cars whizzed past, I watched them, praying my mother would come alone, and that neither Greg nor Sally had tagged along. They always wanted her attention. I rarely got time to speak to her alone. A double decker passed; I watched it until it disappeared. I would have been home by now, if I had been allowed to catch the bus.

Another bus passes by, a single decker this time; the children at the back of the bus waved to me as I noticed the number. If mum hadn't insisted on picking me up, it was the one I would have caught. She had stood there, hands on her hips, blue eyes sparkling, telling me *'you maybe thirteen, but you're not old enough to ride a bus on your own.'*

She was not serious was she? It was a waste of time arguing with her. Once she gave me that look, I had no choice in the matter.

I couldn't blame Wendy for leaving me alone, since she had to go visit her grandparents. She had talked her parents into allowing her to go swimming on the understanding that they would pick her up afterwards. Of course, she agreed. My parents were the same, and since my grandad died, we visited our nan every two weeks.

Steve reminded me that we needed to visit her as often as we could, we had no idea how long she would be with us. When my grandad died, I should have spent more time with him. Steve was right about that. For a brother, he could be so sweet, and often teased me about boys. There was only one boy who captured my heart. I only had to hear his name, or see his face and would melt into a puddle on the floor. *Joshua Lawson*, he was a gorgeous talented young man. He may live in my dreams, but he was real to me.

Biting my lip hard, pushing him out of my mind; I should be concentrating on watching for Mums car.

She was taking forever to get here, where was she? *Come on Mum*.

Four lanes made up the one way system. It was a road I did not like crossing, as it was one of the busiest. Some people did not know what a red light meant, and using the zebra crossing, you did so at your own risk.

My backside felt numb from the cold bricks, and standing seemed like the only way to get my legs to stop shaking. I wrapped my arms around my body to keep warm, inhaling the chlorine in my hair and the fumes from the cars. Wishing I had washed it.

Dropping my bag to the pavement, between my feet, I wrung my hair again; 'the water dripped onto the concrete and created wet droplets around my feet. Staring at them, as my body shuddered again, I felt so cold, bored, and ready to go home. She should have been here by now. *Where are you Mum?* I was searching for our car, jumping from one foot to the other.

There was still no sign of her. I sat down again, and shuffled on the cold brick wall, wishing Wendy had not left me.

Five more minutes pass.

"Come on, Mum," I muttered to myself, craning my neck to check down the road for her again. It's not like mum to be this late. I rolled my eyes, chuckling to myself; as mum hates it when I do that.

More cars pass; one catches my eye, a blue van, weaving across each lane, causing cars to honk their horns. I cannot believe the way he is driving. Watching until it turns left at the end of the road and disappears from my view.

This is so unlike my mother, being this late; I am wondering whether or not to ring home, but that would mean leaving the meeting point and going back into the swimming pools entrance where the phone is. Deciding to wait a little bit longer, I start counting red cars because I am bored. It is a game my family often play on long journeys, but no fun on your own. This was beyond the joke, where was she? Standing, people stare at me as I continue to watch the traffic when I notice another blue van. Realising it's the same blue van. It switches lanes, again and then again. Taking my eyes from the van, I spot my mother approaching. Seeing her face light up as she spots me; she does not wave. I am more than ready to go home now.

Then in slow motion the look of horror is etched on her face. She looked from me back to the road as I noticed that the blue van has switched lanes again. This time right into my mother's path, she has no time to react. I hear tyres squeal as my mother slams on her brakes, but there is nothing she can do, and rear-ends the van. I can't look; I don't want to, I crumble to the floor, my heart racing. Lying on the cold concrete floor, covering my eyes with my hands, I curled up in a foetal position, hearing metal crunching on metal, as screams fill the air. It is only then, I realise that it is me who is screaming. I remain in a heap on the pavement and prise one eye open, not wanting to see. It's as if time has stood still; the sound of sirens fills the air. I open my other eyes; watching people rush to the scene. I feel a hand help me up asking me if I am okay, if I am hurt. Shaking my head, staring at the two mangled vehicles, one of which was my mother's. This can't be real. I'm daydreaming.

As I watch the scene unfold not being able to find but a whisper of a voice and gasping for breath. I stare at my mother as she is slumped over the steering wheel. There is broken glass scattered everywhere on the ground.

"Mum, Mum."

Emergency vechiles approach the scene; the man releases me; sobbing so hard my chest aches. I swallow attempting to make my feet move forward; a police officer walks towards me, and starts to talk, seeing her lips move, but not hearng the words that tumble from them.

Watching the scene unfold as they pull my mother from her car and lay on a stretcher. The whole time the police officer is speaking to me, I mumble that she's my mum as I watch them cover her with a sheet, screaming no. She can't be dead; she can't. They are wrong; they have to help her, pulling away from the police officer she holds me back.

I scream her name over and over.

"She's gone, love; she's gone," the police officer says as she holds me to her, and I sob uncontrollably.

Three days later, the death of my mother does not feel real. A constant flash of the accident plays out in my mind. It's all my fault she's dead. I know it is, no matter what my fmaily tell me. I am to blame.

Dream World

If I had not needed a lift home that day, my mother would still be alive. Refusing to leave my room, hiding in my bed underneath the covers. My eyes red from crying, my nails chewed. I should shower, but that meant leaving the safety of my bed. I don't want to see them, any of them. Knowing they all blame me. I know that everyone blames me; maybe even wishing that I had died instead. I blame myself for the accident.

I've not eaten since my father brought me home from the hospital. I can't eat. My mouth feels dry; my stomach rumbles, but I cannot fill it. I do not deserve food.

Even my best friend, Wendy cannot entice me out of my room. Did they not understand my mother was dead; nothing would be the same again.

If I had ridden the bus home; she would still be alive. Sally being so young to lose mum is lost. And I know that Greg being only ten years old is not old enough to understand. What have I done!

Angry does not come close to how I feel. Throwing back my duvet and standing as fresh tears replace the old ones, and mingle with snot. I wipe them on the arm of my pyjamas and storm across the room. I am angry with myself, the driver, and with my mother. As my anger explodes, I take it out on every poster on my wall, destroying them in seconds.

Sitting among the debris of paper, crying as more tears trickle down my reddened cheeks. It's not Joshua's fault;it's mine. Scooping the pieces up, laying them on the bed. The posters beyond repair, r, I fall back on the bed with a fist full of Joshua Lawson. He is and always will be my favourite character from the show on TV, Victor. I lie down and look up at the only poster of him, which survived, the one on my ceiling. His face stares down at me, smiling; I close my eyes.

Joshua takes one-step towards me and pulls me into a hug, and whispers in my ear.

"It will be okay; I will be here for you, always. It's not your fault, remember that."

Hoping that one day I can believe him. I open my eyes.

Chapter 1
The Funeral

~ Debbie ~

It had only been a week since my world crumbled. Of course, I was taking the death of my mother hard. Witnessing something like that will do that to you. I couldn't care less how I looked and smelt, wearing the same pyjamas all week.

My shirt hung on the back of the door, taunting me. Everyone left me alone, which suited me just fine. I did not want to see anyone. Not even my best friend, Wendy. She tried so many times to entice me out of my room, to take me away from my thoughts. She meant well, but if I wanted to stay in my room and wallow, I would.

I did my best to avoid the family, believing they all blamed me. They were right to. It was my fault. She's dead because of me.

The bluetac on the wall, a constant reminder of where my cherished posters once were, now they were ruined, gone. Just like my mother. I never even had the chance to say goodbye to her. Closing my eyes, the accident replayed in my head, tears streamed down my face, as I attempted to push it out. Losing the battle, my body ached from crying so hard. The pain of losing her would never leave me.

The driver of the van took her from me. I will never forgive him.

Trying to think happy thoughts and that meant Joshua. He always wore a constant smile. Staring at him, wanting to know what made him so damn happy. Of course, he was stuck in that pose. All he had to do was hold me in his arms and the pain melted away. Loving him was so easy. I often imagined him here in this room, with his arms wrapped around me. If I closed my eyes, I could see him clearly. Run to him, throw myself in his arms and have him hold me.

It was harder to imagine mum, without the accident appearing. Helping me deal with my guilt and loss was the image of Joshua holding me; until the image left.

Two knocks on my door told me someone had finally come for me, but I buried myself deeper in my cave, unable to stop the tears from flowing. The voice asked if she could come in, I ignored the question, knowing my nan would enter regardless.

Hearing her cross the room and sit beside me, she removed the duvet from me and wiped the tears from my cheeks, which just made me cry more. I sat up and wiped my tears along the arm of my pyjamas. I knew I looked a mess; my eyes were red from crying.

"Debbie, love," my nan began, pulling me into a hug. "Come on, please. You'll make me cry again. Your mother would've hated that."

"I…" I stuttered. Knowing she was right. Yet it did not stop them from falling, dripping onto my pyjama leg and expanding into large wet droplets.

"I know, sweetheart. I do." My nan, Sophie took my hand. Tears in her eyes, making my own continue to flow. "You know your mother loved you?"

Nodding, I knew she did. She told me all the time; now she never would be able to again.

"Do you think she would have wanted you stuck in here all alone?"

I remained silent, trying my best to stop the tears from falling.

"Debbie, sweetheart, it will get better. When your grandad died, I went to pieces. Your mother was my rock, she helped me through it." She released me from the hug, and stared at me. "I can still hear her telling me how he would be cross for me sitting in the same clothes and crying for days."

"Nan, it's my fault," I mumbled. "She's dead because of me."

"Oh sweetheart," she said, pulling me into her arms again. "It wasn't your fault. How can you even think that?"

"She was coming to pick me up and…"

"Never think it was your fault."

Tears spilled down onto my nan's shoulder. I wished I could believe her.

Twenty minutes later, my nan released me from the warmth and safety of her embrace. She stood, and left me to dress. Wiping the tears from my face, needing to shower, I was unsure if I had time. They could wait. Walking to my bathroom, switching the shower on, I placed a hand under the running water, checking the temperature.

I stood beneath the flowing water, washing away the guilt, hoping it would disappear down the plughole with the dirty water. Rinsing the last of the soap from my hair, I switched the shower off and wrapped a large towel around my body. Hair wrapped in a second towel, I made my way back into my room.

They were waiting for me, but I needed to dry my hair.

"*Your hair was wet that day too.*" *Joshua reminded me.*

He was right, it was. I knew then, I could not leave until every last strand was dry. The only way was to blow dry it.

Once dry, I brushed my hair, and then put it up in a ponytail. Dressing, I wanted to believe my nan, but still it felt it was my fault.

Buttoning my white silk blouse, I reached for the door handle, opening it to find my father standing there on the landing, red eyed. I flew into his arms; he held me and laid his chin on my head. I felt his body heave as sobs came deep within him. How stupid had I been, we were all hurting, I was not alone in this. We had all lost her.

We arrived at the church. Family and friends occupied every

seat. I sat between my father and nan, sobbing silently throughout the service. My nan squeezed my hand. I did not want to think of her body in the coffin. *When would this be over?* Yet, we could not leave, not until the guests had given their condolences to my father, and the family. It was too much for me to bear. Steve slid across the pew and placed his hand on mine. It reminded me once again how selfish I had been. Laying my head on his shoulder, wondering who had arranged everything.

After the funeral we walked to the wake, which was being held in the back of a pub. Why? They never came here, did they? I had no idea, but still we were here now, in this small room, filled with family and friends who had come to pay their final respects to my mother.

They all ate, joked and talked about what a lovely kind person my mum was. Yes she was all those things, the anger boiling up inside me with them and myself.

Leaning on the wall, closing my eyes, unable to look at any of them. I was sick of the looks of sympathy and the whispering. Opening my eyes, listening to them, were they talking about me? I had to get away from them; I'd had enough, pulling on my coat I made my way outside. The cold air slapped me in the face, but not hard enough, I deserved the pain. Taking two steps towards the busy road, not thinking.

"Debbie, don't do it," Joshua's voice said, causing me to stop.

I looked back towards the pub, sighing, I should go back in, but could not. Instead, deciding to go home.

The first droplet of rain hit my face, stinging. Even with the pain, I did not care as my feet hit the tarmac with such a force my legs ached. Moving forward, my eyes filled with tears as the rain belted around me, soaking me to the skin. Somehow, I arrived in town; how I ended up there I had no idea. Walking towards the site of the accident, my head pulled me back, but my feet urged me forward. It was then I saw them, the flowers from so many people. Some who knew her, many who did not, yet they cared enough to lay flowers. Crouching down I read each message. One made my heart stop. Holding it in my trembling fingers my teeth were on edge as I tore it to pieces.

"What the hell do you think you're doing?" a female voice questioned me.

I stood, the pieces floating to the ground, landing in a muddy puddle, the black ink, merging into one big mass as I spun around.

"Doing," I spat.

"Yes. That's disrespectful," the woman began, staring at me. "A woman died here a little under two weeks ago."

"I know!" I said, through gritted teeth.

The woman studied me, her eyebrows raised.

"She was my mother," I sobbed, turning and sitting beside the flowers. "And he left her this…" I indicated to the remaining pieces of paper. "…saying he was sorry."

"He did?" the woman asked.

"Yes, he did. How dare he?" I said, pulling the heads off the flowers.

"Ah. Maybe he's sorry. It was an accident after all."

"An accident," I bellowed. "He was drunk and swerved into her lane."

"Yes, he was." The woman nodded, placing a hand on my shoulder. "He should not have been driving, but he is sorry."

I looked up at her, and shrugged her hand off.

"You're his mother aren't you?"

The woman nodded, I saw tears in her eyes.

"Why was he driving?"

"I don't know, but I do know this; his life is ruined too. He has to live with the fact he killed your mother."

I nodded again. "Yes he does, but…"

"It doesn't excuse it, I know, and I'm ashamed of his behaviour, but he will have to live with this for the rest of his life." She paused and sighed. "Some may say he was lucky for surviving, but he doesn't think so, he wishes he died too."

"Me too."

"You don't think that really, do you?"

"Yes," I snapped. I did. *At least I thought I did.* "No, I don't know what I think. All I know is he killed the most important person in my life. You tell him that. Tell him he ruined my life too."

The woman stood silently watching me, the rain still falling upon us.

"Debbie," I heard my brother's voice call.

I turned; he ran towards me. I saw the look of worry on his face and suddenly felt ashamed for running off.

"There you are! Dad's going crazy, because you disappeared."

"I'm sorry. I couldn't…" I mumbled as he held me.

"Take her home," the woman said. "Tell your father my son is sorry, and so am I."

Steve led me towards his car.

"Was she?" he asked.

I nodded, as I climbed inside and buckled up.

Steve drove us home, where our immediate family now were.

I entered the house, my father pulled me inside and held me. He later ranted about the worry I had caused. I apologised and excused myself, racing up the stairs to the safety of my room. Throwing myself down on the bed, I closed my eyes, seconds later; Joshua's warm arms engulfed me.

"It's going to be okay, Debbie, please don't cry. No more tears." He wipes them away as I look up into those brown eyes and allow a flicker of a smile to appear on my lips.

"I will try," I promise him.

~ *Mark* ~

Loud music played, the band N & N stood centre stage, the crowd went wild. I knew all the words to the songs, but never sang them. The crowds sang along, knowing all the lyrics, thousands of them in unison. Turning from the stage, I walked back to their dressing room, knocking shoulders with my cousin. We stared into one another's eyes, for a brief moment.

"Sorry Mark, didn't see you there," he said.

"Of course you didn't," I muttered reaching my parents' dressing room. He may be my cousin, but how I iwhsed he would go and butter up his own parents.

Chaper 2
In His Arms

~ Debbie ~

Three weeks had passed since my mother's funeral. Family and friends called less often. My nan checked in on us once a week. No matter how much I was told by my family and friends, I still blamed myself.

The accident kept invading my dreams over and over again. Each time I heard the shattering sound of metal causing my heart to break. With tears falling down my face; begging Joshua to hold me in his arms where I knew I would be safe. But it was too late. I saw the image of my mother flash before my eyes. I shut them tight, swallowed and relived it again. My heart raced, as I grasped the duvet in my clenched hand, as tears fell down my cheeks. Switching on the lamp and rolling onto my side I looked at my mother's picture; her eyes staring back at me. Almost like a frozen state, her mouth parted in a smile. Oh what I would do just to see her smile again, to hear her laugh and most of all, just to have her hold me.

Pulling my knees to my chest, I recalled the day it was taken, Steve's wedding. It was the happiest I had ever seen her. In every photograph she wore that smile. More tears threatened to fall. I lifted the photograph down, held it in my hand, feeling her close to me. Was she really looking down on me? Did I believe in such things? Before her death, the answer would have been no, but now, yes I did. I wanted to believe it more than anything. Would she be angry with me for crying? Did she blame me for her death?

Lying back down, with the photo against my chest, I stared up at the poster of Joshua. Hoping he would make my pain go away. I needed him now more than ever. *Oh Joshua.* In that moment, I allowed myself to smile, but felt guilty in an instant. I closed my eyes.

"Debbie, we said no more tears. Come on, dry those eyes."

"I know; I'm sorry," I reply.

"Now come here."

Joshua pulls me close to him. I lay my head on his shoulder. Only then do I allow the smile on my lips to reappear.

Opening my eyes, I took a deep breath and sat up. The image of Joshua vanished as I stared at the photo in my hand, biting my lower lip until I tasted blood.

Another tear made its way down my face. Wishing I could turn back time, and ridden the bus home. Or not gone swimming at all. Then she would be alive. I would blame myself for the rest of my life. No matter how many times I was told it's not my fault. Did they not get it? It was.

Wiping the tears away with the sleeve of my pyjamas, promising her this would be the last time I would cry. Placing the photograph back in its place, I lay down staring up at the poster of him on the beach, wearing red shorts, with the sun glistening in the background. In his arms, I always felt safe. When I needed him, he would be here for me.

Closing my eyes, Joshua lay beside me, his arms wrapped around me.

~ *Karen* ~

I sat in my usual seat with the gang, discussing our last weekend together. We'd had another catwalk show, wearing my latest collection of new clothes. It was now a ritual, and the girls expected it. I of course, was happy to oblige, after all, they were my friends.

Over the years, it had grown from one hour, to a whole day with a catwalk show. I provided snacks, and some weeks they stayed over and watched movies.

"Hey Karen, she's back," Stephanie whispered.

I turned my attention to the girl boarding the bus, with her head down. Debbie Conway was a former friend, now we rarely spoke to each other. I could not be friends with her, not now. Now she had Wendy. She did not need or want me, and I did not want her either.

~ *Debbie* ~

My stomach was in knots with the thought of returning to school. This had not been my idea, but dads. And as always Mondays sucked. I wanted to be with Joshua in the safety of my room. Yet here I was, climbing aboard the bus, as if nothing had happened.

They stared at me as I made my way to my usual seat; Wendy followed and slumped down beside me. She had forgiven me, but remained silent, only a quick hello before we had boarded. I looked at her, but the words I wanted to say were stuck in the back of my throat. She took my hand and squeezed it. It was then; I knew no words were needed.

We arrived at school, it was odd, everything looked the same. The building remained exactly as it had before my mother's death. Why had I expected it to look different, just because my life had been turned upside down? It made no sense, but that is how I felt, like somehow when I looked out the window, life would have stopped, paused maybe, but no, everything continued to move forward. Even though I was not ready to return dad was right, I had already missed too much. And mum said making good grades in school was important, so I will do my best.

As I took two steps towards the school my first day back began.

The day went slowly, and now I was stuck in this old dull classroom. I did not really mind English, but was not in the mood to listen to Mrs Row read a passage from Oliver Twist. Sighing, ignoring all around me, I turned my attention to the outside world, staring out of the window, focusing on the swaying trees. A tiny blackbird caught my attention; I watched it as it flew across the sky and landed on a nearby tree. My eyes felt extremely heavy, from the lack of sleep. Yawning, unable to stop myself; I rarely slept a whole night, because the image of my mother or the accident invaded my dreams, as they threatened to do so now. I closed my eyes as Mrs Row continued to drone on in the background. I tried to keep my eyes open, and failed miserably.

The bird flies over my head and squawks loudly. I watch it continue its journey, as it lands on a low tree branch. Below the tree, I notice a figure leaning against its trunk. Crossing the field towards the tree, my heart races, as I realise who it is.

"Joshua," I say. "You're here!"

Joshua nods stepping towards me, and pulls me into his arms.

"Debbie Conway?" A voice said.

I smile at him. He leans towards me, his eyes sparkle. Will he kiss me? I wait for his soft lips to…

"Debbie Conway," the voice repeated.

I tilt my head, stare up into those eyes, lips apart I will him to lean in and steal a kiss. He opens his mouth.

"Did you hear me?" he mouths in the voice of Mrs Row.

I narrow my eyes as I frown at him. Then something pulls him away from me; he floats backwards across the field, leaving me standing with my mouth open.

Opening my eyes, and adjusting them to the light flooding in through the large glass window, I sighed, d*amn it*, I thought as the dream faded. The classroom came into focus. Staring straight ahead, I noticed two legs stood before me. Swallowing hard, I adjusted myself and sat up on the plastic seat. My backside numb, quickly wiping the saliva off my chin, looking up into the eyes of my English teacher, Mrs Row.

"Are you with us now?" she asked.

I nodded, hearing someone snigger behind me, but chose to ignore it.

"Debbie, I will not stand for this in my lesson. Now collect your books and move to the front," she instructed. One day back and they were not going to let anything slide. I felt close to tears, but held them in.

I let out a groan, and pouted; I felt my face redden snatching up my bag and books off the table. I shot Wendy a look as I stood. Why had she not warned me? Now it was obvious, she was reading.

Eyes forward, I moved slowly towards the front of the classroom and slumped down in the only empty seat. Head down, I sighed; waiting for what must come next, the punishment. I waited, holding my breath.

"Look," Mrs Row begun in a hushed voice. "I know it's your first day back, and that you are grieving, but you really need to pay attention in class. Read the book, and answer the questions on the board. Please don't make me have to keep you here after school."

"Yes, Miss," I replied, biting my lower lip, ignoring the pain it caused.

Removing the book from the desk, I opened it, and found the passage, trying my best to read the words before me. Yet they danced on the page. I tried hard to concentrate on the words, blinked and tried again. It was just no good; I could not concentrate on anything, except the accident. Right now, I needed Joshua to hold me in his arms.

I continued to stare at the page as the words turned into a black mass, creating a silhouette of him.

Blinking, the words dashed back into place. As I removed my pen from the pencil case, I attempted to answer the questions on the board.

Twenty minutes later the bell rang, and the noise level in the classroom rose. All I wanted to do was escape as Mrs Row dismissed us. As I packed my things away, I kept my head down. Leaning towards me, Mrs Row placed her hands on my desk.

"Debbie can I have a quick word with you?"

I nodded, and sunk back in my seat as Wendy passed me, raising her eyebrows as she did. As she reached the door, she opened her mouth to speak.

"I won't keep her long, Wendy," she said.

The door clicked as it closed. Mrs Row turned to face me, and took the seat beside me.

"Debbie, I'm not going to lecture you. I know it's only been a few weeks since...since the accident, but you need to focus on your education. Your mother would have wanted that."

"I'm trying Miss," I began. "I really am, but I just can't. You don't understand. Every time I close my eyes I see..." I left the sentence unsaid.

"I won't pretend to know how it feels to lose someone." Mrs Row paused as she handed me a tissue. "I wish I knew the right thing to say, but I don't."

"How can she be gone? I keep expecting her to walk through the door."

"It's going to get easier; all you can do is take each day as it comes." Mrs Row said as she stood. "You can talk to your father if you need to, or Wendy, or even me."

I wiped my eyes, sniffed and headed for the door, still holding the screwed up tissue.

"Debbie, my door is always open," she said, as I reached the door. I turned and thanked her, but I knew I would not be able to talk to her, my father or even Wendy, not yet.

Chapter 3
The Band N & N

~ Debbie ~

The cool air hit me in the face as I entered the corridor and took one step forward; Wendy joined me from the place she had been hiding, and hooked her arm through mine. I was glad she waited for me. If we missed the bus, at least we would be together.

"Let's get you home, come on," she announced, dragging me towards the bus.

As soon as we approached, I knew they were looking at me; I tried to avoid eye contact with them, not wanting to see the sympathy in their eyes. Knowing it would be there, and once again, tears threatened to fall.

Wendy placed her hand on mine and gripped it. I turned to look out the window, once I gave her a reassuring smile. My first day back was over.

"Do you want me to come over later?"

I wanted to answer yes, but something held me back. She kept talking about watching a movie. I was grateful for her ignoring my silence. She still had her hand on mine. It did not feel odd at all. We were best friends and she was showing she cared and was there for me.

Standing on the grass, the bus pulled away, I stared at my house, at the empty space where my mother's car once stood. Steve's was in his space, but my father refused to drive again. I did not blame him.

"Debbie," Wendy nudged my arm.

I turned to face her.

"I'll see you later?"

I nodded, not giving her a real answer, before running across the grass towards the safety of my home.

Once inside, I slammed the door shut behind me, closing out the world.

The only person I wanted to be with was Joshua, but I needed to spend more time with Wendy. I would try not to push her away any more. I would walk over to hers and watch one movie with her.

Throwing my bag over my shoulder, I entered the house.

"Is that you, Debbie?" my father called out.

I sighed, choosing to ignore him. He had not returned to work, so it seemed. Yet, he insisted, I return to school.

Making my way to my bedroom, kicking the door closed behind me, I threw myself onto my bed, letting out a frustrated scream. Rolling onto my back, looking at the photograph of my mother again. Thinking about Steve's wedding, and how lucky he was having our mother witness it, but she would never be there to attend mine. Guilt hit me; I was wrong to feel this way, but could not help myself. They lost her too. Greg cried himself to sleep every night, Sally asked us every day when mum was coming home. I could barely look her in the eyes; she was so like my mother to look at. At three she was already the image of her. Right down to that sparkle in her eyes. I knew that was the reason my father could not look at her. I understood, but she did not. Many times she had tried to find comfort with him, only to be pushed away. He did not mean to, he was still grieving, and Sally reminded him so much of what he had lost. What we had lost.

Staring up at Joshua, his eyes melting all my fears away, I closed my eyes.

I sit up, hearing him whisper my name, and watch him cross the room. The moment he is beside me, I throw myself into his arms, and sob uncontrollably.

"It's going to be okay." I feel his hot breath on my skin.

I hold onto him. I feel safe. I listen to his heart beating a tuneful rhythm. I relax. The tears dry on my face as he lies beside me, until I close my eyes and fall asleep.

~ *Karen* ~

Closing the front door, I walked down the hallway, poking my head around the front-room door, discovering that as usual no one was home. Of course, I had not expected them to be here, they would be at work.

My father would be operating, while my mother sat at her desk; phone in hand, taking on new clients, or studying her newly manicured nails. She loved working for my father. It was how they made their money. I had a weekly budget, and spent it on whatever I wanted, which was usually on clothes and my friends.

My friends were always there for me, unlike Debbie. Sure, her mother had died, but even before that, she ignored me. I had not changed, she had. We had not been friends for many years.

I removed a can of pop from the fridge, climbed the stairs and entered my huge bedroom. Looking around my room, I could not help but smile, having so much more than I had when living across the street from her, when we were friends. I did not need her, not at all. I crossed the room and switched the tape player on, turning the volume up. Lying on the bed, listening to my favourite band N & N. I loved them, and had tickets for their next UK concert. It would be an awesome night.

~ *Mark* ~

Sitting backstage; listening to the band 'N & N' perform their latest hits, I waited for my parents. They asked me to come along, spend time with them; this was not what I had in mind. Often attending their concerts, more in the past than now, and knowing the songs by heart, but never singing them. Listening to my own favourite band on my Walkman, I stared up at the roof joints, wondering how much longer this set would last. Not hearing the band coming into the room, when the drummer sat at my feet and tapped me. We made eye contact as I removed one earpiece.

"I don't know why you bothered coming, if you're going to listen to that rubbish!" my father, Nigel said.

"I didn't have a choice; take it up with my father!" I snorted.

He shook his head, as he turned to face Nina, my mother and the lead singer of the band.

"Don't look at me; he's your son too!"

I raised my eyebrows. I was their son when it suited them. I loved them, but they rarely had time for me. Sitting backstage at their concert was not exactly what I had meant when I'd said I wanted to spend more time with them, before they shipped me off to the UK. They were both looking at me, as I recalled the chat we'd had.

"Come on, Mark, it won't be that bad, besides you made your choice. You could have gone to boarding school here, like your father."

"Yeah, I tried that, remember."

"Mark, we would have been happy to have played for the prom, but…"

"You let me down, like every other time in my life. No, you're not doing it again. You made me look like a fool. Everyone blamed me, and said I lied about you being my parents, so no. I want a fresh start in a new place."

Taking a deep breath, recalling their words, the hate mail. I could not wait to get out of there.

Next month I would touch down in the UK and spend a year with my grandparents, something I was looking forward to.

Of course, I would miss my parents, even if they would not miss me. Since I rarely saw them while they were on tour, it didn't matter.

The next tour would last a little over a year, taking them all over the world. They did not want me with them. Would I really want to follow them around? Answering my own question. No.

Instead, I would have a fresh start, and I could not wait. I heard my mother speak to my cousin as he entered the room. I ignored him, turning up the volume on my Walkman.

~ Debbie ~

I had slept the best I had in weeks; lying with his arms wrapped around me was how I slept most nights. I knew I had to move forward.

The night before, I spent two hours watching a movie at Wendy's house. Not once thinking about my mother, just enjoying the movie. It did me good I knew that, to not allow that day to invade my head. The moment the movie ended and Wendy's mother asked if we wanted snacks, placing her arm around me, I let the tears fall. She had not meant to make me cry, but it was the closeness of a female adult. She held me for ten minutes and without a word left. I needed that, a motherly hug. Which had brought more tears flowing down my cheeks, and it was Wendy who hugged me next.

Having a best friend like her meant the world to me. Knowing she was always there for me. I regretted more than ever how I had pushed her away, but she told me she understood. She was always there for me, always. Yet, I still needed the comfort of Joshua's arms around me, every now and again.

Days had mingled into one another, and time did not register with me most days. I had woken early once again, ready to get up and head to school, then it dawned on me, it was Saturday. I sat up and selected the most recent copy of my favourite magazine, Hot Gossip. I scanned the pages, when one page made my mouth hang open.

"He's doing what!" Reading how Joshua was going to be joining the band N & N for a few of their concerts. I would love to hear him sing live. A thought entered my head, as I continued to flick through the remaining pages, scanning the articles, wishing I could afford tickets for the concert. I would, of course take Wendy with me. She loved the band too, and a bonus for me would be to see him sing live. Either way, I could not wait to tell Wendy about Joshua performing with N & N. I knew there were many students at our school who loved their music, and those who said they didn't, secretly did.

~ Karen ~

As I reached the window I heard the car engine start. Then the car containing my parents sped down the road: with no, see you later Karen or be back later. My parents don't care about me so stuff them. Besides I planned another shopping spree; just a few pairs of jeans and that pair of shoes that I had my eyes on. I showered, and dressed in the pair of jeans I'd bought the week before, my favourite heels and a button down blouse. I studied my reflection in the mirror. I looked good, I knew that, and today the girls and I would have the best time ever. I still had time to decide who I would take with me to the concert, besides I had not told them, yet. It would be a surprise for whoever I picked. There was no way I planned to tell them, having them suck up more than they usually did.

Today we would shop, and then their usual catwalk. Later we would watch a movie, and order in a takeaway.

~ Debbie ~

I spent an hour lying in bed, thinking about how to raise funds for the tickets, but none came. Too young to get a job, maybe a paper round, but that would take months to save on a small wage. My heart sank, realising I would not be able to go.

I climbed out of bed, tossed the magazine on the floor and dressed quickly. I realised that for the first time since the accident my waking thought had not been of my mother. I had something else to think about. I raced down stairs to fix a bowl of cereal.

After eating, I made my way to Wendy's. Praying she would be up. It was unlikely that she would be, but regardless I had to go see her. I was so excited about the news I wanted to share with her.

I knocked, and Wendy's mother opened the door, still in her dressing gown, her hair not brushed.

"Debbie, come in," she yawned. "You're up early, Wendy's still in bed."

I worried I had got her mother out of bed, but she was dressed, so maybe not.

"I guessed that, but I was up and well…" I paused. "I should come over when she's up."

"No, go on up. It's nine; she should be up anyway, even on a Saturday."

"Thanks."

"Have you eaten?"

I nodded, and made my way up to her room, knocking on her door, before entering. She was still asleep. I tiptoed across the room and gently shook her.

"Wendy, Wendy."

"Go away, five more minutes, please."

"Wendy, it's me."

"Huh!" she said, opening one eye and peering at me. "What!"

"Sorry, I know I am early and all, but I had to tell you something."

"It's okay, I already..."

"No, not that. I was reading Hot Gossip."

"Brilliant, well done," she smirked closing her eyes again, pulling the duvet over her head.

"Wendy, listen, you will want to hear this."

"Tell me in an hour, I'm too tired."

"No, I have to tell you now; it's about N & N."

She sat up, rubbed her eyes, and insisted I continue.

"Well, they're performing in concert in London."

"London?"

"Yes, and guess who will be joining them for a few of them?"

"Who?" she asked.

I was not sure if she was bothered, but told her Joshua was performing with them.

She rolled her eyes, and flung herself back down on the bed.

"Wendy, I thought you'd be happy for me. If we can afford the tickets, I would finally get to hear him sing. How cool would that be?"

"Cool, but you woke me for that?"

"Yeah, oh come on I am so excited," I screeched, unable to control myself. "I really want to go, don't you?"

She sat back up, and smiled at me.

"Of course, I do," she said, shaking her head and looking at her clock. "Is that the time?"

"Yes, now get up. We need a plan to come up with the cash."

Chapter 4
Memories

~ Debbie ~

I could not believe another three weeks had already passed.

The accident continued to haunt my dreams. Sometimes Joshua would take me in his arms and make the pain go away. Other times, nothing could ease my pain.

I scurried down the corridor towards the drama room, with Wendy hot on my tail; I could hear the sound of the others chattering in the hall, not hearing their words, just the sound of their mixed voices.

"I kept my head down, unable to look them in the eye. Knowing what I would see if I did. Sympathy.

We made our way down the corridor towards our first lesson and joined the queue. A posted on the wall caight my attention. I stared at it for a few seconds, reading it twice, titlting my head, smiling. It was the first one since my mother's death. I stared at the pencil dangling on the string. Wendy nudged me; I spun around to find Mrs Duncan beckoning us in. The pencil remained in mid-air; I would think about it. Was I even ready to audition for the school musical? A voice in my head said, yes, but my heart screamed, no.

Debbie, come on," Wendy said, tugging me by the arm of my coat.

Following her, I entered the room, slumped down on the newly varnished floor, and crossed my legs.

Mrs Duncan took the register, hearing my name; I replied yes Miss, but my thoughts were elsewhere, and for the first time in weeks, they were not on my mother, or Joshua.

Instead, the poster on the wall outside had me distracted, and for the remainder of the day it was all I could think of. The accident sneaked inside my head now and again, but I found Joshua forcing it out. Allowing my head to think clearly about the words printed on the poster and the pencil dangling below it, and the decision to add my name or not.

A thought crossed my mind briefly about Joshua, what he would say if he knew I dreamt about him. Would he think I was just a silly little school girl with an obsession for him, or would he be pleased, knowing he had a dedicated fan? Just the thought of his lips sent goose bumps up and down my arms.

Mrs Duncan's voice faded away as I recalled one of my dreams, the one on the beach.

I lay on a red towel on the warm soft yellow sand. Joshua approaches me. I stare at him, wanting him to kiss me. All the time I stare at those deep brown eyes. The touch of his lips on my skin sends a wave of electricity through my body, making my whole body shiver with pure excitement. I hear a voice, I turn to face the owner and frown, why is Mrs Duncan here? My mouth falls open as she repeats my name.

"Debbie, are you with us?" Mrs Duncan asked.

"Um, yes," I stuttered, returning my attention back to the present, the dream disappeared. The room returned. I blinked my eyes fully open and nodded.

"Good, now get into pairs and make your own ending. Come along."

I held my breath. Ending of what? I turned to face Wendy; she shook her head, hands on her hips.

"What?" I shrugged.

"Come on," she said, pulling me to the other side of the room. "Let's discuss our ending."

Thank God for her, again I regretted pushing her away and planned to make it up to her. I had no idea how and told her so; she told me there was no need. To me there was.

She filled me in on the ending we needed to work on. I did my best to pay attention. Praying the bell would hurry up and ring.

Half an hour later, it did.

~ *Karen* ~

The bell rang, thankful that my group missed out on performing our ending. The girls were not the best actresses in the class. I would not shy away from showing Mrs Duncan my talents. Play to my strengths, of course Debbie's group managed to get away with it too. I had been looking forward to watching their train wreck. I could not help but watch her, staring into space for the most part. Bless her; I wondered if she was thinking about her dead mother. Poor Debbie. I shook my head; she was gazing into space for most of the lesson. I guess Wendy would have filled her in, dependable Wendy. If we were still friends, that would have been my job. I shuddered, friends with her, what was I thinking?

I followed the girls towards our next lesson. My least favourite, double Maths. We joined the queue outside the mobile and waited for the large man who taught us. He was odd to say the least. Maybe if he lost weight; he would need my father's help. I chuckled at the thought. Mr Savoy lose weight. That was like me not shopping for a month. Never gonna happen.

~ *Debbie* ~

Finally, the last bell of the day rang. Placing my things back into my bag, I followed the others rushing out of the gates. All I wanted was to get home.

We looked forward to the six weeks holiday. Wendy counted down the days; I personally was not sure how long we had. I had other things on my mind. Days and weeks seemed to all roll into one. Take today, just another Tuesday. I had no idea why those few words on a poster affected me the way they did.

We reached the bus queue, waiting for the doors to open and allow us to board. From the corner of my eye, I saw a figure on the other side of the road. I held my breath. Could it be her? I knew my mother was dead, but for a split second, I could have sworn it was her. I blinked, wiping away the tears. Of course, it was not her. She looked nothing like my mum. Taking a deep breath. I slid my fingers upon the cold metal rail, and boarded the bus.

I attempted to push the thoughts of my mother away, hoping the accident would not appear. Instead Joshua's face floated around, and made me feel better. It seemed some days I needed him more.

Joshua leans towards me his lips apart. I gaze at him, waiting for his lips to land on mine.

"Glad we got away with not having to act out our ending," Wendy said, nudging me, snapping me out of my daydream, just when he was about to kiss me, typical.

"Huh!" I replied.

Wendy shook her head and told me again what she had said.

"Me too!" I agreed. Knowing we would have to run through it, in case Mrs Duncan wanted us to act it out next time.

"Yeah, I don't suppose I have to ask what you were thinking about, do I?"

"I don't know what you are talking about," I said, shrugging.

"Debbie, come on, it's me you're talking to."

"Okay, in that case, I guess not."

"It might be a good idea to practice our ending later Knowing Mrs Duncan, she won't forget."

I heard a snigger from Karen; she was sat in the seat in front of us. She twisted her body to face us; her eyes were wide as she sneered at us.

"You'll need the practice," she snorted.

She was unbelievable. "Whatever!" I said, rolling my eyes.

"Debbie, just face it you should leave it to the professionals."

I opened my mouth to speak, but thought better of it; she was not worth the effort. We stared at one another, as the bus pulled over. Jerking forward, taking her by surprise. I kept my eyes on hers; they matched mine perfectly. Why did her eyes have to be so similar to mine?

"I think this is your stop, Karen," I remarked, smirking.

"I know where I live, thanks," Karen snorted, as she stood, clicked her fingers and every one of her cronies stood and followed her off the bus.

~ Karen ~

I stood on the grass, watching the bus pull away, the girls stood beside me, commenting on Debbie. I listened, agreeing and nodding. Then they took off towards their homes, promising to call me. I nodded, knowing none would, not caring if any of them did.

I crossed the grass and made my way into the empty house.

Can of pop in hand, I climbed the stairs to my room. Closing the door, I crossed my room and pressed play on my tape recorder, the band N & N filled my room. Being alone, I danced to the music, putting another one of my talents to use. I had not attended dance classes when I was younger for nothing. Well, three weeks' worth, but the teacher was useless, she could not teach me anything I did not already know.

Two weeks later, I started singing lessons, but that teacher too was useless. How she got her degree as a singing teacher was beyond me. I attended for a week and in that time; I knew she could not teach me anymore. My mother agreed. Fad she told the woman, fad indeed. Useless was the word I would have used. My mother paid her the remainder of the money she owed and left red faced. I smiled and held my head high.

I then decided to take up playing the guitar, but my mother refused to allow me to take lessons. Instead I found a book in the local library and taught myself the basics. I kept it a secret, as I knew my friends would think it was lame. I played it when I was alone, and hid the guitar in the back of my wardrobe.

I loved having a room at the top of the house, it may not be sound proof, but most of the time I was alone in the house anyway. No one ever heard me play. Which was exactly how I liked it, and being at the top, I could hear and see them coming and going. It helped that I had a window that overlooked the front of the house; it was a floor to ceiling window. It made my room extremely light. I often stood at it watching the world outside.

I considered on taking a swim in the pool no one else in the family used. Why they did not, was beyond me and decided I would use the pool more often, give the cleaning boy something to actually clean.

I stripped out of my clothes and pulled on one of my costumes. Grabbing a towelling dressing gown, I marched down the stairs and made my way to the pool. It was always warm in the pool room. Closing the glass door, I laid the dressing gown down on a sun lounger, and sat on the edge of the pool. Dipping my toes in, I then slid into the water and swam the full length of the pool. Yes, this was a good idea.

~ *Debbie* ~

Lying on my bed, staring up at Joshua, I thought once again about my day. Imagining I saw my mother. I saw her everywhere. Wendy had chased me, once, as I followed a woman who wore a coat similar to the one my mother owned. I knew her coat still hung on the peg in my parents' room. My father was not ready to remove any traces of her, at least not yet. Holding onto them, he felt closer to her.

I understood him totally him totally. I had often sneaked into his room and wrapped myself inside the coat. It still smelt of her perfume; white musk.

Chapter 5
Rudolf

~ Debbie ~

I awoke twenty minutes before the alarm clock was due to go off, and prised one eye open, and then the other, as the numbers came into focus. I wished I'd slept five more minutes, because if I had, Joshua would have pulled me into his arms and laid those lips on mine.

I sat up, rubbing the sleep from my eyes as the alarm clock buzzed into life. Yawning, I hit the snooze button and threw back the covers. Crawling out of my bed and stumbling across the room, I still felt tired. It was the first night I had not dreamt of my mother. The guilt continued to eat away at me, and I missed my mum every day, I had to stop allowing the accident to take over my every thought, and to let it affect me. But I was failing miserably at it. All I could do is take each day as it came.

Brush in hand, I stood before the mirror and attempted to detangle my locks, switching to a comb, before pulling it back into a ponytail. I hated my hair, and how it never went how I wanted it to. Wispy pieces of hair always floated up and framed my oval face. I sprayed a mist of water to flatten them, knowing in a few hours they would rise once again.

I dressed in my school uniform, a plain pair of grey trousers, a white shirt and a red jumper, which once lay on the back of the chair. How I hated the uniform. I despised it, but not as much as one former best friend, who had done her best to get the uniform banned; but she lost. The uniforms were here to stay. Sighing, I checked my tie's position in the mirror.

Dream World

With one quick look at the photo beside my bed, I slipped my feet one at a time into my sensible black shoes. I then left the safety of my room and made my way down the stairs to the back of the house to the L–shaped kitchen. No matter how I tried, I could not get the image of my mother spending hours in there, baking her creations out of my head. A gift, one I had hoped she would teach me, but who would do that now?

She had taught me the basics, but her skills were self-taught, I hoped my own would be too. Just the thought of being in the kitchen baking, brought me close to her, yet made my heart sink at the same time. I missed her every single minute of the day. Taking a deep breath, I stood in the doorway, watching Greg and Sally eat their cereal, the sugar coated kind. My mother would not have allowed them to eat it too often, but right now, they needed it to get them through the day. Both slurped at the milk; I could hear her voice, asking them to stop. I spun around expecting her to be behind me; of course, the voice was in my head. I sighed and entered the kitchen. My stomach rumbled, deciding to have my own breakfast.

I removed my favourite bowl from the cupboard and added cereal to it. Unable to resist a mouthful of it dry, I scooped up a spoonful and munched on it and then added a splash of milk; I had to eat them quickly before they went soft. I hated soggy cereal. Returning the milk to the fridge, I noticed my mother's photograph had slipped, I straightened it. Staring at her face, her name was rarely spoken; I loved her name, and had often wondered why nan chose to call her Alison. She stared back at me, a huge smile on her lips. Once again, tears threatened to fall. I swallowed as a single tear fell down my cheek and quickly and wiped it away, taking one final look at her face.

Breakfast eaten, I made my way out of the kitchen, snatching up my bag as I went, closing the front door on my way out. I made my way out of the garden, threw my purple backpack over my shoulder and made my way to meet Wendy. Her first words to me were not to daydream today. Did she not understand I had to? If I didn't, that scene would replay in my head. A living nightmare and one I wanted to no longer witness. The pain and guilt it caused. What child wants to watch the death of her mother over and over again? I for one did not. If that meant I would daydream of Joshua Lawson, so be it.

"Ready for another fun-filled day?" Wendy said, looping her arm through mine.

Was I? No, not really.

~ Karen ~

The house was quiet; I had no idea whether they were still in bed, or if they had left already. They had sent me to my room after eating our evening meal, which suited me; I had everything I wanted in here.

I had enjoyed the swim the day before, and considered swimming before school. I was up early most mornings, I did not see why not. I had enough costumes. Decision made, I tossed my nightclothes in the wash, and changed into a two-piece and made my way down the stairs, pulling on a clean towelling dressing gown.

Reaching the pool, I laid it on one of the sun lounges and then took a running jump, lifting my knees to my chin, and jumped in, creating a huge splash. I swam a few lengths, before heading to the showers and washing away the chlorine. I needed to get ready for school; the bus would not wait for me. There was no way I was walking.

I dried, dressed and then made my way down to the kitchen, which was empty. I had not expected my parents to be there. I ate a bowl of cereal, before catching the bus. As usual, they were at the back.

~ Debbie ~

Ten minutes later, we arrived at school. Everyone stood ready to get off the bus. I ignored those looking at me; surely, they had other gossip to talk about? *Leave me alone*, I wanted to shout.

Remember today was a new day, I told myself, as I stood, head held high. I walked to the front and took the steps one at a time, landing with a thud on the concrete floor. Together Wendy and I made our way towards the school building.

Mr Williamson stood behind his wooden desk waiting for the last of the students to enter.

The light above my head flickered. I wished they would fix it already. It was distracting. He ran his hand through his hair, as the last two seats were taken. I yawned and placed my bag between my feet. Closing my eyes briefly, as the dream from that morning flashed in and out of my head. Joshua was always there with his perfect hair, white teeth and that smile. I had lost count how many times I had dreamt about him.

This morning's dream we had been dancing. *Joshua,* I thought opening my eyes, hearing the teacher calling out my name. I shook my head, and said I was here.

Mr Williamson held the registration book in his hand as he paced the classroom, before finally perching on the edge of his desk, where he continued to reel off the last of the names.

His voice faded away, until I heard him no more. I faced the window and found myself staring out at the sky, squinting from the sun's rays. The warmth of the sun made me feel drowsy, yawning, I leant forward on the desk and folded my arms. Resting my head on them, closing my heavy eyelids, strands of my hair fell down covering my green eyes.

I stare into his eyes; they twinkle as his sings to me. I love the sound of his voice, and dream of doing a duet with him.

He pulls me towards him, our faces inches apart. I can feel his heart beating, or is it my own? I bite on my lip as he leans towards me. He is going to kiss me, I am sure of it.

"Debbie," he says, before he applies his lips to mine. I am in heaven, until he releases me and repeats my name.

"Debbie. Debbie."

The voice continued. I opened my eyes slowly, instantly realising I was in school and prayed no one had seen me.

The voice of course, belonged to Wendy I swallowed and mouthed the words, 'thank you'. What would I do without her? I turned to face her, wiping away the small amount of saliva, which escaped while I had slipped into my dream world.

"Thanks," I stammered as I sat up in the chair, straightened my tie, and smoothed down my jumper.

"You're welcome," Wendy whispered, "But Debbie; you're gonna have to be careful, about where you daydream," she said, shaking her head. For a moment, I was mesmerised by her perfect blonde hair.

"Debbie, you know I will always look out for you, but one of these days you'll get caught daydreaming and I won't be there to help you," Wendy said.

I rolled my eyes. Problem was, she was right. I bent down and picked up my bag as Mr Williamson continued to call out the remaining few names on the register.

Adjusting the bag on my knees, I searched inside looking for my oval mirror. Finding it, I flipped it open and peered at my face, double-checking for spots.

Satisfied, I closed it, slipped it back in my bag, when a voice called out from across the room.

"If I were you, I wouldn't look in the mirror too long, you might just crack it," Karen snorted.

Karen's cronies sat behind her giggling as she cupped her hand and pretended to check herself out, imitating my actions. I glared at her for the second time that day.

"Get lost, Karen," I said, through gritted teeth.

No one would believe that we had once been friends. The day her family moved into their new house; she changed and ignored me.

Karen continued to mimic me, as I caught sight of the redness on the end of her nose. It called to me. Our green eyes locked. I opened my mouth to speak. Karen glared at me.

"How many mirrors did you break?" I enquired.

Karen snorted. "What are you talking about?"

"You heard me. It must have been a few, Rudolf."

"What!"

"Rudolf, the red-nosed reindeer," I sang. I could not help myself; I began to laugh, as she finally understood my joke.

"Get lost, Debbie. I don't have a red nose," she said, through clenched teeth.

"Yeah, you do." I nodded, tears streaming down my cheeks. I had not laughed in ages.

"Yeah, like I'd fall for that one," Karen said, standing. "You think you're so funny!" she said,

pointing her finger at me, and then I heard it, it was just a whisper, "at least I have a mother!"

My heartbeat so loud in my chest, I swore everyone could hear it.

"How dare you? You vicious foul-mouthed bitch."

"Why, because I speak the truth?"

"Speak the truth, really? At least when my mother was alive she..." I paused; it pained me to speak of my mother.

"*Joshua!*"

"*Ignore her. She may be right, but she will always be in your heart, remember that.*"

"You gonna cry again?" I heard her say.

"No," I stammered. "Not today, but if I was you, I would seriously consider asking your father to fix your nose," I shouted moving towards the door, and took hold of the handle. "Just like your mothers," I said wrenching it open.

Chapter 6
Flashback

~ Karen ~

I opened my mouth to speak, *how dare she speak to me, like that. As if I would sink so low to have my nose fixed, besides there is nothing wrong with it.* I glared at her as she slammed the door, she was unbelievable. I was told to be nice to her, not so much by my parents, but by the teachers. Give her some slack, because her mother died. Boo hoo. Poor Debbie. I could not understand why so many people liked her. What made her so special? Once she had been my best friend, but now she was just so plain and boring. Her clothes looked as if they came from the local second hand shop, and most likely did.

Some of her clothes may have come from my favourite place, Jacobs, but unlike me, she couldn't afford the designer gear. Poor Debbie had to make do with the bargain range, or when things were on sale. Give her slack; no way was I doing that. Ever.

No, she was not getting the better of me, I tilted my head and stared at my reflection in the glass. *What the hell is that?* Leaning forward, peering at myself I turned round to face my friends. The look on their faces told me what I already knew. My first spot, and by the look of it, it was huge. I placed a smile on my face.

"What!" I snapped.

"Um, Karen, I…we…"

"Spit it out, Stephanie!" I demanded, running a hand through my silky brown hair. It seriously couldn't be that big could it? I know it looked big, but the glass distorted it, surely?

"You know we would never usually agree with her, but Debbie

was right!" Stephanie quickly said.

"She was what?" I said.

"You have a huge zit on your nose," Stephanie replied.

"It can't be that big," I muttered, daring to touch it. It felt huge. They tried not to laugh. I glared at them. Wrenching open the door I walked to the girl's toilets. I needed to investigate this thing, as soon as possible.

I could not blame them for laughing; I would if it was on somebody else's face not mine. I'd always had perfect skin, so how and where did this thing come from?

I aimed for the nearest mirror; I was not prepared for the size of it. It was huge.

"Oh, looks nasty," a girl with red hair, said, realising her mistake as I turned and flared my nostrils at her. "I meant..." she stuttered.

"Get out," I screamed, waving my free hand at her.

The girl flew out the door; it slammed shut, echoing in the silence. Why did this happen to me? Should I squeeze it? No, surely, that would make it worse. I needed make-up to disguise it; unfortunately, it was in my locker. Could I leave the safety of the girls' toilets to get it? No one else could see me like this. *Pull yourself together Karen. It's not the end of the world.* Then why did it feel like it was.

~ *Debbie* ~

My blood boiled, I stood shaking from head to toe as Wendy linked her arm through mine, and led me as far away from Karen as possible. *How dare she?*

Pushing past the students mingling in the corridor, Wendy pulled me along; we made our way through the main building and walked towards the canteen. We reached the double green doors, with one hand each, we pushed them open; they clattered behind us as they closed.

Of course we knew the canteen would be empty. Like everyone else we should be heading to our first class. Pulling out a chair and flopping into it at the closest table.

The staff shook their heads and continued their duties behind the counter without saying a word to us. I was so grateful for that.

The smell of freshly baked cakes and bread made my stomach rumble. I knew it was lunch time, as it was making me very hungry.

"Debbie, about what Karen said."

I turned to Wendy; she smiled and took my hand.

"I know I should not let her get to me. I can't help it. She's…"

"…a bitch," Wendy suggested.

"Yeah, she is." I had to agree, but what she said was the nastiest thing I had ever heard. How dare she say that? I could never forgive her for saying it. Knowing my mother was no longer was with us, and that it was my fault. Where was Joshua when I needed him?

Wendy placed her hand on mine; stopping me from tapping my fingers on the table, I was barely aware I was doing it. She stared at me with those eyes and lowered her voice, a serious look on her face.

"You'll always be my best friend, you know that don't you?"

I nodded, finding a lump in my throat and mumbled, "Thanks. You'll always be mine too." I cleared my throat. "I just knew we were going to be friends from the moment I saw you."

"Me too," she replied.

"I hoped we'd be best friends."

"Really?"

"Yeah," I said, it was true. Recalling the very first time I saw her.

'I was seven; playing Barbie's sat on the floor of my room, dressing them up in ball gowns. I jumped to my feet when a rumbling sound caught my attention. Dropping the doll to the floor, I raced to the window and peered out. I saw a large removal truck parked outside the house; which had been empty for some time. My mother had hoped a nice family would move in. That day, she got her wish.

I stood transfixed at my bedroom window, watching as the new family carried boxes and furniture from the back of the truck. The two boys who looked alike fascinated me. I could not help but watch them; they were identical in every way.

I watched them, staring at the woman with the swollen tummy. My mother informed me later that night, she was pregnant, which meant a baby was growing in her tummy.

I continued to watch from the safety of my room with fascination and anticipation of new friends. I watched a young girl with a skipping rope in the front garden. Now, I knew the girl was Wendy. I, of course, could not make my mind up if I should go down and say hello. Finally deciding I would, I ran down the stairs to the front door.

I stood in the front garden searching for her, but the girl had gone.

Disappointed, I sat on the little brick wall outside my home and watched the others as they came in and out of the house opposite.

I stayed on the wall, waiting for the girl to return. It was half an hour before she did. I stood, our eyes locked. I waved; she waved back, it was the beginning of a great friendship.

The following week, Wendy joined my school and class, cementing our friendship.'

I stared into space as she waved her hand before my face.

"Earth to Debbie."

"Sorry."

"Thinking about you know who?"

I shook my head. "No, not this time. Actually, I was thinking back to the first time I saw you."

"You were?"

I nodded. "Do you remember?"

"Of course, it was the day we moved in."

It was also the day my brother first saw Carol.

"Who would have thought they'd end up married," I said.

"I never would have."

"They used to hate each other. He had no fashion sense, greasing his hair back, 'cos he thought he looked cool."

We laughed at the image of Steve. Glasses, slicked back hair and attempting to grow a goatee. Carol saw something in him and they fell in love. I sighed, at least my mother saw her firstborn get married, but she would not be there for my wedding. I pushed the thought away as we stood, picked up our school bags and made our way to the double doors. I pushed them open and together we stepped out, the cool breeze, stinging my face, at the sudden change in temperature.

"I'd never get married at their age, would you?" I asked as we walked towards our first lesson. Knowing we were going to be late.

"No way, seventeen is far to young," Wendy said, quickening her pace. "We all thought he'd gotten our Carol pregnant, when they told us they were getting married."

"Us too, we would have been aunties. That would've been so cool," I said.

"It would have," Wendy agreed.

I thought about my own wedding dress, the one I had imagined for the past year, when I walked down the aisle with Joshua.

"Earth to Debbie."

"Sorry, I was…" I paused. "One day I'll have a white wedding."

"You want that for real?"

"Yeah, I do. Don't you?"

"I don't know."

"Come on, who doesn't want to be a princess for a day."

"I guess. I've not really thought about it. Maybe in a few years' time I will. Maybe then I'll want the big white wedding."

"True. I know I want a big white fancy dress, and arrive by horse and cart."

"Debbie, trust me, I know you and if you dream it, it will happen. Besides, we all know who to, don't we? I can see the headlines now." Wendy used her arms to motion this. "Joshua Lawson marries his long-time girlfriend, Debbie Conway. You'll have a double spread centre page of all the top magazines. Maybe it will even be shown on TV," Wendy said as she closed the door behind us and checked her watch. "We'd better get to class."

"Yeah you're right," I said. "Anyway it might not make it on TV, just in a few magazines," I chuckled I gently elbowed my friend in the side and shook my head. *In my dreams.*

We continued to walk as we heard the second bell; we were going to be really late if we did not hurry. The doors leading us back into the school swung open as we walked quickly towards our first lesson.

"I wonder if she'll have a nose job," Wendy said.

"Maybe after turning into Rudolf, she might need one."

"You know you're cruel," Wendy said shrugging.

"Me, never," I said, shaking my head. "Anyway she asked for it."

"True. It wasn't like you could miss it. My God it was huge."

"Any redder and it would be the colour of her sweatshirt."

I nodded, straightened my jumper and eyed my reflection in a classroom window. I felt my skin; no redness or bumps had appeared. I dreaded the day I had my first break out. Wendy tapped her watch; we were going to be really late if we did not hurry. We sprinted down the corridor towards our first lesson with Mr Travis.

~ *Mark* ~

I would be flying to the UK in less than three weeks, and my suitcases still remained empty. Mom insisted that I start packing; I tossed a pair of socks in the open suitcase that sat on my bed.

"Made a start," I announced to the empty room. Shrugging my shoulders, going towards my closet I pulled back the doors, studying the clothes hanging there. I had too many clothes. Some I had hardly worn. Going to the UK with no idea what I needed to take with me. Selecting several pairs of jeans and t-shirts, folded them and adding them to the suitcase. Soon it was half-full.

I closed the closet, studied my reflection in the long mirror on the back of my door. I ran a hand through my hair. My mother begged me to cut it, but I refused. I had been mistaken for my cousin, Joshua. I saw no likeness. If he could have long hair, why couldn't I?

Chapter 7
Another Side Of Karen

~ Debbie ~

I pushed all thoughts of Karen out my head, as we raced down the corridor and threw my bag over my shoulder. We moved quickly, dodging students who got in our way. We had never arrived late for his class before, but Wendy had a crush on Mr Travis and often sat ogling him. I did not blame her; he was a good-looking man, but neither of us were fans of Religious Education.

Finally, we stopped to catch our breath, as we approached the classroom. I felt a sharp pain in my side; and winced, it was rare for me to get a stitch, but we had raced across the school grounds, in the attempt to arrive on time. Of course, we were far too late. Class had started, and we discovered that Mr Travis was not teaching. Instead, Mr Miles our Science teacher stood at the front of the class. He had seen us as we approached and beckoned us in.

We entered with our heads down. Even though we had never been late before, I knew we would be punished, especially by Mr Miles, he was mean. I had been right; he did. Telling us, he expected a hundred lines from each of us. I heard Wendy groan. I remained silent; as he informed us he wanted them handed in the following morning. I shuffled towards the back of the classroom and slipped into a seat. Wondering where Mr Travis was? Wendy grunted as she sat down. Should I offer to do her lines, would she accept? I was all ready to say just that, when Wendy whispered.

"I wonder where Mr Travis is?"

I shook my head, saying I had no idea. And why would Mr Miles take his class. Wendy tapped my arm.

"Do you think he'll really make us do those lines?"

I nodded. Even with my mother's death still so recent, teachers were not being gentle with me anymore; to them enough time had passed.

I told Wendy I would do her lines; she shook her head and told me I would do no such thing. Turning my attention back to the lesson, Mr Miles ran through the lesson plan, left by Mr Travis. Mr Miles looked at me and seeing the flash of sympathy. I smiled, showing him I was healing, even though the thoughts of that day would be with me forever. I sighed, *Joshua I need you*.

Feeling a sharp pain in my ankle, I yelped. Rubbing where Wendy's foot had hit.

I glared at her, she mouthed sorry.

Mr Miles continued, I sighed as my thoughts turned to doing those lines. They would take ages to write, and I did not intend to take them home. I would have to explain why Mr Miles had given me them. Telling Wendy, I would rather do our lines in school than at home. She agreed.

At least, Mr Miles had not given us a standing parade. How we all despised them. Standing in the centre of the school hall for all to see, and laugh at. It was true I had giggled at those unfortunate to be given a standing parade. Thanking my lucky stars that I had never been given one. I would rather do lines any day.

The bell rang; Mr Miles dismissed us. I stuffed everything in my bag and stood, following everyone as they made their way towards the door. Just as we reached it, he reminded us about handing our lines in the following morning. How could I forget?

"Don't be late to class again. Otherwise next time it will be two days of standing parade," he said, raising his eyebrows.

Wendy pushed me out the door, slipping into the crowds.

"Who does he think he is…" she began.

"I don't know. We better not be late again, I don't ever want to have a standing parade," I paused. "Come on; let's go to the canteen, after being in there this morning I fancy a bacon roll."

"Oh, that sounds good to me. I think I'll have one, too, smothered in brown sauce."

"Brown, ughh, it has to be red." How could she smother it in brown sauce? It was so wrong. It just had to be red, or barbecue.

"Brown."

I shook my head. "Red. Anyway," I said changing the subject. "I also thought we could make a start on those lines."

"You really want to start them now?" Wendy moaned.

"Yes I do. The sooner we get them done the better."

"I guess we should make a start."

~ *Karen* ~

Hearing the bell, I slipped into one of the toilet cubicles. The make-up I managed to collect from my locker, so far had no effect. Nothing would cover this damn huge zit. I had to face defeat. There was no way I was leaving this bathroom. Not until I knew the coast was clear. I cursed sitting inside the cubicle. Hearing laughter as a group of girls entered.

"Did you hear," one of the girls said.

I imagined them staring at their reflections, applying another layer of make-up, as I had so many times in the past. The girl continued, but I did not recognise her voice.

"Amy's now dating Craig?"

"You mean they were," the other girl informed her.

"She broke up with him this morning. Good thing too, have you seen him?" She chuckled.

"Yeah, I have. He's cute, but there is something weird about him." The third girl admitted.

"You're telling me. I wonder what it was she liked about him?"

about him?"

"I don't know, anyway…"

I sighed, rolling my eyes and attempting to recall just who Craig was. Not being able to place him, waiting for the girls to leave. Resting my bag on my lap, I fished out another foundation to try next. This was the last chance I had to cover it. Nothing else worked and this stuff was the most expensive foundation I owned.

As the girls left the bathroom the second bell rang. The coast was clear as I unlocked the cubicle and stood before the broken mirror. I placed my bag on the side of the sink and removed the bottle of foundation. Twisting the lid off, I then applied some to the back of my hand, before blending it in. I usually had flawless skin, so why had this spot appeared? I used the best cleanser, and until now, I had never had a pimple.

Staring at my reflection, recalling Debbie's comment about my nose; she was wrong, I didn't need it fixed. Until today, I had a perfectly shaped nose. Besides in a few days it would go away, at least I hoped so. I leant forward, the huge red lump was staring back at me. Yup, it was still there but not as red. The hot salty tears ran freely down my cheeks until they reached my chin and trickled onto my white blouse. Another five minutes wasn't going to hurt.

~ *Debbie* ~

Making our way to the form room and sitting at the back of the room. I pulled out a pen to write the lines with. After writing two pages my hand began to cramp. Dropping my pen and rubbing my hand; I put my lines away. While Wendy continued with hers, until the bell rang.

Scanning the room with my hands on my lap I did not notice that Karen had entered. She now sat by the window with her back to everyone, her hand covering her face. I turned to face Wendy and shrugged. She shook her head, folded the paper with her lines on, before shoving them in her bag and looking over to

Karen.

"Where's she been?" she whispered.

Again, I shrugged and pushed ot my lower lip. I hated her, I thought we were friends once, but she didn't care who she hurt. I thought I knew her, but I guess I really didn't. She was a bully.

I did my best to shake her from my thoughts; I lifted out my notebook, with his name scribbled all over it and opened it to a clean page. I took out a red pen and drew a heart in it, placing Joshua's name in the centre, adding smaller hearts to the page while we waited for our form tutor to arrive.

Hearing Wendy's sigh, I felt my cheeks redden and slipped the pad back in my bag, as the room began to fill with our classmates. Only two chairs were empty as we waited.

In my first year of high school, there were around twenty-eight in the form. Over the past two years, two had moved schools and three new pupils joined us.

I saw the smirk on my friends face as she looked over at Karen. She was trying not to laugh, but it was no good. The giggle erupted like a volcano. Like an infection, I too joined in. Tears trickled from our eyes as Wendy frowned at Karen, pouting.

I pulled myself together, wiped my mouth and eyes.

"Oh, Karen, what's wrong?" Wendy began. "Are you okay?" her voice mimicking a younger child.

Karen's face drained of all colour. Her hand remained in place. "Nothing's wrong," she mumbled through her fingers, as she turned her head to look back out the window.

"Sorry, what did you say? I can't hear you with your hand over your mouth," Wendy said.

"Nothing," she snorted.

"It's rude to mumble you know!" Wendy shouted.

I tried to stop myself from laughing, turning my attention to the playing field. Walking across it was the male P.E teacher, Mr Kross. He carried a bag to the goal post.

I understood why so many girls liked watching him. He was

well-built and played rugby for the local team, he had a nice bum, at least from what I had seen, but he was not Joshua.

Turning my attention back to Karen, who was peering over her fingers, I saw a flicker of the old Karen, at least in her eyes as she stood and raced out of the room. Could she still be in there somewhere? No, this may be another side of her, but she was still the girl she had turned into. A bitch, but for a second I swore I saw tears in her eyes.

"Leave me alone," she yelled, slamming the door shut behind her.

"Something I said?" Wendy shrugged.

For a moment, I hoped Karen felt the pain she had caused many over the years. Maybe then she would know how it felt and understand how she made other people's lives a misery.

I had witnessed first-hand one of Karen's outbursts. It was when a girl had looked at her the wrong way. After that, she set in motion rumours which turned her group of friends against her. The girl ended up leaving school, and it was all because of Karen.

~ Karen ~

That's the first time I have had no control over a situation. I knew I should not have returned to class, I thought as I stood in the corridor. *Damn it. Why do I let her make me so mad?*

Kicking a nearby bin, it tumbled over, the contents spewing over the floor. Heart thumping, I raced outside and hid behind a large oak tree. I would not cry, even though I felt the tears sting my eyes. I would not give Wendy, the best friend stealer, the satisfaction.

Should I head home now, or wait to catch the bus as usual? I could not decide, but the sound of a whistle bought my attention to the P.E teacher escorting the Year Sevens onto the field. Choice made for me; I slipped down the trunk of the tree and closed my eyes.

Listening to the groans of the students as the teacher split them into teams.

~ Debbie ~

In our next lesson, we were seated at the back of the classroom; I stared at the empty board. Empty, apart from the date. Mrs Row stood at the front and began to explain we were doing GCSE mock papers. Not many understood what a GCSE stood for. One of the boys asked that exact question.

Mrs Row paused, placing one more paper on one of the table's and addressed the class.

"It's simply stands for a General Certificate of Secondary Education," she said, continuing to hand out the worksheets and instructed us to work in pairs.

I looked over to Wendy and rolled my eyes. This was going to be a fun lesson and one where I should not let my mind wander. Briefly, I wondered where Karen was. Nobody had seen her since lunchtime registration.

Chapter 8
Happy Families

~ Debbie ~

Our final lesson of the day, and the rain had fallen heavily for the past hour, but that did nothing to get out of having our lesson outside. Instead, we now stood on the muddy field; dressed in a short pleated grey skirt and white t-shirt. I hated the P.E kit, more than I hated the uniform. It meant showing my legs, and I did the best I could to cover them whenever possible.

I hid behind the others, praying the heavens would open and we could go inside. Jenny was chosen as one of the team leaders, and chose who she wanted on her team. I knew neither girl would pick me first, second or third. I was proven right, when I was picked fifth. I walked over to my team, feet sinking in the mud, as Wendy joined my team. I felt better about the game, not that we had any chance of winning. I prayed for the lessons when Wendy and I were on the same team.

I preferred playing hockey, not that I was any better at it, but I was rubbish at rounder's. And everyone knew it, but with the weather the way it was, would any of us play well. Our teacher blew her whistle to start the game, we were about to find out. Gripping my bat, ready to hit the ball, but not feeling at all confident. I watched the ball as it flew towards me and swung the bat, missed, *damn it*. Running to the first base. The game was on.

Finally, the game was over, as our teacher blew her whistle again. We were all covered in mud; I seemed to be covered in more than the others. I had slid across the field, doing my best to get the ball. After an hour of laughing at ourselves, slipping and sliding the teacher gave up and sent us in. Usually I would skip the shower, but for once, I needed one, and was glad I had a towel in my bag.

Showered, changed and ready to head home, we chatted about the game and my skid across the grass, almost causing me to do the splits. They'd laughed at how I had not managed to hit one single ball. I nodded, in agreement; as usual, my mind had been elsewhere. They praised Wendy, who had hit three of hers and made it back to base. Of course, whatever team I was on, it was a rare thing for us to win. Wendy often told me I daydreamed far too much. She might be right, but I was not a sporty person, and to be fair I usually played better in team games. It was not my fault my daydreams seem to come to me when I should be concentrating on other things.

Pulling my bag over my shoulder, I raced down the steps, hoping that taking the shower had not cost me my ride home. Wendy had showered too. I had not meant to, but on passing her on the field, I had pulled her down onto the mud. Covering us both. It had taken us a few minutes to stand up, as we were laughing so hard.

I made my way down to the back of the bus with Wendy. Falling into our seats as it pulled away. Lifting my bag up onto my lap, searching inside, I removed my notebook, and began adding more to the larger ones. I changed to a green pen and added twirls to the page.

"Aww, that's lovely," Wendy teased.

"I can't help myself," I muttered. She had pulled out her latest novel and opened it to the page with the corner turned down and began to read. I continued to draw, knowing her lips would be moving as she read. It was something she always did. It amused me, and even though I had told her she did it, she never believed me. Looking up I saw her, catch her reflection.

"Told you."

"Oh my God, I do don't I?"

I nodded. "It's kind of cute."

"No it's not." She closed her mouth firmly shut.

"Okay, it's not." I offered to kick her in the shin if I saw her doing it, of course, she declined. I was joking, Wendy knew that, and chuckled as she turned her attention back to her book. She accused me of daydreaming, but she became sucked into her books, thinking about the blossoming romance of the young couples in them. We were very much alike, but our dreams came from different places. I liked reading, but rarely picked up a book, unless it was for school.

The bus pulled over at the first drop off point, and came to an abrupt stop. I stared out the window, one house caught my eye. Until then, I had forgotten all about Karen Langley. Scanning the rows of seats, I found her, two seats across from us, with her head down, hiding. She had a book in one hand, which I sensed she was using to shield her face. She attempted to join the others getting off the bus. I watched as she stumbled into the aisle and I gently elbowed Wendy.

"Am I doing it again?" she asked, looking up.

"No, look!" I said, gesturing over to Karen.

The bus fell silent as everyone realised it was her. Those heading off the bus, rushed off to escape. The rest of us were trapped. No one looked at her, except for one boy who stood at the front. He was collecting his bag. Karen stopped beside him and with her free hand pushed him. He landed on a girl sat at the front. Without stopping, Karen stormed off the bus. I opened my mouth to speak, but no words came. I watched her until she reached her house. I could not believe it, but then again I should not have been surprised, this was Karen all over. She could be so nasty.

I turned back in time to see another student help him off the girl. He then, quickly made his way off the bus.

~ *Karen* ~

I ran towards the house, and pulled out my key I kept in my purse, and desperately tried to put it in the lock. Why would it not go in? Taking a deep breath, I tried again. Finally, it slid in and unlocked. I pushed the door open and fell into the house. Slamming it shut behind me, I slipped down it. Grateful I was alone. As usual, my parents were not home. It was rare for them to be home before me.

I closed my eyes, before standing and running up to my room, where I knew I would be safe.

Dumping my things on a chair, kicking off my school shoes, I entered my bathroom. My nose felt sore and although I knew I should not do it, I had to. Leaning towards the mirror, I placed a finger on each side of the massive lump and squeezed. Pop. The pus hit the mirror, my stomach churned. *Gross*, I thought. Now the red spot was bleeding, surely it looked better now. How wrong was I? Instead, the spot bled and no make-up was going to cover it. No way in the world was I going to school, at least not until it had healed. My parents would never know; they left before I did, and arrived home after. Unless of course, the school contacted them, but would they care? Most likely not. That was it, I was staying home for a few days, at least until the spot healed enough to be covered by make-up.

I had of course overreacted on the bus, but the boy, whatever his name was, deserved it. I had a reputation to uphold. And, of course, Debbie had to be there to witness my meltdown.

Dabbing the spot with a tissue, I walked out of the bathroom and flung myself on my bed. Hoping it would look better in the morning, which reminded me of the comment Debbie made earlier. Nose job indeed, I was not my sister, Jackie, or my mother. I was perfect just the way I was.

~ *Debbie* ~

Twisting the handle on the door when I arrived home, I entered the hallway. Turning around almost knocking over my little sister Sally, as I closed the door. Her sweet face beamed up at me. I could not look her in the eye, not today. Her little fingers tugged on the hem of my coat as she dragged me into the front room, which had been recently decorated cream. Except the wall we stood opposite, it had a coal fire and a lick of rich red paint. Pointing at the painting lying on the wooden coffee table, I looked at Sally.

"Wow. Did you do that?" I asked, taking in the display of splattered red and green paint.

"Yes. I did!" she replied.

"It's brilliant." I patted her on the head, crouched down to her level. "When it's completely dry, I'll put it on the wall in the kitchen, okay?"

She nodded with a smile, her eyes lit up, reminding me once again how much she looked like Mum. I swallowed, thinking about her hurt, it made me remember everything, and the guilt returned.

"Debbie, it's not your fault. Please, stop thinking it is."

Little arms wrapped around my waist as far as they would reach, snapping me from my thoughts. I gave her a squeeze and kissed her softly on the top of her head. *Thanks, Joshua.* Sally pulled free; giggled and wiped away the kiss, before running off to play. I loved her dearly, yet looking at her still caused my heart to ache. Bless her she had no idea the effect she had on us. It was not her fault.

I sat on the sofa and admired my sister's artwork. Sighing, I slipped my backpack off and tossed it on my favourite chair and removed my shoes, wriggling my feet into my slippers. Standing, I went in search of my brother Steve and his wife, Carol. My shower could wait until later. I entered the kitchen and found Steve, flicked on the kettle, turning my back to him, my mind wandered once again. I squealed as he crept up behind me, and put me in a headlock. Laughing as he gently rubbed his knuckles on my head. I fought to free myself. My chest hurt from laughing so hard. Steve released his grip, setting me free. I should have seen that coming, he was a goofball, but he was a married man, too. Was it about time he grew up? I looked at him, wondering where his wife was. It had only been six months since the wedding and they were living with us, so they could save enough money for a deposit on their own place.

"She's at the doctor's," he replied.

I frowned; she had looked fine this morning. I knew there was a bug going around, and I for one did not want it. I assumed neither did Carol. "Is she okay?" I asked, concerned.

"Yeah, she's fine."

"Right!" If it was not a bug, I had an idea what she had gone for. I raised my eyebrows. Was he going to be a father soon? "Glad it's nothing serious," I said.

"It's not." Steve shook his head.

"Good," I paused, removing a mug from the cupboard, pouring milk into it. "You should go and pick her up. I mean now I'm home."

"Do you mind?"

"No, now scoot, besides I wouldn't have suggested it otherwise. Off you go," I said, gently pushing him towards the door. Some days, I liked having the house to myself, and Sally was no trouble you hardly knew she's there, so I could let my thoughts wander.

Chapter 9
Dream Invader

~ Debbie ~

It was not very often I was home alone, and I stood for a moment enjoying the silence, staring out of the kitchen window. Wrapping my hands around the mug of hot tea, I thought about getting the washing in, wondering if the rain would return. The clouds were darkening out there; the washing blew gently in the cool breeze. As the first droplet hit the window, the decision was made for me. I placed my mug into the sink, and dashed outside with the basket.

It took a few minutes to remove the damp clothes, and return them to the house. I hung the few pieces on the airer by the back door. I had many years of enjoyment using it for a tent. Now it was Sally's turn.

I returned to the kitchen and switched on the radio. Since my dad, Steve and Carol were out; I decided to make the evening meal.

As the radio played one of my favourite songs, my hand was on the door of the fridge and I froze staring at mum's picture. The last word I sung hung in the air as I looked into her eyes. Mum's praise replayed in head. I snapped my mouth shut, as the memory knocked the breath from my lungs. I rarely sang now; even though I knew that she would want me too. But it was our special thing. As I was looking at the picture of mum, I suddenly saw the white sheet they placed over her. I stepped backwards. Finding the wooden chair and slumped down into it. Focus, I told myself. Leaning forward, I rested my head on my arms, and closed my eyes, drifting off into my dream world.

I spin around to face Joshua. Lost in his eyes; yet easily distracted by his hair, which blows gently in the breeze.

"Debbie," he says. My heart misses a beat. My knees are weak as I listen to the sound of his voice. "Debbie," he repeats, but this time his voice sounds more like Sally's. This is odd, and I wonder why Sally is here? I spin around looking for her, but she is nowhere to be found. I turn back to Joshua, as he repeats my name in her voice. I tilt my head, feeling a nudge in my left side. What was that? I frown.

Opening my eyes, Sally stood with her arms crossed, and told me she was hungry. I handed her a small box of sultanas, which she opened and began to eat.

Fifteen minutes later, the meal was ready; I removed it from the oven, and set out plates for Sally and Greg, dished up and called them.

I pulled out a chair and helped Sally into her seat. Greg sat in the seat beside her, as I joined them; I tried not to look into Sally's eyes, but it was no good. She was so much like my mother. Pushing her image away, and willing that last image not to invade my head, but of course, I had no control over it. Closing my eyes, Joshua's face floated before me. I needed him. To be held in those strong arms. Blinking a few times, trying to keep the tears from falling, I called to him. *Joshua I need you.*

He stands before me and tilts his head as the breeze continues to toy with his hair. He takes my hand; the heat of his touch sends electric shocks through my whole body. My heart races, as he takes one-step closer to me. So close, I can feel the heat radiate off him. Any second now, I will be in those arms, resting my head on his shoulder. I step forward, my eyes on him, when I hit something, solid and red. He releases my hand, as I stumble back. Realising the red something is a someone. She turns to face me and smirks. Flicking her perfect hair over her shoulder as she moves closer to Joshua. I open my mouth to object. Peeling my eyes from him, I hear her cackle and turn her full attention back to him. My Joshua. I watch in horror, unable to move.

My dream vanished as Sally's voice brought me back to the present once again. *Thanks Sally, saved me from watching her take my man.*

I swallowed. "Sorry, would you like me to cut it up for you?" I asked.

Sally nodded. "Daddy home soon?"

"Yes, Daddy home soon." I repeated. She was so cute, as long as I did not look into those eyes.

"Daddy home soon," she repeated.

I nodded, watching Greg push the food around his plate. I knew he was hurting as much as the rest of us, and out of the blue things would set him off. I tried hard not to let him upset me with his cruel words. Greg was ten after all. He had lost her, too, I understood that, but I had witnessed her death, and watched her being pulled from the wreckage. I had been the one, and I was the reason.

"No, you are not, stop thinking like that," Joshua tells me.

"Go back to Karen," I snap. "Go on."

I did not mean it; I sighed, turning back to Greg, his eyes on the window watching the rain. The droplets hit the pane and trickled down to the base. I watched them for a moment, unable to look at him, without wanting to shake him. To snap him out of it, tell him it's all my fault, not his.

"Greg, are you okay?" I asked.

He ignored me. I understood his pain, and wished I could take it all away. If only I had taken the bus home. I looked at him; his eyes filled with tears. I fought to keep my own at bay. He was hurting, and needed our father more than ever. I wished he spent more time at home. I understood why he was not here, but we all missed her.

I ignored Greg's silence, praying he would not throw the plate across the room; it would not be the first time.

"Would you two like a drink?"

They both nodded. Just like that the moment passed. I moved

to the sink and poured squash in and then added water to two plastic glasses. Placing them on the table, I heard Carol and Steve return.

A check up, I smirked. *Yeah right, I had a feeling I was going to be an aunty soon, but I decided to keep it to myself.*

"Dad not back yet?" Steve asked.

"Not yet," I replied. "I've left the rest in the oven. Help yourself. Make sure you leave some for Dad, not that he'll eat it," I mumbled. He often played with his food too, like Greg. "Do you mind if I head up to my room?" I no longer felt hungry.

"Did you eat?" Carol asked.

"Yes." I lied. "I'll have an apple as afters," I added, removing a red one from the dish.

"Okay, and don't worry about cleaning up, we'll do it."

"Thanks," I hurried out of the kitchen, apple in hand.

I lay on my bed with the apple beside me. Moments ago, found I had soon devoured it. Maybe I was hungrier than I thought. Tossing the core in the bin, I intended to make a start on my homework, but my thoughts turned to Joshua. I lay back; staring up at him, taking in those dimples. Closing my eyes, I focused on where I had left him. Regardless of Karen being there, I attempted to push the girl far from my mind.

I watch Karen place her hand on Joshua's arm and pull him towards her. My mouth drops open. I tap my foot before moving forward, ready to reclaim him, just as the song changes. I stand behind her; worrying Joshua may prefer Karen to me. After all, she has a perfect figure, and that dress just proves it. Revealing she has an hourglass figure. I knew mine was not in the same league as hers.

Joshua places his hand on Karen's waist. I want him to push her aside and scoop me into his arms, but instead I witness him kiss her.

"No," I scream. 'Joshua'.

Hearing laughter in the kitchen, I returned to the real world. Even in my dreams, Karen I was a nasty piece of work. I sighed, and rolled my eyes. *Homework*, I reminded myself. Knowing my mind would wander again if I stayed where I was. Instead, I made the decision to go to Wendy's.

Opening my school bag, I slipped the books I needed in. On my way out, I popped my head around the living room door and told my father where I was going.

"Okay, Dad?"

"Of course," he replied, staring at the television. I knew he was not watching it.

Closing the door behind me, I walked over to Wendy's. Crossing the road, I passed Wendy's twin brothers, David and Dean. They were playing a game of football. The rain had let up, but the puddles were still on the ground. The ball rolled towards me, through a puddle, flicking up dirty water. I gently kicked it back to one of the boys. They thanked me, and continued their game.

Playing football in the road had been something their older twin brothers, Ryan and Ricky had done years before. Now they were all grown up with girlfriends, swapping playing childish games with necking in the back of the cinema.

I swung open the wooden gate and stepped inside their garden. I waved to the boys, knowing they would continue to follow in their brothers' footsteps. I was sure of that. I knocked on the open door, before entering.

"Hello, only me," I called out.

"In here, Debbie," Wendy replied.

Entering the living room, I found Wendy and her parents watching the news. The images flickered on the large television screen.

"Door was open!" I said. "Hi, Mr and Mrs Allan."

"Hello, Debbie. Take a seat, love!" Mrs Allan said.

"Thanks," I replied as I perched on the edge of the sofa. "I thought we could do our homework together, if you haven't already done yours?"

"No, not yet," Wendy replied. "We'll do it up in my room."

"How about I fix you two a snack?" Wendy's mother asked.

My stomach rumbled, reminding me just how hungry I was.

"I made a fresh batch of cookies, what do you say to a few of them?"

I smiled. She made the best cookies. I missed my mother's baking. Emma, Wendy's mother moved towards me and patted me lightly on my shoulder.

"Please tell me they're your chocolate chip cookies?" I enquired, biting my lip. They were my favourite. Mrs Allan knew that.

"Why, of course they are. Tell you what girls. You go upstairs and I'll bring them up with something to drink. Some squash, maybe?"

"Squash!" Wendy wailed.

"Okay. I think I may have some cans of pop, will they be okay, Wendy?" she asked as she walked towards the kitchen.

Wendy agreed that would be fine, and winked at me.

We thanked her as we made our way upstairs. Unlike my tidy room, I knew Wendy's would be a mess. Clothes lay on the floor, catalogues and magazines were strewn across the room. I helped her tidy up once, but three days later it returned to this state. I gave up.

"I cleaned up in here yesterday. Honest," she tried to tell me.

I knew her too well. I smirked, of course she had.

"'ll believe you. Come on," I said, moving across the floor, stepping over the piles. "We have homework to do."

"In a minute, I promise, but first my mum got that new tape I wanted. We could listen to it?"

"Sure," I said, picking up a pile of clothes and moving them to the left of me. A few minutes of distraction would not hurt.

The sound of our favourite band, N & N filled the room.

"Listen to this one. I love this one," Wendy said, turning the volume up.

The door swung open, and Wendy's mother carried in the tray of goodies she promised.

"Turn that down a little," her mother said, placing the tray on Wendy's desk. "And don't forget to do your homework." Emma looked around the room and shook her head. "One day I am going to come in here and be shocked that I can see the floor."

"Mum!"

"It's true. I don't know how you can sleep in here, in all this mess. You know when you're older you'll be like one of those hoarders?"

"I won't," Wendy said, defending herself.

"She might, don't you think, Debbie?"

"Maybe."

"Hey, you're supposed to be my best friend. I just like to keep things. I may need them again, you never know," Wendy said, rolling her eyes.

Her mother left the room and closed the door behind her.

I turned the music down, not wanting to upset Wendy's mother. Walking over to the desk, I removed one of the cookies and bit into it. "Mmm these are the best. I wish my mu—" the word mum stuck in my throat. I could not even say it, without choking on it. A single tear trickled down my cheek; I wiped it away and took a deep breath, blowing it out noisily. I saw Wendy staring at me. "I'm okay."

"Are you sure?"

"Yeah." I sighed. "I just wished she was still with us. I miss her so much."

"I know you do. She'll always be in here," she said, pointing to my heart. Wendy pulled me into a hug and held me tight.

"Thanks, it's just sometimes I think she'll walk through the door. You know what I mean?"

"I do," she said, releasing me.

"Thanks," I said, changing the subject, refusing to allow more tears to fall. "I wish I could make them as good as your mum does." I removed another from the plate.

"You will do. You're a much better cook than I am."

"Anyone's a better cook than you." I chuckled, stuffing more into my mouth. Wendy's cooking left a bad taste in the mouth. I never tried anything she made, unless we made it together. I could not work out what she did to food.

"Funny ha ha," she mumbled, knowing I spoke the truth. "I think we'd better get this homework done. Promise me you won't disappear into one of your daydreams?"

"I'll try not to," I said, meaning it. *You are always in my thought's Mum. I miss and love you, always,* I thought as I turned to face Wendy. She sat on her bed, ready to concentrate on the homework.

I brushed the crumbs from my mouth, took a long drink from the can, and then set it down, wiping my mouth. The next song began and I found myself singing along.

"I'd forgotten how good you were," Wendy said, standing, turning the music off.

"Thanks, I feel odd singing without her."

"I know, but you have a fantastic voice. Now if I could sing."

I nodded, if she could, she would never shut up. Even though she could not sing, it did not stop her. I picked up my pen, and opened my book.

"Guess we'd better get this homework done now," I said.

"Yeah, we should," she agreed.

Wendy lay on her bed, and made a start I lay on the floor, my feet swaying as I looked up at Wendy, she was already scribbling away. I grasped my pen tighter and began to write.

~ Karen ~

I heard the car approach the house; my parents were home. I stood at the window, watching them climb out and walk towards the house.

I could just make out their chatter as they went into the kitchen; not even calling out to see if I was home. Of course, I was home it was five past seven. Where else would I be?

I had fixed my own evening meal, a microwave dinner. I

could have cooked a homemade dinner, but not tonight. I was not in the mood to cook, and with this thing on my face, I was more than happy to hide out in my room.

My bag lay on the floor, the contents spilling out. I had homework to do, but it could wait. Since I had no intention of going to school the next day, I would take my time. I could spend an hour in the pool, and then do it, or whatever I liked. With no one here to watch over me, I could do as I pleased.

Chapter 10
Daydreams

~ Debbie ~

The next morning, not wanting to get up, just another few minutes lying in bed would not hurt. I closed my eyes, whispering his name.

"Joshua."

I see those eyes, reducing me to a puddle at his feet. He moves towards me. My knees shake. He holds out his hand and I gladly take it, allowing him to pull me towards him. I rest my head on his shoulder. My heart races as I look up at him, music starts to play as we move. I close my eyes, enjoying being close to him. I inhale: he smells nice. I open my eyes as the song changes. Light flashes in the distance, once, twice, and then dozens of times, blinding us. I realise they have found us, the paparazzi. He spins me again; I fly towards them, they catch me, arms hold me. I cannot break free. I struggle against them, and plead with Joshua to rescue me. When I see her, a face so familiar and hold my breath. As Karen takes his hand, and places it around her waist. She stands on her tiptoes, their lips inches apart. My mouth drops open.

Waking abruptly from my dream, I throw back the covers, and sit up. The dream instantly replays in my head. This should not be happening. Why did she keep invading my dreams? I was not about to let Karen have my man. These are after all my dreams. Miss Perfect better watch out.

Before dressing for school I set my bed straight and glanced at the photograph of mum. Sighing I crossed the room and stood before my mirror, staring at my reflection, I put my hair into a ponytail. I turned sideways; pulling my tummy in and sticking out my slow growing bust. It was time to get my very first bra, but asking dad was out of the question. I was gonna ask mum about buying my first one. As I took a deep breath I allowed Joshua's face to swim before my eyes. I moved towards the door and made my way downstairs to the kitchen.

I stood waiting for the bus, my dream still fresh on my mind; I wondered if I should tell Wendy about it? No, she already thought I was mad for daydreaming about him. If she knew, Karen was invading my dreams too. What would she say, then?

It was not until we reached the school, I realised Karen had not boarded the bus.

"I wonder where she is?" someone asked.

I wondered if anyone really cared where she was. Did I? No.

~ Karen ~

I had eaten breakfast and now sat on the edge of the pool, my feet in the water. I looked up at the window, the sky outside looked grey. I had a feeling the rain would fall again. I was grateful I was home all day and could enjoy the warmth of our heated pool. Slipping into the water I swam to the other side. Placing my arms on the edge of the pool, pushing my hair out of my eyes, and wiping the water from my chin, I knew staying home had been the right decision. I had plans for the rest of the day, watching a few movies, and maybe doing my nails.

Staring at my reflection in the mirror the following morning. I covered the spot with foundation even though the spot was just a tiny pinprick. As my parents' car roared to life, I watched them drive away.

Once again, they didn't stop and say good-bye. I should be used it by now. I had intended to go to school, but as one tear fell then another, more raced down my face. Soon I was sobbing, unable to stop. I threw myself onto my bed and cried until my chest ached.

~ *Debbie* ~

Tuesday morning arrived and with that came my favourite lesson, Drama. The door to the drama room was open, but no one was sure if we should enter.

Stephanie marched to the front, and entered, everyone else followed her in. The room was empty apart from a few chairs lined up against the back wall. Mrs Duncan entered the room from the cupboard she used as an office and removed a seat down from the back wall, and sat on it.

"Morning class." She smiled, scanning the room. "As you know, we have the end of year musical coming up."

Musical, I had intended to audition last year, but with the talent so high, I chickened out. Could I be tempted to join this time? Time would tell. Mrs Duncan continued.

"So, if anyone wishes to sign up. You need to do so as soon as possible."

The noise level rose again, as we discussed the musical. Mrs Duncan raised her hand, which silenced us instantly. "Now, I have your attention again we'll proceed. Simon, take these and hand them out."

Simon stood; I watched him as he flicked his head, sending his wavy blond hair out of his green eyes. He did as instructed, taking the sheets from Mrs Duncan. He handed me one, and I studied it.

"Everyone got one?"

A loud reply of 'yeses' filled the room.

"Good. I thought we could get you guys worked up ready for those who want to audition. Now, I want you to act out the scenes in groups of four, and we will then perform it to the rest of the class at the end."

I looked back down at the piece of paper in my hand, as the others in the class began to discuss who they would be grouped with. I looked over to Wendy, secretly hoping I would be with my best friend, but knowing my teacher that would not be the case.

"Not now!" she bellowed, taking me by surprise. I watched her take a deep breath, before speaking again, "I will tell you when."

We all fell silent; I looked down at the piece of paper once again. I really wanted to be with Wendy, it made the lesson more fun. Instead, Mrs Duncan informed us we would each be given a number, and that would determine who we would be with. *Great,* which meant it was unlikely I would be in the same group as Wendy. I heard the others groan, feeling the exact same way I did. Wendy sat motionless; I knew she dreaded being with anyone else.

I prayed I would not be with any of Karen's cronies. Musicals were my favourite. Grease, being at the top of my list, but teamed with them would be no fun at all. I waited for Mrs Duncan to tell me the number I would be assigned.

Luck was on my side; Mrs Duncan gave me the number three, and none of Karen's cronies were in my group. Sighing I made my way over to my group, and we set to work on the lines. I looked over to Wendy. She looked uncomfortable. I however was in my element. I would not allow my mind to wander.

Without Wendy, I knew I could not let myself think of Joshua. Not even for a second.

Half an hour later, the bell rang, ending our rehearsals.

The teacher clapped her hands together and told us we had done well, and we would be carrying on next lesson. Standing, I pulled on my coat, and joined Wendy by the door.

"Glad that's over," she said. "But you looked like you enjoyed that."

I had, it was true. "Yeah, it was fun."

Wendy pushed the doors open and I followed her out. Once in the corridor, I pulled out my timetable, reminding myself what lesson we had next. I let out a long sigh, *Maths, brilliant.* A lesson I was not in the mood for. We made our way across the school towards the Maths block.

Reaching the classroom, we joined the queue and waited for our teacher to let us in. I stuffed the timetable back in my bag, pulling out a bottle of water. I placed the lid back on, as the door swung open and Mr Savoy told us to enter. One at a time, we climbed the metal steps, which led to the classroom and slumped into our seats. I fumbled in my bag searching for my book; I found it and placed it on the desk, adding my pencil case beside it.

"Come on now, quietly please," he said, sternly as the rest entered the classroom.

I watched him from my seat as he stood before the class and peered at us from over the top of his glasses, which rested on the end of his nose.

"You can put your books back in your bags," he informed us, smirking.

I let out a groan, not liking the sound of this. We all did as instructed.

"I have a surprise for you," he announced.

A surprise? I really did not like the sound of that.

"Yes, you're going to have a test," he said.

"Sir, we haven't revised for this!" one of the boys said.

"I know that's the point," he declared, clearly happy with himself.

I looked over to Wendy and frowned. Her pencil held firmly in her hand, as she nibbled on the tip. Usually I would escape to my dreams, especially in Maths, but not today, and never in a test, especially a surprise test.

Mr Savoy handed out the papers, placing them upside down on our desks, before heading back to his. He sat down and smiled. "Okay, you have thirty minutes from." He paused. "Now."

I glanced up at the clock, half an hour; surely we were entitled to more time. I quickly looked around the room. Everyone else had begun to write. I took a deep breath, and then made a start on my own paper. Only looking up when Mr Savoy announced we had ten minutes left.

I put my pencil down; he collected the papers before allowing us to leave. I dreaded the results, sighing as I placed my things back into my bag.

We both stood and made our way out of the classroom, my head down, with equations running through it. I hated maths. Now my head was full of it. I willed Joshua to take them away, and lock the information up, until I needed it again. Which I hoped would not be for some time. We left his classroom, and made our way towards the field.

We sat down on the grass, I removed my lunch and perched it on my lap, clearing my throat, turning to Wendy I had been meaning to ask her for days, but had not had the courage to do so.

Knowing that there would be no easy way to ask Wendy, I swallowed, "Wendy, can I ask you something?"

"Sure!"

"Are you wearing a bra?"

Wendy's face turned red, "Sorry, maybe I should have talked to you about this at your house or mine."

"No, it's okay, and yes, I am. You're not?" she said frowning.

"I had planned to ask...and you know it's just something that I can't ask my dad" as I shook my head. I wanted Joshua to swoop down and take me away.

Wendy had her hands on her lap as she began to talk, "Tell you what, we could go together, if you want?"

Liking the sound of that, and turning to face her again; "Would You?"

"You Know I will, Debbie!"

I sighed, knowing that I wouldn't have to ask dad or Carol to take me to buy my first bra.

Finally, the last lesson the day arrived. Sitting in the classroom looking out the window, mesmerized by a young man in the field; I had no idea who he was, or why he was even there. Yet, I focused on him, paying no attention to Mr Banks, the Geography teacher as he waffled on. I could not take my eyes of him; he had familiar wavy brown hair. I allowed my mind to wander.

I perch on the ledge of the open window, watching him as he walks across the field. His hair blowing in the wind with each step he takes. He lifts his head and catches my eye. I wave. He nods. I smile, as I watch him beckon me down. He does not have to ask me twice. I sprint to the door and tear down the steps. The corridors are empty. Of course they would be, everyone else is in class, where I should be. I reach the double doors; open them as the wind hits me in the face. Joshua is a few feet from me as I race towards him…

"Debbie," a voice whispered in my ear.

I felt someone gently nip my arm, snapping me out of my daydream. I sat up, looked at Wendy and mouthed the word thank-you to her. I had done it again; I looked out into the field. The young man had gone.

I turned my attention back to the teacher as he continued to explain how map skills would be useful. I doubted they would be, and was thankful when the bell rang telling us the lesson and day was over.

It had been the best day I'd had in months, even after a boring Geography lesson and a Maths test. It was no wonder I drifted off. Half the class wore the same expression. At least I had not snored in class, like one of the boys had. He had been frogmarched to the head teacher's office. I needed to be careful.

Chapter 11
Arriving In The UK

~ Mark ~

The plane hit the tarmac with a thud, waking me from my dream. I wiped the sleep from my eyes as I landed in the UK, and wondered if my grandparents would remember me. I had not seen them since the age of ten. Now, being thirteen, I had grown a few feet taller, my hair longer, much to my mother's disgust. It was acceptable for my cousin. He could do as he pleased. How many times my mother insisted I cut my hair, but I chose to keep it long.

Now here in the UK I may decide to have it cut, for me and no one else.

I was nervous, for a few reasons, but starting a new school was the main one. I was a Hobson, and my parents told me I would succeed at whatever I decided to do, including starting another new school.

I stood, waiting for the passenger sat beside me to exit the seats.

Pulling down my overnight bag, a green backpack, I followed the last few passengers off the plane. My feet hit the ground, the cool temperature bit at my arms. The sun had been shining back home, now I felt the goose pimples rise on my arms. I would have to seek out a sweater, before travelling any further.

I pulled the sweater on and waded through the tourists, those arriving home from vacations and business trips. I collected my two suitcases and walked out the gates to find my grandparents.

Entering the terminal along with the crowds, I felt my cheeks redden as I saw my name in large black letters on a white piece of card, which they were waving over their heads.

I rolled my eyes. *Welcome to the UK.*

~ Debbie ~

I lay on my bed, staring up at Joshua, as the aroma of the evening meal drifted up the stairs.

A gust of wind toys with my hair, running my fingers through the sand. The scenery is beautiful. I sit up; scan the beach, and there he is. He walks towards me, dressed in a pair of royal blue shorts. His bare chest glistens in the sun's rays. I cannot take my eyes off him.

"Tea's ready," my father called, taking me from my dream.

"Coming," I sighed.

Opening the door to the kitchen, I eyed the large oven dish, which overflowed with minced meat and onion, topped with mashed potato. My stomach rumbled. We ate our first meal as a family. Had things really moved that far forward already? On one hand, I was happy we were all eating together, but it also hurt.

The seat, which was once occupied by my mother, remained empty.

"Smells good, Dad," I said, and meant it.

Later that evening, I arranged to meet Wendy outside mine. The wind was warmer than it had been for days. Leaving our coats hanging on the wall. We climbed on our bikes; setting off down the street.

Riding towards the park, taking us past Karen's house. Reaching her driveway, Karen stormed out, placing her hands on her hips. She must have seen us coming.

"You better watch your backs?" she snorted.

"Why?" I asked.

"You know why! Besides this street, is my street!"

I looked up and down the street; it was nothing like where we lived.

I sighed. "This may be where you live, but you don't own the road!"

"Well, you two have a nerve coming down here."

"Why?" I asked.

"You—" She pointed her finger at me. "You know why!"

"Right," Wendy said.

I could have answered.

Karen narrowed her eyes, glaring at us. Her mouth opened to say more, just as a large black jeep pulled up into their driveway. I watched as the door flung open and an attractive young woman climbed out, waving over at us.

Karen rolled her eyes. "Damn it, Jackie. Not now," she said, gritting her teeth.

"Who's that?" Wendy inquired.

"Is that?" I began, recognising her. It couldn't be, could it?

"None of your business. Why don't you two just go away."

If she was Jackie, she had grown into a stunning looking woman. The look on Karen's face, told me she was. I hadn't seen Jackie for years.

Noticing her hospital pass clipped to her blouse, I could only assume she worked there.

"Hello girls. Is that you, Debbie?" she asked. "My you've gotten tall." She paused. "I am sorry to hear about your mum."

I opened my mouth to speak, but words failed me.

"Are you girls going on a bike ride?" she asked, looking from us to Karen.

Surely, she knew we were not friends any more. We remained rooted to the spot, holding onto our bikes, I forced myself to smile, and nodded.

"Are Mum and Dad in the house?"

Karen nodded.

"We best be off," I said, not wanting to talk about the old days.

"You're not going with them?" Jackie asked. "Why don't you

run along like a good little girl and get your bike. I'm sure your friends will wait."

Karen looked at Jackie and mumbled something we did not catch, before she raced to the house. Slamming the door shut behind her.

Jackie looked at us. "Something I said?" Shaking her head, she continued. "Nice to see you again, Debbie. Please send my condolences to your father and the rest of the family."

I nodded and looked over at Wendy.

Jackie said good-bye and walked towards the house.

~ *Karen* ~

I slammed the door hard behind me, knowing my mother would rush to welcome good old perfect Jackie. I entered the kitchen, grabbed a drink from the fridge and made my way to the living room. I stopped in the corridor, as I watched her enter the house. My mother ushered her inside the living room. Something was up and I had no intention of going up to my room. I followed them in, half expecting them to close the door before I could enter. They paid no attention to me.

Jackie sat perched on the edge of the brand new sofa. My mother decorated this room annually, changing the furniture to suit the new décor.

It had taken two years for them to get to my room. After all, I had outgrown the 'My Little Pony' wallpaper.

I considered heading up to my room, but if I left now they would not tell me the news Jackie was bursting to share with them. I fell into the large chair, waiting for the news to erupt from my sister's mouth.

"Your father won't be long, he's just finishing up a call in his office," our mother announced.

Jackie sighed; neither my sister nor mother spoke or paid any attention to me.

Swinging my feet and clicking my fingers did nothing to distract them. I thought about the day Jackie moved out and hoped they would finally take notice of me, but that never happened.

Instead, my mother redecorated Jackie's room, two months after she moved out, and turned it into her office. She filled it with all her favourite things, including a family photo, a rare picture, as I was in it too. One we had posed for over ten years ago. Why had she bothered to place that one there? Guilt I expected. The rest were of Jackie and all she had accomplished. Had I really disappointed my parents that much?

Jackie had not lived at home for months, having bought a small place near the hospital where she worked. Visiting us regularly, and as usual, she was the centre of attention the moment she stepped into the house. I hated her.

The door swung open, our father bounded in, and joined our mother on the sofa and took her hand in his. He nodded at Jackie, who lit up like a Christmas tree.

"Come on, Jackie, you can spill the beans now. He did, didn't he?" Saffron, our mother said.

"Yes, mother!" she screeched.

"Oh my goodness! When?"

"Next year. We need time to plan and--"

"Yes, we do! I think we should open that bottle of champagne your father has been saving for such an event," our mother said. "Show me the ring!" she insisted.

Jackie's eyes widened as she held out her hand. Our parents peered at the ring. Our mother hugged Jackie. She had not held me like that, since before I started high school, three years ago.

Released from our mother's grasp, Jackie sat back and admired the ring. Slipping forward on my seat, waiting for her to show me, of course, she ignored me. What did I expect?

"Can I--" I began, our mother interrupted me.

"We're so proud of you, Jackie, first training as a doctor, and now you're to marry a surgeon." our mother paused. "I'll go get the glasses!" She stood and left to fetch them.

I perched on the edge of the seat as my family ignored me. I would have liked to see the ring, after all Jackie was my sister. Most sisters bonded and shared everything. Then again, Jackie was older than I was, and never had any time for me. Why should now be any different?

She continued staring at her ring, fiddling with it.

Our mother returned with the glasses, smiling. I slid back on the sofa, crossing my arms, staring at the wall.

I wanted for nothing living here, except their attention. Would I ever get that?

Jackie sat back, her hands on her lap; the ring on show for all to see, not that I was one bit interested in seeing it now. No, she could go to hell. Jackie made it clear I would play no part in their celebrations. Should I make my way to my room? I knew they would not notice if I did.

"We have to celebrate tonight. Don't you think, dear?" my father said, pouring out the champagne into three glasses.

"We should," my mother agreed. "Invite Dean and his parents, we'll make this the first of many. We have a lot to arrange. Dresses to shop for, cakes to taste," my mother babbled.

"Yes there is," Jackie stood, smoothing down her trousers. "I'll phone him now."

"Use this phone; I'll use the one in my office to book the table." He placed his drink down on the coffee table.

Jackie downed the remainder of hers and picked up the phone.

"Hi," Jackie began. I rolled my eyes. "Yes, they're over the moon. I think so...my parents thought it would be a good idea, if we went out for a meal tonight. Do you think your parents would come?" Jackie nodded. "I'll tell him to book a table for six, yes for six." Jackie paused. "No. We don't need her there, do we? This is about us--" Jackie sighed. "Dean, she'd be bored, besides she has plenty to do here. She could have her friends over."

I could not believe what my sister was saying. My bottom lip trembled as I heard her dismiss me just like that. *It's as if I don't exist.* I looked at my mother, her eyes fixed on Jackie. *They all ignore me, but more than usual when Jackie is here.*

Jackie re-joined our mother on the sofa as I stood, picked up my drink and slipped out of the door. Making my way up to my room, it was the only place where I could escape. My parents rarely came in here, and I liked it that way.

I opened the door and slammed it shut; using my foot. Stomping across the floor, I made my way to my double bed and dived onto it. Lying face down, tears slid down my cheeks. I heard their excited raised voices downstairs.

~ *Debbie* ~

We giggled as we set off, peddling towards the park. Out of breath, Wendy said.

"You didn't tell me her sister was stunning!"

"She wasn't. At least not the last time I saw her," I replied, picking up pace as we reached the park's entrance.

"I guess we all know what Karen will be when she grows up!" Wendy said, propping her bike up against a tree. I placed mine beside it, as Wendy handed me the ball, as she got into position with the bat.

"Ready?" she asked.

I nodded. Throwing the ball in the air and attempting to catch it, and missed. I picked up and took aim, and then tossed the ball towards her. Wendy hit all three balls, we then switched places. I missed all three. We continued to switch back and forth until the last ball flew past me, and landed in front of a group of girls.

Together we made our way to retrieve it. When we reached the group of girls, it was then we realised, they were Karen's cronies.

One of the girls, Tracey, scooped the ball up and put it in her bag.

"Can we have our ball back?" I asked.

"Your ball? Haven't seen it," she said, shaking her head. "Have you girls?"

"Forget it, Debbie. It's only a ball. Let's go." Wendy said, tugging me by the arm.

"That's right. Listen to her; now run along to your Mummies."

My mouth fell open, my heart raced, as I stared at Stephanie, she nodded, a huge smile spread across her face. Who was she trying to be, Karen? Trying to take her place? Not that Karen would allow that, yet her words stung. I did my best to hold back the tears, clenching my fist.

"What! You gonna hit me are you?"

I continued to stare at her.

"I don't think you have the balls," she informed me.

"No," I began.

"I do," Wendy said, moving forward.

"Wendy, it's fine."

Wendy stepped back.

I swallowed. "No, I'm not going to hit you, I don't need to."

"Really?"

"No."

Stephanie stepped towards me, I held my ground. I had done nothing wrong, yet she moved closer smirking.

"Go on, then," I dared her.

"Not today, next time, I'll get you next time."

I nodded. All talk, most girls like her were.

"Why don't you run home, like good little girls."

"We will, and then we'll have cookies and milk, too." I added sarcastically.

I felt their eyes on us, as we mounted our bikes. My heart hammered inside my chest the whole time. I sounded a lot braver than I felt. I peddled as fast as my feet would allow.

"Debbie!" Wendy called as I sped off.

"What!"

"Slow down."

"Sorry," I replied, as she reached my side. My heart slowed down too.

We rode towards Karen's street, debating whether to take that route or another. As it was getting late, we chose to ride pass Karen's. Passing her house, something made us both stop. We stared at the house from the end of their drive; and witnessed her parents hugging Jackie.

"Wonder what's going on in there?" I asked.

"No idea," Wendy said.

I shook my head, and pushed forward, as we raced each other home.

Arriving home, Wendy won.

~ *Karen* ~

It took over an hour for them to remember me. In that time, they had all changed ready to go out for their meal.

I guessed my mother would be wearing her new dress; the one with the plunge neckline, and spaghetti straps. My mother knew how to look good and spent as much time as she could on her appearance. Every week she insisted on having her hair and nails done, and once a month, she spent a weekend at a health spa.

At the age of fifty-five, my mother was attractive, looking younger than all the mums at the school. She did have the best surgeon in town, her husband, and my father.

My mother had often been mistaken for Jackie's older sister, which my mother loved. My father loved it more. He too had cosmetic surgery. And why not since he owned the practice where their procedures were being carried out. With all the work my mother had done, she was a walking advert for his surgery.

Jackie got her looks from our mother, which meant she needed a nose job at eighteen and six months later, a boob job. I was lucky; I took after my father's side, and everything was natural. I would never allow my body to go under the knife.

A sound in the hallway told me someone was outside my door. It opened and my mother stood in the doorway with her hands on her hips; it was very rare to see her up here, which is why it startled me at first.

"Ah, there you are?" my mother said.

"Where else would I be?"

"Have you been crying?"

"No. I had something in my eye," I lied.

"Well let me have a look!"

"It's gone; I don't need a doctor or the secretary to one."

"There is no need to be so cheeky, young lady," she said, taking one-step inside my room. "Since you disappeared I thought it was best to inform you, we're going to dine out to celebrate."

I nodded. I had been in the room, when they discussed it, had she already forgotten I was there too.

"Now," my mother continued. "I've left you some money by the phone. Order something in if you like; you may invite one of your friends over."

As my mother turned to leave not saying goodbye, I nodded my head again.

As I waited for them to leave, I made my way to my bedroom window. My father only drove his pride and joy Jag on special occasions or on Sunday mornings. Tonight was no exception, five minutes later, they all climbed in and drove away.

~ *Mark* ~

"Mark, oh come here, let me look at you. Oh, my goodness you have grown into such a handsome young man," my nan gushed.

I groaned. Grandparents could be so embarrassing.

"So, tell me all about your trip here?" Vic, my grandfather inquired.

I thought about what to say, as we approached the waitng cab.

"Where's your old pickup-truck?" I asked, recalling the last time we had visited. Travelling in his old pickup-truck, Betty had to be one of the highlights of the stay.

"Oh my goodness, you're remember Betty."

"Yeah."

"Well sadly, your grandma made me sell her, something to do with me not being safe on the road. Tsk."

"No," Alice, my nan interrupted. "It was not safe for everyone else on the road."

"So you say."

Vic opened the back door, allowed my nan to climb inside, and closed it behind her. "Truth is, even though I'd had old Betty a long time, these old eyes ain't what they once were. Don't tell your nan," he said with a wink.

I nodded, as my nan from the back seat winked over at me. Maybe staying with them, would not be as bad as I had first thought.

Suitcases in the trunk, the cab drove us to their hometown.

Chapter 12
A Fine Young Man

~ Karen ~

I continued watching the Jag, until I could no longer see the taillights of his beloved car. A tear trickled down my cheek as I stood alone in the house. I wiped it away, angry with myself for allowing them to make me cry. I was strong and happy, and rarely, no, I never cried.

Looking around my room; I had everything a girl could wish for, and more. I have my own bathroom, a living room with a sofa and a large television; and a wardrobe full to the brim with clothes. I knew they tried to buy me, and I allowed it, but only because it was the only attention I got.

I wiped away the tears, closed the handmade curtains and made my way to the desk where my phone sat. I snatched it up, calling my friend's number. Each button brought me closer to a night of fun. Stephanie answered after two short rings. Inviting her over for the night, she instantly accepted.

I hung up, and slid open the door of my wardrobe. They moved smoothly on the runners as I chose an outfit to wear. One I had seen in my favourite magazine and just had to have. The jeans were designer; the top matched perfectly, made in a velvet material.

I laid them on the bed, and made my way to the bathroom and switched on the shower.

Showered, dried and dressed, I applied make-up, before slipping my feet into a pair of my sister's old heeled shoes. A pair Jackie had never worn, purchasing them just because she could. The pair I had wanted and begged for. I had already spent my allowance, but wanted them badly. Jackie knew that, and bought them to rub my nose in it. She gloated at how she bought them in the sale. Without trying them on at the time, but once home, she did, and it was then, she realised she had picked the wrong size. With a grunt, she tossed them in the bin outside.

I could not let them go to waste, that evening even though it was not my job, and would normally protest about taking the rubbish out, I agreed to do so. I hid them, ready to collect the next day. They had remained hidden in my room, and tonight was the first chance I had to wear them.

Studying my reflection in the mirror, I spun around inspecting the outfit. *Looking good*, I thought, taking a deep breath, and stuffing the money my parents left me in my bag. Taking the stairs two steps at a time. *I'll enjoy tonight. Thanks Mum, Dad, Jackie and her Fiancé, what's his name.*

Hearing the doorbell, my company had arrived. I opened it, Stephanie stood smiling back at me; she wore jeans and a silk blouse with a jean jacket over the top. We told each other how good we looked. She was right I did look good. I smacked my lips together and suggested we head out.

We made our way to the pre-ordered taxi, climbed inside, and told the driver our destination, and then we were on our way. My parents assumed I would stay home, order take-away, but I had other plans.

The club was busier than I had expected, but now we had arrived, I was not in the mood. Yet, we joined the long queue.

"I can't believe this line, can you? " I said, hoping she might suggest we go elsewhere.

"I know," she said. "I mean we could try and jump the queue."

I had thought about doing that, and then I spotted two good-looking guys. Placing a smile on my lips, together we sauntered over to them.

Dream World

"Hi," I purred. "I'm so sorry; I thought you were someone else!" I stuttered, knowing that sounded like the worse pick up line ever.

"Hi," Stephanie said, fluttering her eyes.

"Hi," one of the two boys said.

"Would you like to join us?" his friend asked.

"If you insist," I purred, thinking the night may not be too bad after all.

We slotted ourselves between the guy and his friend.

"So, do you two come here often?"

"Odd weeks," I informed him. "I'm Karen and this is Stephanie."

"Tom and he's Ryan."

The doorman allowed us to enter. We followed them inside, and then to the bar. We ordered cokes, since alcohol was bit served on the under eighteens night.

I watched the dancers as I sipped my drink. Stephanie handed me hers, dragging Ryan onto the dance floor.

"Do you want to?"

"Dance?" I asked. "Maybe later. So Tom, you look like you work out, a lot!"

"Oh I do, three times a week. My father owns a gym."

"I can see that," I said, feeling his biceps.

"I spend hours in the gym."

Tom continued to talk about himself. Nodding
hoping they were in all the right places. *Oh, my God this guy talks about nothing but himself.*

"Shall we dance now," I asked, downing the last of my drink. *Anything to stop you talking.*

We joined the others. Noticing a mirror behind us, it was not long before he checked himself out. Was he that vain?

I rolled my eyes and turned my attention to a guy beside me, our bodies briefly touching as we moved in time to the music. I turned, saw his eyes sparkle and without warning, his lips were on mine, but not for long. I discovered Tom had pulled him off me. Then a fight broke out between them. I slinked off the dance floor. Boys were so predictable.

Finding Stephanie, we left, laughing all the way to the kebab shop.

"Oh my god, did you see that?"

"What the hell did you do?" Stephanie asked.

"Nothing." He was more interested in his own reflection, I informed her. She shook her head. We ordered, ate, and made our way home.

We crashed on the sofa in my living room. Lying her head back, Stephanie belched, *classy girl.*

"You know a night out with you is never dull."

"You can say that again. It's not like Tom was really interested in me. Not until that guy stuck his tongue down my throat."

"I know. I saw him lunge at you."

"I had no time to react," I said, defending kissing him back. "Okay he was cute, but come on. I don't think that was called for, do you?"

"No, but put it this way, it's a night neither of us will forget in a hurry."

"Don't think I'll be going back there for a few weeks." I chuckled.

"I agree." She yawned. "I'm shattered. Think I'm ready to go to sleep."

"Me, too. I'll get your blankets."

Removing them from the hall cupboard, I heard my parents and sister return. Their voices travelled up the stairs.

"I think you made a wonderful choice, he is perfect and his parents..." their voices trailed off as they entered and shut the living room door.

I sighed, walked to my room, handing Stephanie the bedding before climbing into my bed. *Think about something else,* I told myself, but nothing came to mind.

Dream World

~ Debbie ~

I entered my room and climbed into bed, pulling the duvet up to my chin. Closing my eyes, thinking how going to bed was my favourite time of the day. Being able to escape and join Joshua in my dream world. I snuggled further beneath the duvet, opening my eyes and took one final quick look up at his face on the poster.

The warm breeze blows the sand gently around my toes as I walk along the beach, scanning the water and sand for him. I see gleaming bronze-skinned bodies lying upon the sand. I feel my sunglasses slip down my nose, when I realise they are all female. Feeling the wind against my skin, I notice I am wearing a two-piece suit. My flat chest lost in the top half. My heart races as I look desperately for something to cover my child-like body. I spot a towel lying on the sand; snatch it up and wrap it around myself. In unison, the women all stand and look at me. They point and laugh. I step back, my mouth open, I close and open my eyes willing them to disappear. Every face morphs into Karen. They part to reveal a young toned man walking towards me.

'No, please not now'.

I pull the towel up to my chin; step backwards and lose my balance. I feel myself falling in slow motion down onto the soft sand with a thud.

I awoke, feeling my body jump beneath my sheets as I left my dream. Once again, Karen had invaded them. It was time to take a hold of my dreams; after all, they were mine. Wiping sleep from my eyes, I peered at my clock; it was six-thirty, far too early to be awake, but I knew I would not go back to sleep. I yawned, stretching my arms above my head, in one movement swinging my legs over the side of the bed, and placing my feet straight into my slippers. I padded across the room and stopped at my window, suppressing another yawn. I still felt tired and thought about climbing back into bed, but instead, looked out the window over to Wendy's house. Her curtains were closed.

Meaning she was not up yet. The sky looked clear and bright. I slipped my dressing gown on, tying it in a knot. I took the stairs two at a time, reaching the last step; my brother Steve entered the hallway.

"Morning Steve, it's a beautiful day!" I said.

"Sure is." he nodded.

I made my way down the hall and entered the kitchen. Slipping the tips of my fingers onto the side of the kettle, and flicking it on. While the water bubbled furiously, I pulled a cup from the cupboard, dropped a teabag in and added a splash of milk.

Ten minutes later, I pulled my bag up onto my shoulder, slamming the front door behind me. Wendy was already standing at the bus stop. I checked the road was clear, crossing the road, I joined her.

"Morning," we said, in unison.

"Ready for round two?" I asked. I was not looking forward to it, but I had a feeling we were in for more tests.

"Round two?" Wendy frowned.

"I assume we'll be having more tests today."

"Oh, no, please don't tell me that, we have R.E first thing."

"I know, let's just pray he's back. After all there is only one reason we pay attention in R.E."

"Mr Travis," we said, together.

"Yeah, you really have to start taking notes, instead of watching him all lesson."

"Moi?" Wendy said, placing one hand on her heart.

"Yeah, you!" I chuckled.

"I'll try," Wendy promised.

She may have promised, but I knew her. Many of us had a crush on him. Even though he isn't Joshua. He still is a very good looking man. I found it hard to concentrate in his lessons. Which is why I always made notes to refer to later. Plus I shared them with Wendy.

The second bell of the morning rang; our form tutor excused us.

We entered the corridor, and made our way to our first lesson, with Mr Travis. We arrived in plenty of time, not wanting to be late, and praying Mr Miles was not standing in again.

The door opened, I sighed with relief as he told us to enter. We hurried inside; I noticed those kind eyes, which made the girls swoon. I caught Wendy gazing at him, her eyes shining. It was my turn to nudge her back into the real world.

"Good morning class, I can see you are all happy to have me back" he said, taking a seat on the desk at the front of the class.

Everyone nodded as we took our seats and replied, "Morning."

I placed my bag on my lap and removed my books, unable to take my eyes off of Mr Travis as I laid them on the desk. I noticed how his blue eyes sparkled; he smiled as he walked down the aisle of the room. As he stopped at our desk, both Wendy and I looked up into his eyes.

"Wendy," he began. I turned to face her, as she turned crimson. "Would you take out your books, please?" he asked.

I did my best not to giggle at her embarrassment. She would never have done that to me. I tried my best to keep a straight face, holding in the laugh that really wanted to escape, as she dove under the table in search of her bag.

"Who needs who now?" I whispered, her eyes shot up at mine and she stuck her tongue out, rolling her eyes, her face remained red.

He turned his attention back to the class as he walked towards the front, and perched on his desk. Wendy shrunk down in her seat and listened to his every word. I hoped she would make notes, but her pen remained on the desk. I lifted mine ready, as he addressed the class.

"Right, now I have everyone's attention. I thought it was best to inform you, that we will be going over a few of the things we have already learnt for a test on--"

"Oh no," groaned some of the other students.

I joined them. *I knew it.*

The last session ended. Chairs scraped on the floor as we followed the others out of the classroom and into the corridor. I followed Wendy, passing the Drama room. The wall outside it had been covered in posters. I stopped and looked at the wall where the latest list for the drama club had been posted. *Should I sign up? I don't think I'm ready. Was I ever going to be?*

~ Mark ~

Three days later, I lay on my bed in my new room. Much smaller than I was used to, but it would do. After all, I only planned to be here for the next year. Even I could manage that. School on the other hand would be another matter. I would take each day as it came. I did choose to come to the UK. I knew it had been the right decision, but it just did not feel like it, not yet. It had only been three days, and I had not left my grandparents' house.

A light tap on the door alerted me either my nan or grandfather was on the other side.

"Come in," I called. As the door opened, my nan entered the room.

"Hi, just wondered what you fancied for your tea tonight?"

"Oh, I'll eat whatever you cook!"

"Oh, that's good to hear. Even if I serve up liver and onion, it's your grandfather's favourite."

I wrinkled up my nose that sounded gross, how anyone could eat liver; I could not hide my disgust for my grandfather's favourite meal.

"Thought as much," she began. "Tell you what, we'll have a little chat about what you do like and then we can do some shopping."

I nodded. I hated shopping, food shopping anyway. However, I could spend hours looking at new outfits and charging them to my card. My parents allowed me to spend my allowance on whatever I wanted. The same rules applied while I was in the UK, but there was no way I was going to make myself out to be the rich kid in school. I wanted to be accepted for being me, Mark Hobson. I would not need much money here, I had a closet full of clothes and shoes, and my parents were paying my grandparents for my keep.

I looked up at my nan, the thought of food shopping had an appeal to it. One, I would get to choose the food I liked, and two; it would get me out of the house.

An hour later, my nan selected a large grocery cart and walked towards the entrance of the grocery store, which she informed me they called a supermarket. I had no idea what made it super, but liked the name they called it. The place was not much different to the ones back home. Not that I went food shopping with my parents. After all, it was rare that they shopped themselves. It was more of the job of their assistant, or my once Nanny. Of course, I outgrew the Nanny years ago.

I followed close behind, not wanting to get lost.

"Oh look they have a sale on, brilliant. We can stock up. I hate shopping."

I chuckled. It looked as if I was not alone in my thoughts.

"What?" she asked.

"Nothing," I replied.

"Come on, or all the sale items will be gone," she said, as we turned a corner her grocery cart smashed into another, causing her to stumble back into me.

"Sorry," my nan and the other shopper apologised in unison.

"Oh Alice, it's you. Oh and who is this fine young man? Finally ditched old Vic and replaced him with a younger model?" the woman chuckled.

I stood opened mouth, feeling my face turn crimson.

"Oh look, you old bat, you made him go red. She's only joking," my nan said turning to face me.

"I..." I mumbled.

"So this is the famous Mark?" the woman questioned.

My nan nodded. "Indeed, as I told you, he'll be staying maybe a year or so, depending on how things go with his parents. He's a good lad."

"Is he now?"

I wished the floor could swallow me whole. I looked from one to the other as they continued. Hearing nothing, they said, until I heard my name.

"Mark, you're settling in aren't you?" my nan's voice interrupted my thoughts. I turned to face them and nodded. She smiled, before turning her attention back to her friend. I took a step back as the pair continued to talk, gossip more like. What they found to talk about once they had moved off the subject of me, I had no idea. I realised we were going to be here some time and headed over to the magazine stand, and selected one. I pretended to study it, as a young girl caught my eye. She had an amazing smile; I had to get a closer look, but did not want to appear as if I was staring at her. I scanned the store, there were many others wandering up and down the aisles, but only one girl had caught my eye. I noted the toddler by her side; she was too young to have had a child, surely a younger sibling? The girl looked to be about my age, I could never correctly guess ages.

I continued to stare at her, and found myself smiling. My heart did a double flip. I continued to watch as they waltzed over to a young guy who I could only assume worked in the supermarket, if his shirt was anything to go by. I watched them as the toddler lifted her arms for him to lift her, which he did and smiled down at the young girl.

I liked how she was dressed, in jeans and a top, even if I recognised the logo printed on it. It seemed to follow me everywhere I went, typical. Taking in her dazzling smile, I tilted my head and studied her. I could overlook the t-shirt; the girl inside it was someone I would like to get to know. I edged closer, the magazine held high, but I could still peer over it.

I watched her as she spoke to the guy, she nodded and turned to leave, holding the hand of the toddler. I continued to watch the girl as she left the store and vanished from sight.

~ *Debbie's* ~

I took hold of Sally's hand and led her towards the exit, glancing back I noticed a guy standing by the magazines. I felt myself blush as he caught me staring at him, but then he was looking at me too, or had I imagined it? Lost in my thoughts, Sally loosened her grip, bringing me instantly to the present. I tightened the grip and in a stern voice told her how dangerous it was to let go of my hand. Sally whimpered.

"I'm sorry; Sally, but you scared me. If anything happened to you…" I left the sentence unspoken.

Chapter 13
Star In The Making

~ Debbie ~

A few days later, passing the drama room, as I made my way to our next lesson, French, I found myself stopping, staring at the posters on the wall.

"Are you thinking about signing up, Debbie?" Wendy asked me.

"I don't think so."

"You should."

"I don't know. I'm just not ready." I paused. Was I really thinking about this? "If I did decide to I'd only want a small part."

"Come on, you could have the lead role, if you wanted it."

"That would mean kissing the male lead."

"You see that as a problem?"

"Well, kinda, yeah."

"Sorry, I forgot you're waiting for your dream guy."

We stood outside the French classroom, our second lesson of the day, ready to be tortured by our next teacher. I did not like French, and wished the lesson to be over before it started. I placed a smile on my face and entered the room. My thoughts elsewhere, until I heard the word, test. *Great, here we go again.*

An hour later, we rushed out glad to be speaking English again, and not looking forward to Friday, when we had the test. I knew I would fail and Wendy said she would too. Walking towards our next lesson, art, I wondered if we would be drawing fruit again and asked Wendy if she thought we would be too.

"I hope not. Let's hope we get to do something more interesting."

"I agree."

We had drawn so much fruit I was sick of it. I bit my lip thinking about what else I would love to draw. We turned the corner, and made our way towards the art block.

Seated in class, luck was on our side, not one piece of fruit sat on the table. Instead, Mr Jolly informed us we were making a poster for a pop star's concert; and this would be part of our exam. A smile spread across my lips, as I knew exactly what I would draw. *For once, I would not get into trouble for thinking about him. Perfect.*

The French test arrived sooner than any of us wanted, and no matter how much studying I did, the words would not stay in my head. We arrived and saw the same fear in everyone's face as I had on my own. For once, there was silence as we waited.

Wendy looked at me, as our eyes locked; knowing how badly we both were at French. Our teacher called us in, and told us to take our seats. Mrs Norris stood at the front and waited for silence. I waited for the test to

begin; knowing once it was over; the verbal test would be next. To me that was far worse.

Before she could even ask me a question, I informed her she might as well fail me. I had no idea what she said half the time, and would not now. She turned to me and smiled, a real smile, causing me to stare at her. Surely, she had not just given me a genuine smile.

"Debbie," she began in English. "I know this is hard for you, and you have had a lot to deal with. I won't pretend to understand how you feel, but I know you can at least try, after all you might surprise yourself."

I sat opened mouthed. Had I just heard right, surprise myself? I had never thought of it like that. Surely, I would not get a huge score, but if I did not try, I would never know.

"I know I'm seen as an ogre, but really I have my students best interests at heart. I know those who are capable of trying harder, but don't want to," she continued, lifting the question paper in one hand and a pen in the other. "I think it would be an idea if you just tried, what do you say?"

She was right, I had nothing to lose, nothing at all. I nodded as she began.

~ *Mark* ~

When I had first seen the single bed, I had wondered how anyone slept on it. Now I liked it. I would not say I preferred it, but it was comfortable. I looked up at the newly painted ceiling, my thoughts on her, the mysterious young girl who had caught my eye at the grocery store.

That day I also discovered my nan liked to talk. Fifteen minutes after the brunette left me with my tongue practically on the floor, I located my nan. Her friend had left her and she continued adding shopping to the grocery cart.

Placing my hands behind my head, I closed my eyes, attempting to picture her. I would recognise her when I saw her again and prayed it would be soon. I heard a tap on the door.

"Are you okay in there?" I heard my nan ask.

"I'm fine," I replied, sitting up.

"That's good," she said as she pushed the door open. "The sun's shining. I wondered if you fancied going out and taking advantage of this fine weather. You could visit the sports centre, the swimming pool or the local park. Knowing our luck it will rain tomorrow."

I nodded. It was warm out; maybe I could have a swim and then hang out at the park on the way home. The more I thought about it, the more it appealed. I may even find her. She could be at the pool or the park.

"Tea will be ready at a little after five."

I nodded, pulled on my sneakers and tied the laces. I removed my trunks; my nan laid a beach towel on the end of the bed. I placed them both inside a bag and headed towards the kitchen, where I picked up a bag of chips and added them too. I had a general idea where the pool was, and with the thought of her on my mind, I made my way down the road.

I hoped to bump into the girl from the grocery store. Maybe this time I would say hi. I had not wanted another girlfriend, but I was only thirteen. When a girl had that kind of effect on me, what could I do? I was done for. Then again, would I ever see her again? It was a small town and I had to hope I would, it kept me going.

I found the pool, paid, handing over the correct money. It turned out there were two main pools, one with lanes and one where the youngsters could play. An inflatable ran the entire length of the pool, and I could not resist having a go. We never had anything like this back home. It was fun, even if I did spend more time falling into the water, than being able to stay on it, but then again was that not the point of it?

For the first hour, I was the only teenager. Having the pool to myself, except the odd adult who tutted if I accidentally splashed them with water. What were they worried about? They were already wet.

The first teenager arrived just a little after four.

I perched on the side of the pool, my feet dangling in the water. I watched the others swimming, wondering whether it was time I got out. I decided on one last swim, as a lad swam past, splashing me.

"Sorry," he said.

"That's okay," I replied, slipping into the water.

"You're American?"

"Yeah."

"Cool. You over here on your hols?" he asked.

"Not quite."

We chatted for a few minutes; I discovered his name was

Simon. I informed him I had to go as I was expected back at my grandparent's house.

"It was nice meeting you."

I nodded and agreed it was nice to meet him too. After all, he had been the first person, except the girl, I had met.

I dried and quickly dressed, exiting the pool building. Happy to have found a possible friend as I headed towards home, as I did I heard my name. I turned back and saw Simon. He caught up with me.

"Looks like we're going in the same direction," he said.

I nodded. "Looks that way." I wondered if he knew who I was, and decided to stalk me. I shook that thought out of my head, how could he?

We chatted all the way, until we parted. I had a friend, and we arranged to meet up again.

~ Debbie ~

The following week, more tests popped up in other lessons. We were thankful the French one was over, but my teacher had been right, it was not as bad as I had thought. Trying meant I had achieved something, and my father would be proud of me. That alone was worth it.

Having completed tests in our worst lessons, all that remained was Drama and Home Economics. Both I liked, and there was little to revise.

Passing the drama room, Mrs Duncan stepped out the door and handed me a script for the musical. I thanked her, and stuffed it in my backpack as we continued walking towards our next lesson.

"So, you decided to sign up then?" Wendy asked as we continued down the corridor.

"No, I'm still thinking about it, but she said I could read over the script if I changed my mind."

"I hope you do. I think it would be good for you," Wendy said.

"I don't know. Maybe you're right. I just don't feel ready."

"I think your Mum would be proud of you. Remember she knew you were a star in the making."

"Don't say that, I'm not that good." Hearing those words brought a lump to my throat. Tears trickled down my cheeks. Times like this hurt the most, not that Wendy had intended to make me cry. *You're a star in the making.* I quickly wiped the tears away, sniffling.

"You are, believe me," she said, turning to face me. "If I could sing like you, I would be in there demanding they gave me the lead role." She stared at me. "Oh Debbie, I am so sorry, I never meant. I forgot..." she paused.

"It's okay," I swallowed. "It was nice, but hard to hear. Mum always said that to me, remember?"

She nodded. "I do, I should never have said it."

"You should have. Its fine, little things like that still hurt. I know the pain will ease, but I won't ever forget her, ever."

"Of course not, and no one would expect you to, she was your mother."

"Thank you for being there, and for always understanding." I paused. "I am sorry for shutting you out when it happened."

"What did I tell you, forget it? I am here whenever you need me, no matter when or what time of the day, okay?"

I nodded and pulled her into a hug. Maybe she was right it was time to get back out there, joining the cast of the musical might be just what I need. Taking on a small part might be the right thing to do. I could take small steps, until I was ready to take bigger ones.

A few days later, I discovered the main part went to Mary. Danny, who already shared his name, had the lead male role. I had heard rumours he had soft kissable lips. They considered him a hunk. If I had gone for the main part, kissing him would not have been too bad. However, to share my first kiss in the musical was not my plan. I turned to Wendy.

"Thank you for pushing me."

"No problem, like I said you could have had the lead, but right now any part is a step in the right direction."

"It is," I paused. "Thanks again, you're right." *There is no way I could play the part of Sandy. Having all eyes on me. I'd be too nervous, and what would happen if I froze on stage?*

"Of course I am. You should start off small and work your way up."

"You know Karen really wanted the lead role," I said, changing the subject.

"Yeah, but come on, she can't even sing."

"True," I agreed. "She just thinks she can."

"She's lucky she's still in the musical."

"Yeah, she is."

"And now the rehearsals can begin," Wendy said. "I'm just glad they let me help out with the scenery. That way we can still spend time together. While I remember, I'm sorry I had to cancel our shopping trip. We'll have to reschedule it."

"It's okay," I said, nodding. Buying a bra was on the list of things I needed to do, but it was not at the top.

I took a deep breath and let it out noisily. My thoughts were on learning the few lines I had, and all the songs. Luckily, I knew many of them already and secretly looked forward to singing them with the rest of the cast. Knowing my mother would be watching over me, helped make the decision.

Chapter 14
Acting Out

~ Debbie ~

The day was finally over; together Wendy and I made our way to the bus.

Staring out the window, I thought of my last dream, and vowed to rid Karen from them.

I cross my legs as I sit on the soft sand, look up and stare at every one of those Karen's. They are all smirking at me. I stand, close my eyes, and wish them all to go away. As I open my eyes, every one of them disappears in a puff of smoke. Then, I am finally alone with him. He smiles and takes one-step closer towards me.

Wendy nudged me, bringing me back to the present. It worked. I did it. I had rid myself of Karen. Wishing it were that easy in the real world. Standing, I floated off the bus. Not recalling if I said goodbye to Wendy or not.

I entered my room, tossed my bag on the bed and moved towards the desk, where the script lay. Being part of the cast of Grease meant a lot to me.

The next morning, I woke early and climbed out of bed. I opened my curtains allowing the light to flood in, lighting up the whole room. Pulling out the chair from under my desk I sat down, tapping my fingers on it as I hummed 'totally devoted to you'. Picking up the script, I read from the start to a few scenes in. Glancing at my clock, the red numbers showered that it was eight o'clock, far too early to head over to Wendy's.

Leaning back in the chair I stretched out my whole body, before standing deciding to get dressed. I opened my wardrobe, took out a pair of jeans and my favourite t-shirt with a logo of Victor and slipped it on.

With the script in my hand, I scanned the lines one more time before making my way down to have breakfast and a cup of tea.

Back in my room, breakfast eaten and a mug of tea on the side. I lay on my bed and held the sheets of paper in my clammy hand. I re-read the lines for what seemed like the hundredth time.

"Maybe I could have tried out for Sandy. Doesn't every girl want to play her?" I asked myself. "Guess they do." *I did. I do. One day.*

I switched on my small television set, which sat on a cabinet on the far wall, placed the tape of Grease inside and pressed the play button. I added the empty case to the others, before settling back on the bed to watch it. Singing the songs as I sat in the safety of my room was one thing. I just hoped I was ready for the show, when we had an audience.

The film drew to the finale as I jumped up and sang louder to 'You're the one that I want'. Hairbrush in hand, I belted out the tune as my door opened. Steve stood in the doorway, hands on hips wearing a large grin. I swung around upon seeing him; the brush flew from my hand. I stood there in an open-mouthed surprise. Red faced.

"You're singing again, that's great," he said.

"Thanks, I…" I had not realised how loud I had become.

"I don't want to stop you, but could you keep it down a little, Carol has a migraine."

"I'm so sorry," I said, turning the volume down. "I didn't think. I guess I got carried away."

"That's okay. Any other day I would not have a problem with it. You know I love to hear you sing. We haven't heard you since." Steve paused. "I'm glad you've found your voice again." He nodded and took me by surprise and hugged me, really hugged me.

"Me too." I said, meaning it.

"If mum was here she would be very proud of you," he informed me, a tear trickled down his cheek and landed on my forehead. I pretended not to notice.

"Thank you and if she was here, she would tell you not to keep secrets," I said, hoping he would confide in me with what I already suspected.

"Debbie, I don't know what you're talking about." He smirked.

"Okay, if you say so."

"Anyway how come you're singing along to Grease, and not your favourite band, or him?" he said, pointing to Joshua.

"Didn't I tell you?" I frowned and thought for a moment. Had I not told them about it? I sighed; realising I had not. Now I had the perfect opportunity to tell him, not that I expected any of my family to come and see it. "I have a small role in the school musical of Grease," I informed him.

"You didn't go for the lead role then?"

"No. I'm not ready for that." I said as I leant on the wall. "Besides, you know me. I don't like being centre of attention, but I do get to sing in all the songs."

"Debbie," my elder brother started to say then shook his head.

"What?"

"You were made for the role of Sandy!"

"Thanks, Steve. I'm just not ready for a lead role, not yet."

"Debbie, I'm just proud of you for getting out there and taking part, no matter how small or big the role is. We're all proud of you."

"Thanks, Steve." I needed to hear that. I really did, he knew how much this meant to me. How hard it was to take part in this. Baby steps, I reminded myself.

"You're welcome," Steve said as we heard the doorbell chime. "Can you get that?"

"Sure," I said, as I rushed to the base of the stairs, jumped the last two steps and opened the door, Wendy stood on the other side.

"Morning. You're up early," she said.

"Yep, I've been watching Grease. I'm going to fix myself a hot drink. Would you like one?" I asked.

"Go on, then. Hot chocolate?"

I nodded, as she followed me into the kitchen. I opened the fridge and made the hot drinks.

Once they were ready, I sat opposite Wendy.

"Two tests left then!" I informed her.

"Yeah," Wendy said as she wrapped both of her hands around the mug.

"I'm going to take Home Economics next year." I said, lifting the mug to my lips and sipping the hot liquid. "What are you going to take?"

"I don't know. I can't make up my mind, but there's one subject I am NOT taking--"

"French!" we said together.

"I just can't decide between cooking or working with children," Wendy sighed.

"Hard choice?" Really, was it that hard? Not for me. I had already come to my decision on that one.

"Yeah. Nappies versus cooking."

"Ah, but at least you can eat what you make with cooking. Trust me, what a baby makes, you don't want to eat."

"True," Wendy said, screwing up her face.

"Then again, with your cooking who can tell the difference?"

"Hey, not funny."

"It's a little bit funny," I remarked, sipping at my drink once again.

She shook her head. "Some best friend you are."

We both could not help but laugh; knowing after all, I spoke the truth.

Monday morning I met Wendy at the bus stop. We were relieved as the last of the exams were soon to be over. I wasn't too worried about the last two tests.

Walking down the corridor, my thoughts were elsewhere, but this time not on Joshua. I had my head down, thinking about the musical. I looked up briefly as my shoulders hit against another student. Staring at his deep brown eyes, I became lost in them. He hurried away. I watched him disappear from my view. An image flashed in my head; surely I had not just seen him not Joshua. *It couldn't have been*. I thought. *I imagined it*. I decided.

"Sorry," I called out, but he carried on walking, ignoring my apology.

It was then I realised he was not a student. He was not in uniform; he wore dark blue jeans and a checked shirt. He was tall with wavy brown-cropped hair. I did not recognise him, but I had seen him somewhere, but could not place it.

Reaching the other end of the corridor, I looked back. The guy stood watching us leave. Wendy tugged me by the arm and led us towards the main doors, not giving me the chance to look back one last time.

"Wendy!"

"What!"

I shook my head. "Never mind."

"Sorry, did you want to be late for our next lesson? After we've already had lines for being late."

"No, but—" I sighed.

"I know that look. Trust me, that guy was not Joshua. Yeah he was cute, and all, but he was not your man. Now get your head out of the clouds and let's get moving."

I sighed, how well she knew me, but he did look familiar. Where had I seen him before?

~ Mark ~

I marched down the hallway in the attempt to keep up with the head teacher, as my shoulder bumped against a student. I looked back briefly; saw the flash of green eyes. I recalled the girl from the grocery store. Could that have been her? I hoped so, but if I did not follow the head teacher, I would soon become lost in the maze of students and hallways of the school. He continued, discussing my future at the school, unaware that I was lagging behind. Hoping to get another glimpse of the girl, but she was gone. It turned out I would join after what they call the six weeks holiday, since the term and year was almost over, which suited me just fine. I was not looking forward to joining a new school, but maybe it would be okay. Now I knew she attended this school and if she was in my year, I could not wait to start.

With the thought of the girl being at the school, things were looking up. It would be a coincidence if Simon attended here too. When I saw him, my heart flipped, as I was thankful I knew someone else here.

Things were going to be okay. Simon walked towards me, a smile on his lips.

"So, you'll be joining us here, then?"

I nodded.

"Ah, Simon, just the lad I was looking for," the head teacher announced.

Simon stared at him.

"How would you like to give young Mark, here, a tour of the school? I have a few things to discuss with his nan."

"What about class?" Simon asked.

"I'll deal with that, off you go. Be back here in an hour."

Simon walked down the now empty hallway and I followed him. We reached the Drama room, the posters filled the walls, and one stood out. I found myself staring at it.

"We put on a musical every year. They're a bit lame, but you know, if you like that kind of thing. I can get you a ticket."

"Actually I'd like that."

Dream World

"Really?"

"Really!" I said, as Simon continued his tour.

I smiled; tempted to join next year's cast. Going to this year's performance would make my decision on that.

~ *Debbie* ~

Friday finally arrived; I looked forward to the weekend and the fast approaching six weeks holidays. They gave us freedom from lessons and early mornings.

With the subjects chosen I would be taking next year, I was happier than I had been in a long time. I had been carrying this scrap of paper around half the morning before I dared to look at it.

"Did you get what you wanted?" I asked Wendy.

"Yeah," she replied. "How about you?"

"Pretty much. Let's see what you chose?" I said as we swapped papers.

Discovering Wendy had chosen childcare, and I had decided on Home Ec. I scrunched up my nose and told her, rather you than me.

Sat on the grass, Karen passed us, sneering at us.

"Guess she's still fuming then?"

"Just a bit."

"It's her own fault, she's lucky they allowed her to remain in the musical."

"Yeah, true, but she hates the fact she has the smallest part of all."

"I know. Oh well, she'll get over it."

"She'll have to."

~ *Karen* ~

I stormed into the house, furious with the day's events. The girl playing Sandy deserved what she got, and they had the nerve to tell me, I was lucky to have a part in the musical. Stuff them; I should have been cast as Sandy. I had the body, the looks and the talent. If they could not see it, they were blind. As I entered, I heard voices coming from the living room. It was unlike my parents to be home.

In the living room sat my sister, a huge smile plastered to her face. I turned and left, stomping up the stairs to my room. I hated her so much.

Ever since she got engaged, everything evolved around her. Tasting a variety of wedding cakes, choosing the perfect wedding dress, this would now have to be handmade to her satisfaction. The worst thing ever to happen to me was being a bridesmaid. They assumed I wanted to be one. No one even asked me. I dreaded to think what the dress would be like. Bright yellow, green, or pink all puffy and frilly, I imagined.

No one ever asked me anything. Fresh tears spilled down my cheeks. I held a pillow to my chest, hugging it. How I hated my family, most of all Jackie. Perfect Jackie.

~ Debbie ~

Ten minutes later, we arrived home, stood on the grass. Before leaving, we discussed opening night, which would be here before we knew it. I felt the nerves kick in; knowing my mother was watching over me meant everything. Steve and Carol had tickets, my father too, but if he came to watch me, that would be another thing.

Chapter 15
Greased Lightning

~ Debbie ~

The lights shone brightly centre stage; we had less than one week before opening night. Today we were having our last dress rehearsal. I waited in the wings. My hair pulled back in a ponytail, and face made up. I felt nervous, but each time we ran through the musical, my confidence soared; now I sang as loud as the rest of the cast.

Staring at my reflection in the mirror, Karen walked past, scowling at me.

"Ignore her."

I nodded, I knew I should, but she got my back up. Wendy rested her head on my shoulder, and pulled a funny face.

"Wendy, what are you doing?"

"Making you smile."

"Thanks," I said, turning around, shaking my head.

"Places everyone," our drama teacher bellowed.

I looked back at Wendy, smiled, and then made my way onto the stage as the music began.

~ Mark ~

I stood in my room, secretly pleased that I would be watching the musical. It would take my mind off the girl from the grocery store and my parents. I had not heard from them since arriving in the UK, not that I expected to. They were far too busy.

Slipping into a pair of freshly washed and ironed blue jeans, I buttoned them up. Selected a dark red shirt and then fixed my hair. I was still thinking about on having t cut, before I started school. I would sleep on it.

Entering the kitchen, my grandfather tilted his head and smiled.

"Someone's keen. Don't suppose you have a date with a young lady afterwards then?"

"Grandad."

"I'm only teasing," he chuckled. "Fancy a mug of coffee, before we leave?"

I pulled out a seat and sat down. "Sure."

~ Debbie ~

The first performance in front of a live audience was only two hours away. I stood script in hand, not that I needed to read it. I knew all my lines. Taking a deep breath, I looked around at the others. They were all reading their scripts. I felt my stomach churn. I felt sick, but I knew once we were out there, it would leave me. At least, I hoped so.

One hour to go and then the curtains would rise. My stomach felt no better.

I was ready to give the performance of a lifetime. I joined the others back stage. The curtains swayed as the audience arrived and took their seats. The sound of their chatter travelled backstage to our ears.

My nerves were getting the better of me. Mary looked pale and sat with a bag covering her mouth. I watched as the bag filled up with air as she breathed into it. I felt no better than Mary looked. Although I had a small part, I still felt sick. My stomach gurgled as I looked out beyond the curtain, which would soon be going up. I scanned the sea of faces, looking for my family; they were there, except my father. He had time to arrive, but I had a feeling he would not come. I continued to scan the sea of faces, so many had come. Then I saw him, the young man in the front row.

I could not take my eyes of his mop off brown hair, and those dark brown eyes. He had the broadest smile I had ever seen. I could have sworn I had seen him before; I could not shake the feeling. As I attempted to get a better look, the lights dimmed and I could only just make his silhouette out.

He had not seen me, I was sure of that; after all I was hiding in the wings. I was unable to look away, even after the lights dimmed. I was sure his eyes were on the stage, but mine remained on him. I held the curtain in my hand, gripping it more tightly than I intended. My nails dug into my hand. Any harder and I would have drawn blood.

I closed my eyes, trying to remember his face, his features. The more I tried, the less I could recall. All I remembered was his mop of brown hair and dark brown eyes. *Damn it*. I scolded myself and took a long deep breath. Mrs Duncan called us ready for the opening act. I tore myself away from the curtain and headed backstage.

"Places everyone," she hollered, sounding slightly frantic and we had not even started yet.

I looked over to Mary with her light blonde hair half tied in a ponytail. The rest hung loose around her shoulders. Mary did not move. She held a paper bag in her hands, as she looked down at the floor. She closed and opened her eyes, taking long deep breaths and blowing out the air noisily.

I tilted my head, and watching her, realising she wasn't going to move. *Come on Mary, it's show time.*

"Mary!" I whispered.

As I called out her name, what colour remained in her cheeks vanished. Mary's vomit hit the floor, creating a large puddle.

Don't look, I told myself. I knew there would be carrot looking things in it. My stomach twisted as I briefly glanced towards it.

"Miss," I called, looking away. My own stomach churned, my lunch threatening to join Mary's.

Our teacher hurried backstage, and looked at Mary, shaking her head as she made her way over to her.

"Mary, oh dear, I don't think you'll be able to go on stage like this. Are your parents here tonight?"

Mary nodded as more vomit hit the floor, inches away from the teacher's shoes.

"Oh, okay," she said, placing a hand on her shoulder and turned to look at me. "Debbie, change into the Sandy spare outfit."

"But--"

"We have no time to argue," Mrs Duncan said, helping Mary to her feet. "I've seen you, don't deny it. You know all her lines, and we all know you can sing. Please, we need you. Her understudy hasn't turned up. Don't look so worried, when she arrives, she can take over after the first act."

I looked at my teacher as if the words she'd just spoken were in another language.

"I can't," I began.

"You can and will. Debbie, please, the show must go on. We have people who have paid to watch this performance and--"

"Okay," I found myself saying. "I'll do it, but--"

I stood stunned by the events, which had just occurred. With no more time to waste, I transformed myself into Sandy. Luckily, I was the same size as the understudy, and the outfit fitted me perfectly. With a quick glance in the mirror, my smile vanished. *Oh my God, I can't do this, all those people!* I took a deep breath, as my teacher ushered me onto the stage. Too late now, I had to go through with it.

The crowd were becoming restless, as I rushed to the centre of the stage. I swallowed hard as the lines rushed through my head. The faces of the cast were priceless as Danny mouthed, 'where's Mary?'

I gulped in a large mouth of air and shook my head. "She threw up."

"Really?"

I nodded as the curtain began to rise. My heart raced.

~ Mark ~

I watched the curtain as it rose into the air, my mouth open as the first scene began. I could not take my eyes from the girl on the stage. I knew who she was. She was the girl from the grocery store. I watched only her as the cast sang the opening song.

~ Debbie ~

The music began and the curtains opened, the audience cheered. I looked out again at the sea of faces. I searched for him; he was still there in the front row. His eyes were on me, his lips parted in a smile. I looked back to Danny and the show began.

We started the opening scene with the young couple on the beach. I had watched Mary time and time again practice this sc ene. My nerves stayed with me as I realised there was a kissing part any moment. I swallowed hard as Danny held my hand in his, and then lifted my chin, the audience cheered. I did my best to forget that this was my first kiss. Not the person I had wanted it to be with, but he was gentle with me. My nerves left me as we parted. I had no time to think about it. As soon as the kiss began, it was over.

I looked out at the audience. The guy was sat in the front row was smiling up at me. My first solo was due, and I did what was expected of me and took centre stage. I saw my mother's face, smiling up at me as I sang. I relaxed into the part of Sandy.

The audience sang along with each song, and then, it was the last scene; the understudy had still not arrived. They transformed me into the new improved Sandy. Curled my hair, and then I pulled on the skin-tight trousers. The image I saw in the mirror was shocking. I did not look like me at all. I looked good. My cheeks flushed red. Could I go on stage with my body feeling so naked?

"Wow!" Wendy gasped.

"I know right! Do you think I can go out there in this?"

"Of course you can."

"Tell me honestly, how do you think its going?"

"I told you, you were born for this part. Don't let Mary know, but you make a better Sandy than she does," Wendy paused. "How was it kissing Danny?"

"It was okay." I felt my skin prickle again. "Not that I have anything to compare it with."

Wendy nodded.

"When she told me to take Mary's place, I never even thought about that—"

"Don't worry. Your dream guy won't mind. You were only acting."

"Wendy, I know you'll think I'm nuts, but I swear he's on the front row."

"Joshua's here? Really here?" she scoffed.

Wendy looked out into the audience to where I had seen the young man in question.

"I don't see him. All I see is some guy covered in spots. Tell me it's not him."

I peered around the curtain.

"No it's not. He was there, he was," I said as I searched the front row for him, but he had gone.

"There was a guy, and he could have been Joshua. I think!"

He was there, wasn't he?

~ *Mark* ~

I wanted to watch the remainder of the musical, but after the kiss with the lad who played Danny. I had to get out of there. I lied to my nan, told her I needed the toilet. Instead, I stood outside, just as she joined the cast for the last scene in those skin-tight pants. I had to look away. How could I be jealous? After all, she may already have a boyfriend. This was crazy. I had not even spoken to her, yet.

She had a beautiful voice, but watching him put his hands all over her, I had to leave. I marched towards the exit and paced up and down the hallway. I could still hear her; she had the voice of an angel. The way she looked at the guy playing Danny, they had to be dating, I was sure of it. If not, she was a bloody good actress.

I couldn't understand how one girl, who I had never spoken to, had made me react the way I did. Love at first sight. I never believed it.

She was just a girl after all, and if she was taken, I would find another. There had to be another girl who made my heart race, my skin tingle. I would make damn sure to shake this girl from my thoughts.

Having Simon as a friend would be good. Surely, he knew some fine girls I could date, to take my mind off that girl. The girl from the grocery store, who I had now nicknamed, my supermarket girl.

Chapter 16
Karen Free Day

~ Debbie ~

After the first performance of Grease, I was the talk of the school. Taking on the role of Sandy, the first night surprised most of my school friends, as only two people, before the musical knew I could sing. Walking down the corridors, I had never felt so popular. Everyone stopped and congratulated me.

Mary returned to the role of Sandy on Saturday and Sunday night, with no sign of any illness.

Even though playing Sandy had been the highlight of my year, playing her for more than one night was something I was not ready for.

My thoughts turned to opening night. How I had no choice, but to play the lead, becoming Sandy for one evening had boosted my confidence, but I felt more comfortable playing the small part I had.

The thought of having my dream guy watching me, made my stomach churn. I knew Wendy assumed I had been daydreaming, but I could not shake the thought of his eyes on me. Eyes so much like the ones in my dreams. Maybe Wendy was right, my mind was playing tricks on me. Yet, I wanted to believe he was there.

I thought about my first kiss. Not the kiss I had always imagined. Nice enough, but I had fantasised about it for so long. The kiss should have belonged to Joshua. Instead, it had been on show and belonged to Danny. His soft lips pressed against mine and I had responded. Would I have kissed him, if we were not pretending to be in love? No. Plain and simple, no I would not have. It was true he was a good kisser, and while my eyes were closed, I imagined him to be Joshua Lawson. The fantasy dissolving the moment I opened my eyes, and looked at Danny.

During the final performance, I checked the front row for the guy of my dreams. Hoping he would return, but there was no sign of him. Had I closed my eyes and imagined him to be there, as I had so many times before. No, I told myself, he had been there. I was positive. Yet, I could not shake the thought I had dreamt it. Wendy told me time and time again, how I let my imagination run away with me. Maybe this time

I had. I sighed and laid my head back on my pillow, staring up at his poster.

Tuesday morning, I woke up early and put all thoughts of my dream guy to the back of my head. I had to stop thinking about him. With that, I changed into my uniform.

Entering the kitchen, I found Steve buttering toast. I inhaled and licked my lips, taking a piece covered in butter and jam. Steve shook his head and tutted. I smiled at him, before taking a bite. There was nothing like hot toast with melted butter and jam.

The cool air hit me full in the face as I stepped out of the house, joining Wendy at the bus stop.

Taking our seats a few minutes later, Wendy hummed the tune to a Grease song, while my thoughts were on Joshua.

He stares up at me with his big brown eyes as I sing to him. He stands, moves towards me, and climbs the wooden steps. He gently pulls me towards him. I stop singing as he takes hold of my hand, our fingers entwine and then...

"Debbie, we're here!"

"Huh!" I said, turning to face her. "Sorry."

Wendy shook her head and grabbed her own bag as we got off the bus. I swung my bag over my shoulder, missing Karen by inches.

"Hey, watch it, Debbie. Or should I call you, Sandy?"
Here we go, I rolled my eyes. "What!"
"You heard me."
We stood on the path outside the school.
"What's your problem now?"
"You," she said poking her finger into my chest. "How come you got to play Sandy?"
"Look, it's really none of your business. After what you pulled--"
"What I did! She deserved, I--" Karen began shaking her head.

~ Karen ~

I choked on my words, as I stared into those eyes, which were identical to my own. I recalled how years ago we were joined at the hip. Now, we were not even friends. I tried to remember why things changed, before Wendy could speak. I interrupted her.

"Doesn't matter what I said, or did. She had it coming!" What she had done; she had pursued Danny while we were dating. Now I had my payback. It was a shame, she only bruised herself. I had been hoping she would not be able to continue to do the musical. I had hoped to take her place; after all, I should have played Sandy. Danny was born to play the lead in Grease; he already shared the same name.

Playing Sandy, would have meant I was able to kiss him again, but it was my own fault. If I had not spent my time checking out the new talent, maybe we would have stayed together. Turning my attention back to Debbie, I smirked.

I looked at Debbie, and recalled her kiss with him. They had only been acting, but I knew she had her first kiss with him, and couldn't resist saying something to her.

"Anyway, I heard you had your first kiss with Danny!"
"No! I--" Her voice faltered.
I raised my eyebrows and placed my hands on my hips. "Thought so. You're a freak!" I shook my head once again,

calling out 'freak' as I walked away.

~ Debbie ~

I watched her walk away.

"Ignore her. What does she know?" Wendy said.

"She's right though. It was my first kiss. That makes me a freak!" I answered as we entered the school.

"No it doesn't, besides your first kiss was in front of everyone. When I have mine, it won't be so public," she began, instantly making me feel bad. "I'm not as nervous about it now."

"You're not!" I stopped walking and turned to face Wendy.

"No, if you can do it in front of an audience, then, I will be just fine."

"Wendy. Sorry I--"

"It's okay. Anyway, changing the subject, has your dream guy turned up again?"

"No," I sighed. "I am beginning to think he was not there at all."

"I know I said I thought you were daydreaming and all, but if you really believe he was there. I believe you."

"Thanks. I don't know if he was. I just hoped he was!"

Arriving at our form room, we waited for the register to be taken.

The last day of the term arrived; we had been looking forward to this day for weeks now. A day when we chose activities which we could spend the day doing. Some would be travelling on a bus, which would take them to the ice, or roller-skating rink. Some students remained in school and played games in the sports hall, or spent the day cooking. While some used the school computers and played video games all day.

Wendy and I chose roller-skating. Besides, ice-skating cost twice as much and we knew Karen had applied to ice-skate.

I stood behind a girl dressed in pink leggings as we waited for our skates. The girl took her pair and walked over to the hard plastic chairs. I turned my attention to the man behind the counter. He smiled and asked what size shoe I wanted. He handed me an old brown pair of skates with black laces and only one stopper. The skates had seen better days, but it made no difference to my mood. Nothing could change it.

Joining the girl on the plastic seats, I began tying up my laces as Wendy joined me. I looked at hers; they were in a similar state to the ones I now wore.

"About time this place replaced these. If I'd remembered, I would have bought my own," Wendy said.

"Yeah, me too."

The wooden floor beneath my feet felt smooth as I glided along. Wendy held onto me, as we skated our first lap. We had not skated in a long time and after a few laps, our skills reappeared.

The teacher who volunteered to accompany us stood on the side of the rink, watching as the students whizzed by him. A smile appeared on his lips as he made his way to the entrance of the rink. I nudged

Wendy as I realised he was wearing skates. We stopped to watch him, holding on to the side. I held my breath. Wendy held on tighter to me. Mr Miles stood unaided and pushed his feet back and forth in unison, as if he were getting the feel of the skates. I watched him turn in the direction the skaters were going, and joined them.

I waited for him to fall and the sound of laughter, but neither came. He whizzed in and out of the skaters as if he had been skating all his life. We smiled at one another, pushed off and joined the others. I watched as he showed the younger students how to skate.

Gliding to the side of the rink, we made our way to our lockers. Removed our lunch boxes and headed to the first available table. Half an hour later, food eaten, we re-joined the skaters back on the rink.

Just gone three, our teacher beckoned us all over.

"Time to leave," he announced.

I removed the skates and changed into my own shoes. My feet still felt as if I were wearing them.

I floated to the bus. I had enjoyed the day, a Karen free day.

Chapter 17
The Climbing Wall

~ Debbie ~

The bus returned us to school. Our last day was over. We made our way to catch the school bus home.

"Not long now and we're all free," Wendy said.

"Yeah I know, just think no more homework for six whole weeks."

"Heaven and best of all we get to have a lie in every day."

I nodded, as we waited for the bus. Next time we rode it to school we would be Year Tens. Now the holidays had begun.

Standing on the grass opposite my house, I faced Wendy.

"I was thinking you could sleep over at mine, or vice versa."

"I like the way you're thinking."

"Yeah, and we could dig out our old skates and maybe go to the rink again. I really enjoyed today."

"Me, too."

"Although I'll only be able to go now and again since it's not cheap."

"Who says we have to skate at the rink. We could skate at the park. Its free, and the paths are nice and smooth now."

"True."

"Want to hang out tonight?" Wendy asked.

"Tonight? Sure. My house or yours?"

"Mmm, good question."

"Tell you what, come over to mine. Mum won't mind."

"Are you sure?"

"Yeah, come over around seven."

Dream World

I lay back on my bed, my thoughts on the Karen free day.

Stretching my arms above my head, I realised I needed a shower. Peeling off my clothes, I added them to the laundry basket, turning around I caught my reflection in the full-length mirror. Running my fingers along the lace of the underwear, the ones Carol bought me for my thirteenth birthday. I could not thank her enough for buying me them. She handed them to me later that night, when I was alone in my room. I opened the package and hugged her tight, whispering my thanks.

Dried, I stood at my wardrobe and picked out a pair of jeans and a top. Re-tying the belt on my dressing gown, I laid the clothes on my bed, before drying my hair with a second smaller towel.

Dressed, I slipped my trainers on, tied the laces and went down to the kitchen. Where I found Carol preparing the evening meal, I offered to help. Carol accepted.

Meal eaten and dishes washed, I walked over to Wendy's. Knocking on the door, Wendy answered and together we made our way up to her room.

"What film do you want to watch?" Wendy asked as she handed me several.

I shook my head looking through them.

Movies selected we headed back down the stairs and slouched on the sofa in the living room.

"Hi girls, thought you'd like some snacks," her mother said as she placed a tray of goodies on the coffee table.

"Thanks, Mum."

"Wow, thanks, Mrs Allan. They look fantastic."

"You're more than welcome, enjoy, but don't stay up too late will you."

We shook our heads, and turned our attention back to the television.

With a few weeks to fill before Wendy went on holiday with

her family, we planned to spend every day together.

The first week, we rode our bikes and skated at the local park. We went swimming and continued to sleep over at one another's houses.

On one of the bike rides, we rode over to a larger park near the sports hall. It had a climbing wall and even though neither of us had attempted the wall before, we decided this holiday we would.

"We should make a day of it, bring a picnic," Wendy suggested.

"Good idea, climbing that wall will be fun, but scary at the same time."

"I know. Whose idea was it again?" Wendy chuckled.

The day arrived when we planned to climb the wall. Picnic made, we mounted our bikes and took off towards the other side of the town, passing Karen's house.

~ Karen ~

I watched out of my bedroom window, just as the two girls I hated rode past on their bikes. My mouth tightened. I thrust myself back. I needed to get out of the house. I would have to call one of my friends. They would cheer me up. I needed to shop. Maybe a new jacket or shoes, or both.

Picking up the phone, I dialled the number and waited for Stephanie to answer. Once she did, I heard the words I knew would come.

"Yes."

I quickly changed into my favourite jeans, purple top and black shoes. Reaching the front door just as Stephanie and Anna arrived.

"Ready?"

Both girls nodded.

~ Debbie ~

Arriving at the sports hall, we paid at the desk and headed out to the wall.

We handed our tickets to the member of staff, and then were helped into our harness by a grey haired man with a moustache. He instructed us on how to climb safely. We nodded as we listened, taking it all in. Ready, I placed my foot into the first hole, gripping the hole above my head and began the climb. I took a deep breath, I did not have a fear of heights, but my heart was racing. I looked up, imagined Joshua at the top. Checking on Wendy on the other side of the wall, we smiled at one another and continued to climb.

Reaching the top, I saw Joshua appear before me. *Thanks, Joshua.* I could see for miles. In the distance, an elderly couple were walking towards us and *Joshua was with them.*

"Wendy," I said, as we reached the top.

"Made it."

"Yes you did, and look over there." I pointed to the couple and Joshua. "I'm not going mad. I'm really not. Look, Joshua's over there!" I squealed.

"Where?"

"There," I said, continuing to point in the direction of where he stood.

"Are you sure, I can barely make out it's a guy, let alone Joshua!"

"I know it's him. It is. Just look at his hair. The way he walks." My heart raced, I almost lost my balance as I watched the guy of my dreams walking away from me.

~ Karen ~

I tossed the new jacket on my bed. In the shop, it looked stunning. The two girls agreed. Now I was not so sure.

"It's really nice; I mean it's perfect on you."

"Nah, I don't like it. Since you love it so much, call it an early birthday present."

"Really?" Stephanie's eyes lit up.

"Really."

Stephanie and Anna exchanged looks, had I just seen that? Had they played me? No, I imagined it. They were my best friends; they wouldn't do that, would they?

~ Debbie ~

Over the following few weeks, we spent every day together. Each day brought us closer to Wendy and her family leaving to go on their holiday.

We discovered Carol was pregnant. I had been right. The first scan revealed they were expecting twins. I could not believe it, twins. I was so excited I hugged Carol tight, Wendy too. It was a double celebration. The thought of my mother not being here to meet them made me sad.

Pushing all thoughts out of my head, of my mother and the driver, who was to be sentenced for his part in the accident. I took a deep breath and joined in with the family celebrations. Knowing mum was looking down on us.

The next weekend we spent our time putting up my brother's old tent. The blue material had seen better days, but neither of us cared. Sally wanted to join us, but our father dismissed the idea. Besides, she would have wanted to go in an hour later, after being out in the cold and dark garden.

We sneaked out snacks from both of our homes, a few packets of biscuits, crisps, cans of pop and a big bar of chocolate.

Finally, the tent was up. It took us most of the afternoon. It was almost dark by the time we were able to climb inside. My brother had offered to help, but we told him we had it under control. Secretly, I wished we had accepted. Pulling the sleeping bag up to my waist, Wendy handed me a can of pop.

"I cannot believe it took us nearly all afternoon."

"I can," I replied.

"Okay, me too," she began, opening her can. "I wish we'd accepted Steve's help."

"Me, too, but at least we can say we put this up all by

ourselves, even if I'm knackered now." I pulled the ring pull on the can, and drank from it. "That's better."

"You hungry?"

"Yeah, I've worked up an appetite, you?"

"Are you kidding, I'm always hungry."

Wendy opened the bag of crisps, cheese puffs. I loved them, even if they did make my fingers turn orange. They tasted so good.

We spent the night talking about my obsession for Joshua, Wendy's crush on Mr Travis, and tucking into the snacks we had sneaked out.

The next morning we awoke early. I stretched; the sun was already out and beaming down on the tent. Warmer than I thought it would be. We decided to have a water fight.

In my room I changed into my swimming costume. Wendy popped home, to change into hers.

"Are you going swimming?" Sally asked.

"No. Wendy and I are going to have a water fight."

"Did I hear water fight?" Steve asked.

I nodded.

"Oh, count me in," he replied.

"I'll watch from here," Carol said.

"Towels, you'll need towels," my father informed us.

I smiled at him.

"Are you going to join us, then?" I asked.

"Maybe," he said, heading back into his room, closing the door.

I rushed to fetch towels, just as Wendy returned, along with her brothers and parents.

"Guess who wanted to join us? You don't mind do you?"

Wendy's parents passed us and joined Carol in the kitchen.

"Mind, are you kidding. Besides, Steve, Sally and I think Greg maybe joining us, too. Did you bring a towel?"

Wendy shook her head.

"Give me a hand, Wendy, we may need more."

We returned with our arms filled with large and middle-sized towels. I fitted the hose to the tap, handed out jugs, bowls, anything that would hold water. Steve collected our old water guns from the shed and the battle began.

It was the first time since the accident we had come together and laughed. My father joined us, and the smile on his face would be etched into my memory forever. He joined in and soaked me from head to toe. Not that I minded, it was nice to see him smile. I had missed that smile, and the sound of his laughter. I had forgotten how it sounded. I imagined my mother watching us. For a second I was close to tears, but looking back to my father, dripping wet, I picked the hose up, and aimed.

"Debbie, you…" my father screamed, and chased me until he held the hose and got his revenge.

It was one of the best days of the whole holidays. I managed to soak Wendy. I had hidden behind a tree, and as she approached it, I jumped out and threw a bucket of water all over her. Wendy attempted to get her revenge.

The day ended with our two families having a bar-b-que in Wendy's backyard. Due to our garden being water logged. It was a perfect day. We ate and talked about the arrival of another set of twins in the family.

We planned to camp out for a second night, but the ground was far too wet. Instead, we slept over at Wendy's and told ghost stories as we ate the remaining snacks.

~ Karen ~

After the jacket thing with the girls, I decided to think no more of it. They would not do it again, and with that, I decided to go shopping on my own.

Treating myself to a new top and a skirt, and one more two piece swimming suit, which I planned to use the following morning.

With the wedding plans in full swing, my parents were home

even less. That suited me fine. I ordered to order take-out most nights, used the pool twice a day, sometimes three and even found my skates, and spent a whole day at the rink. I was running out of things to do on my own, and considered calling up the others to see what their plans were. It was, then, I realised none of them had called me.

Chapter 18
Looking For Joshua

~ Debbie ~

The sun continued to shine. The third week of the holidays arrived, meaning Wendy would be leaving to go on her family holiday.

I watched from my window as they loaded the car. I was happy for her, but also a little jealous. I did not mean to be, but I could not help it. I wondered if we, too, would go away, even if it were for a few days, but no, not this year. My father promised that next year we would.

The last holiday we had was the year before my mother passed away. I pushed those thoughts from my head, raced down the stairs, out of the house, and over to Wendy's.

"I'll phone you every day." she promised.

"Make sure you do," I told her. "And have fun!" *But not too much.* I thought, nodding as I released her. She joined her younger siblings in the back of the car, while her parents closed her door and then the boot. I stepped back, as her father started up the car, pulled on his seatbelt and set the car in motion. I stood on the path, waving as they disappeared into the distance.

I stood for a few seconds staring down the empty road. My heart sank. I hated being on my own. I knew I would be bored without her, and willed this week to end, before it even started.

I entered the house, found my brother and Carol in the kitchen.

"Are you okay?" Carol asked.

"Yeah, I'll be fine. She's only going for a week."

"We know, but we thought we'd bake you a cake to cheer you up."

"Thanks. Is it going to be chocolate?" I asked, sitting down at the table.

"Of course," Carol said. "Would you like a tea, or maybe a hot chocolate?"

"Hot chocolate sounds good."

Drink made and cake in the oven, Steve and Carol joined me at the table.

"We have something to tell you," Steve announced.

"You do? Please tell me the babies are okay?"

"They're fine. No, what we have to tell you is, we've decided," Carol began. "We would like you and Wendy to be the babies' God parents!"

"Are you sure?"

"Yes, of course we are," Carol said.

"Does Wendy know?"

"Yes, of course. We had planned to tell you together."

"It doesn't matter," I said, hugging them both. It was fantastic news. Ten minutes later, I left them in the kitchen and went up to my room. I was going to be a Godparent, scary.

A few hours later, I stood in my bedroom, staring out the window. All the lights were out in the Allan's house. Of course, they would be, no one was home. It was then I realised night had descended upon the street. Staring back at their empty house, I wondered what Wendy was doing. Had she unpacked? Knowing Wendy, she would leave it until she had checked out the site. I missed her so much, and she had only been gone half the day.

The phone rang, taking me from my thoughts. I raced to the phone in the hallway at the top of the stairs. Answering it, I discovered it was Wendy. I trailed the wire to reach my room, and sat on my bed, bent my knees to my chest, as we talked about becoming Godparents. Ten minutes later, I wished her a good night.

With my arms above my head, I stared up at the ceiling. I closed my eyes, and once again stood centre stage.

I stare down to the row of chairs. Joshua is on one of them. He smiles up at me. I take a deep breath, open my mouth, and begin to sing. I step to the edge of the stage, sit down as our eyes connect. I reach out...

Thud. I opened my eyes; I had fallen onto the floor in my room.

"Ouch," I said, sitting up, rubbing my thigh. *That's going to leave a bruise*, I thought. *Thanks Joshua that was your fault.*

A few days later, moping about the house was doing me no good. The truth was, I missed Wendy and without her, life was dull. That morning I decided to head over to the sports hall, hoping I would see Joshua again. I had a mission. Find Joshua.

Arriving at the sports hall, I locked my bike to a post and walked around the outside of the complex. There was no sign of him. Maybe I really had not seen him at all. Wendy told me the person I saw was not him, and how I just wanted it to be him. Maybe she was right.

"What was I thinking?" I said out loud.

"Talking to yourself? They lock people away for that kind of thing."

I turned around and came face to face with Simon.

"Yeah, I guess you're right."

"On your own today?" he asked. "I always thought you two were attached at the hip!"

"No and funny. Wendy's on holiday as it happens."

"Ah, I see."

"So what are you doing today?"

"No idea!" It was not quite true, but there was no way I was telling him anything. "I was bored, so decided to get out of the house, and ended up here."

"Oh, well I would offer to let you join us, but not sure you want to watch a us skateboarding?"

"Not really, but thanks."

"Another time, maybe?"

I smiled." Another time."

I watched him walk towards the skateboard park, before making my way towards the climbing wall. I had no plans to climb it again, but this was where I had last seen him. My stomach was in knots with excitement. I felt scared and nervous at the same time. Truth was, I knew in my heart, Joshua would never really be in my hometown, but I could dream, and I did.

Simon was quiet, shy maybe, behind that blonde wavy hair and dazzling eyes he was not bad looking, not my type of course. I had not really seen him up close before, and to be honest I had been surprised how cute he was. I knew he would be Wendy's type. She had a thing for blonds. An idea formed. I was going to try and fix them up when Wendy returned. I would accidentally bump into him again. Hopefully he would invite us to join him. I liked the sound of that plan. I made my way back to my bike, unlocked it and rode home. I had a few more days until Wendy returned.

~ *Mark* ~

I had plans to spend the day with Simon, but a few minutes before he arrived, my parents rang. I told him I would meet him there. He nodded and headed back out. I turned my attention back to my mother. The tour was going well. They never once mentioned him. Good.

An hour later, they finally hung up, and I was ready to leave. I had wanted them to call, but they never really asked how I was. More about what they had done, where they had been. I was happy for them, but they forgot to ask me how I had settled in. I would have told them; so far, I was doing well and even made a friend, which reminded me, I had to get going.

I grabbed a piece of fruit, before making my way to the sports hall, found Simon, and his cousin. I perched on a ledge and watched them. I dared not tell them I had never been on a skateboard, and to be honest, Simon looked like it was his first time, too.

Once his cousin was done teaching him, we made our way into the town. Where I had my first taste of fish and chips, they tasted so good. I knew I would have to have them again.

~ *Debbie* ~

Another two days had passed since I had seen Simon at the sports hall. I spent one day taking Sally to the park, and another taking Greg swimming. I was running out of things to do on my own.

The moment Wendy returned, we would head over to the climbing wall. Fingers crossed, Simon would be there. Of course, I had no idea if he would be there or if he would like her.

If I knew my friend, as well as I thought I did, I knew she would like him. All I needed now was Wendy. I counted down the hours until she arrived home. We had chatted on the phone every evening, but it was not the same.

Chapter 19
New Guy

~ Debbie ~

Wendy's arrival was only a few hours away. I pulled out my seat at the desk and planted myself in position, watching her house. Opening the drawer, I removed a notebook and began signing my name as Debbie Lawson. Busy practicing my signature, I did not notice their car arrive.

Running out of room on the page, I looked up and saw the car parked in their drive.

Their door opened. I watched as Wendy headed over to the family car and removed a suitcase from the boot. I waited fifteen minutes, unable to stay away any longer. I rushed out the door and over to Wendy's.

"Wendy!" I called, racing across the road.

"Debbie!"

We hugged.

"Did you have a good holiday?"

"Yeah, as much fun as it could have been without you."

"Really?"

"Of course. The boys had a great time too. They made some new friends."

"Did you?" I asked.

"A few. Don't look so worried, you're always going to be my best friend," she said, with a coy smile. "I even met a few boys too!" Wendy said, dragging her suitcase up the stairs, as I followed.

"Really?"

"Really!"

Wendy threw her suitcase on the bed, unzipping it, as I sat on the end of her bed.

"Were any of them cute?"

"Yeah, one of them was totally cute. He was nice at first, but he was only after one thing. There was no way I was…" she paused. "Anyway, after that he moved onto the next girl."

"Oh!"

"It's okay. I did have my first kiss though."

"You did!"

"Yeah." Wendy nodded

She turned the conversation to the possibilities of having a boyfriend when we returned to school. I nodded, I had someone in mind for her, but for me, no one measured up to Joshua.

The remainder of the holidays flew by, but we never managed to get back to the sports hall. I was disappointed; some plans never went the way they were meant to. Simon did attend our school, so I could set my plans into motion there.

The last week of the holidays meant we would go on a shopping trip. I had more than just school shopping on my mind. Since we had not managed to shop for my first bra, I was hoping to get one, while we were buying things for our return to school.

The lady in the shop looked at us, as we eyed the bras on the hangers.

"Can I help you?" the lady asked in a posh voice.

"Um--" I said.

"Yes. My friend needs to buy her first bra."

"Wendy!" I said as I elbowed her in the side.

"No problem. Come this way," she said, her half-circled glasses perched on the end of her nose. She pushed them up, as she led us to the back of the store.

"Don't look so scared. We have plenty to choose from."

The lady measured me; I felt my cheeks flush, as she placed the tape around my chest. I held my breath; she removed it and disappeared. Returning she laid out a selection for me to try on. Wendy left, leaving me alone to decide which ones I preferred.

Half an hour later, we left with four bras in a bag, and then went to buy school provisions.

Two hours later, we had everything we needed for our return to school in a week's time.

Later that night, I stood before my mirror and tried the new bras on. My developing body filled them well. I might need new ones in a few months, if they continued to grow. Secretly, I hoped so. Didn't all girls wish for more than they had?

The last week flew by. My school uniform hung on its hanger. I went to bed early, ready for the first day back to school.

The following morning waking up early, my stomach growled. I felt hungry, however, when I tried to eat, I felt sick. I knew it was nerves, so grabbed a snack to eat on the way. Meeting up with Wendy I hoped the nervous feeling would disappear.

I pushed my arm through my coat sleeve, zipped it up as I stood outside the living room door. Bag in hand; I said my 'good-byes'.

The air had a slight chill to it, and the sky looked clear. I prayed it would stay dry. Even though there was talk of rain.

I crossed the road and joined the others who stood at the bus stop. Wendy arrived a few minutes later.

We boarded, showing the driver our new passes.

~ Mark ~

"Are you ready?" My grandfather asked.

I sighed. That was a good question; I thought as I stood before the mirror, and ran a hand through my hair. The decision to cut it had not been because my mother wanted me to. I decided a fresh start included a new haircut. Now I knew it had been the right thing to do.

"As ready as I will ever be. Don't worry I'll be fine," I

said, walking into the kitchen, following my grandfather.

"Oh I know you will be, take this," he said, placing a few coins in my hand.

"I don't need that," I replied. "I have a packed lunch."

"Take it, and promise me one thing."

"One thing?" I said, raising my eyebrows.

"Yes. Keep your head held high and walk into that school like you own it."

"I don't know, I…"

"Trust me, it will be fine."

"Thanks…."

Still feeling nervous, I poured out a small portion of the cereal and nibbled at it. Done, I placed the bowl in the sink. Collected my bag and pulled it up onto my shoulder. Hugged my grandfather, I then headed towards the door.

I thought the school looked nice enough, and knowing she attended it too made it better. I recalled bumping into her, hoping we were in the same year.

Closing the door, I made my way over to the bus stop. My heart raced as I took a seat, staring down at my hands.

"Is that seat taken?" a voice asked.

I shook my head, indicating it was not. Looking up I realised it was Simon. I smiled, thankful for meeting him before starting school.

"Simon!"

"In the flesh."

"Ready for your first day, then?"

I remained silent.

"I'll take that as a no then." He paused. "Can I ask a favour? I wondered if I could have the window seat."

I stood, and switched seats.

~ Debbie ~

I watched as Simon stopped half way down the bus. A guy I did not recognise stood, and they switched places. Wendy nudged me, and whispered in my ear. I had already noticed the new guy, and could not help, but stare at him. From the side he looked good. What the school needed was some new guys. Most of them were not in Joshua's league. Would this one be? I had no idea. I would have to wait and see. I had only seen him from the side, but something about him had me captivated.

I knew he would not be interested in a girl like me, as one of the most popular girls spotted him and pounced. I watched her stand, apply lip-gloss before walking down the bus towards him. She pretended to be jerked by the bus's movement and fell into the seat in front of him. She giggled and purred like a kitten as she turned to face him. Her lips wet as she ran her tongue along them. She asked him his name as she continued to stare at him. The girls on the bus turned to listen to his reply. I did not mean to be one of them, but I found myself leaning forward, listening.

"Mark. It's Mark Hobson," he said, in an American accent.

My heart missed a beat. I loved his accent; I could listen to him forever. I watched him squirm in his seat as the girls around him giggled at anything he said. They all then began firing questions at him. Their eyes fluttering like a swarm of butterflies.

Wendy and I looked at each other and shook our heads. The girls all continued to swoon over him, right up until the bus pulled up outside the school.

I watched him with Simon; exit the bus, the girls following close behind. Stepping off, we too couldn't help, but stare at him. He was cute; almost perfect. All the other girls were around him like bees around a honey pot. It was degrading, but did I wish I was over there with them? Maybe! I took in his dark hair and chocolate brown eyes. Oh yes, he was a good-looking lad. Who was I kidding, he was gorgeous. Not that he would look my way, not with the others around him.

No, I was not in with a chance. I rolled my eyes and continued to walk past him, with Wendy whispering in my ear, about how gorgeous he was.

~ Mark ~

I held my head high, just like my grandfather told me to. It turned out I did not have to worry, girls already surrounded me, and they were stunning. The one girl I wanted to acknowledge me, walked past without even looking at me. I watched her enter the school grounds and become lost in the crowds. I moved forward with the group of girls and Simon behind me, as the sound of a bell rang out in the distance.

Chapter 20
Back To School

~ Debbie ~

He flashed his amazing white teeth at the girls, making them all drool. I shook my head, as the girls giggled at every word he uttered.

"Can you believe those girls? I mean he's cute, but..."

"I know, he's dreamy," Wendy said as she stared at him too.

"Wendy!" I giggled looping my arm through hers, as we walked through the school gates. For a moment, I thought about my mother. Starting Year Ten meant a lot, a new journey. I still cried, but not every day. I thought about her all the time, and today it hit me hard. I held my head high, stared at the new guy, and blinked. Imagining Joshua stood there smiling back at me.

I followed Wendy through the double doors and headed to our new form room. We sat, and waited for the new form teacher to take the register. No one minded Mr Banks replacing our old form tutor. Mr Williams needed to retire. We moved to a new form room too, no longer in the main building of the school.

The mobile remained set out as it always had been and one light above me flickered on and off. I gazed out of the window, my thoughts on the new year ahead.

I stand centre stage; stare out into the audience below me. Scan each person, until I find him. Even in the dark, I know it's him. I feel his eyes on me, as I lift the microphone to my mouth, and sing. Joshua stands, claps along with the audience. The lights flick on. I keep my eyes on him. In an instant, the remainder of the audience vanish. I remain on the stage; he shuffles towards me, his eyes twinkle, his smile widens…

"Debbie," Mr Banks voice said, bringing me back to the present.

"Huh!"

"You are here, correct?"

"Yes, sorry sir," I said. The dream vanished. I sighed, shook my head, looking over at Wendy, she shrugged and rolled her eyes. It was in that moment, I realised all eyes were on me. My cheeks flushed, the sound of the door creaking drew their attention away from me.

I turned to look in the direction of the door, and silently thanked him for taking the limelight away from me. As our eyes met, I realised it was the new guy from the bus, Mark, and he was going to be in our form. The first day back to school just could not get any better.

The new guy smiled, flashing his perfect white teeth. I tried desperately to look away, but my eyes betrayed me, and I too continued to stare at him. I noticed his huge smile, soft lips, deep brown eyes, and a mop of brown hair and skin, which had a tanned complexion. I could not help, but allow myself a longer gaze at Mark. This time I had a clear view of him, he looked just as good from the front as he did from the side. The glimpse of him as I passed earlier did not do him justice. My mouth gaped open. Wendy was right. The boy was cute. Something about him had my heart racing. Mark was very good-looking, right up there with Joshua. The way the girls hung on his every word made me sick to the stomach.

Usually, the good looking ones were already taken. He probably had a girlfriend. Not that it seemed to bother the other girls in my year, or Mark by the way he reacted to the attention they gave him.

Forcing myself to look away from him, I heard Mr Banks clear his throat.

"Take a seat young man," Mr Banks said as he continued to call out the register.

Dream World

Mark did as instructed as Mr Banks stood before us and he put a hand up to silence us. He sighed heavily as he twiddled his moustache. I stared at him trying hard not to look at the mole, which lived above his lip. He then went on to explain the timetable on the board, and that each student should make their own copy. Everyone groaned as we pulled out pencil cases and began to jot the lessons down.

I took out my new cartridge pen, looked at the board and began to fill in the lessons. The new pen floated across the paper as I wrote. Timetable filled in, I replaced the lid and waited for Mr Banks to dismiss us.

Ten minutes later, he announced we could leave.

"Quietly," he barked.

I placed the new timetable inside my homework book, as we followed the others out of the mobile. Outside we stood at the base of the metal steps, and studied our timetables. I realised my first lesson was maths, not my favourite subject. We looked at one another and together said.

"Maths."

I rolled my eyes, placing the book in my bag, just in time to witness Karen follow Mark down the steps. He continued walking, looking down at the timetable in his hand. Karen wet her lips, ready to pounce as she fell into step beside him.

"Come on, Mark, I'll show you to our first class!" Karen purred.

"Um…thanks, but I…!"

"No buts, come on or we'll be late," Karen said as she took hold of his arm and led him towards the maths block.

I shook my head; realising Karen was getting the man of her dreams, as usual. Most of the guys in our year had dated her. Mainly, the popular guys. If they were good looking and had money, she was there.

Shaking Karen from my head, I decided this year I would forget about her, and move on with my life. After all, we were in Year Ten, older and wiser, and ready for the new challenge we faced.

"Do you think he'll escape her venom?" Wendy whispered.

"If, he's lucky. If not, one bite and…" I said, giggling at the thought. Really, I knew she was right, one bite and he would be hooked, just like the rest of them. She would get the guy just to prove she could.

Karen would date a guy for a few months and then move onto a new challenge. Mark was her next victim.

We walked the short distance across the grass to mobile eight and joined the queue. We stood in our usual groups. Karen sidled up to Mark, whispering things in his ear. The look on his face, told me he was not happy. Had Karen finally found a guy who could resist her charms? This thought put a smile on my lips. I noticed Simon stood alone in the queue and nodded over to him. He nodded back.

"What was that?"

"What was what?" I asked, innocently.

"You and Simon."

"Oh that!"

"Yes, that."

I opened my mouth to speak, but the maths teacher Mr Savoy opened the door and beckoned us in.

~ Karen ~

I fancied him, and planned to make it clear.

"You're going to love it here, and if you stick with me, we will be the most popular couple in the whole school."

He remained silent, but that made me want him more.

"This is the maths room, bit of a drag, but it's only for the next hour, and then we can go out on the field or somewhere more private." I said, raising my eyebrows seductively. I watched Debbie, and tightened my hook on his arm.

No way, Debbie this one is mine, all mine. There is no way in this world Mark would be interested in you, I thought smiling.

As instructed we filed into the classroom, Mark unhooked

his arm as I tried to keep hold of him, but as we moved inside, he slipped from my grasp. I placed a smile on my lips, realising all the seats beside him were taken, I was forced into the row behind him. I pulled out my pencil case, and concentrated on the back of his head. I could not wait to run my hands through his hair. That thought alone, kept a smile on my lips.

~ *Debbie* ~

I attempted to escape the question and took a seat at the back of the classroom as Wendy sat beside me.

"Oh no you don't, Debbie, spill the beans?"

"Silence please," Mr Savoy ordered as he waited for everyone to take a seat. His nostrils flared as his patience wavered. "Thank you. Now, welcome to the beginning of working towards your GCSE's. We are going to begin with a few simple lessons to get you back in the saddle after a long holiday."

Everyone groaned as he handed us each a textbook.

"I thought that would thrill you guys. Now, of course, we have a new student. Mark, welcome, if you have any problems, do not hesitate to ask me or someone sat beside you. Now, turn to page fifteen, we're going to start with Symmetry properties."

I sighed, opened the book to page fifteen as Mr Savoy stood at the front, hand on his large hips, swaying left and right. His glasses slid down his nose as the rocking continued. I looked at him and then to Wendy.

"Do you think he's okay?" I asked.

"Not sure, but he's making me dizzy."

"Be quiet, girls. Time for chatting is for outside my classroom," Mr Savoy announced, as he continued to sway.

With his eyes on us, Wendy did not have a chance to question me again. Looking back up, I could not help but watch him. *Maybe he's exercising!* I thought. Taking my eyes off him, I found Wendy staring at me.

"What! He's putting me off."

"Me too, but you better get on, before he comes over here."

I worked on the problems from the textbook, as he continued to sway; right up until the bell rang.

"Homework will be to finish the problems on page fifteen, and if you have already done these, move on to page sixteen."

I sighed, looking down at the five remaining questions. *Homework already and it's only the first day. Great!*

We left the classroom. Karen remained glued to Mark. *Should I go over and help him?* Just as the thought entered and left my head, Simon came to his rescue.

"Mark, I thought I would introduce you to the guys."

"He's coming with me, aren't you, Mark?" Karen purred.

"Actually, I thought Simon and…"

Karen pouted. "You'd rather be with him, than me?" she questioned.

"Karen, why don't you leave him alone," he said as he led Mark away.

I heard Mark thanking him as they dashed off.

"Looks like Karen wants him to be her next boyfriend."

"Yeah, as usual. Then again, it looks like she is going to have competition. Every girl looks as if they want him, too."

"That won't matter. Nothing ever stands in her way, not when it comes to guys."

"True."

I rolled my eyes, watching as they passed the other girls, their mouths literally dropping open. I shook my head, and followed Wendy onto the field. She bent down and felt the grass before sitting down. I joined her.

"Don't think I have forgotten!"

"There isn't much to tell. Not really."

"Come on, we have half an hour before our next lesson."

"I was going to tell you, honest, and before you jump the gun, no I did not hook up with him."

"Oh, okay!" Wendy said. "Why not?"

"Not my type."

"I think he's cute. I never realised how much, until now!"

"That's nice, but you know blond isn't my type."

"No of course not, no guy can compare to Joshua."

I rolled my eyes; she apologised and begged me to tell her. Really, there was not much to tell.

"You mean you went Joshua hunting!" she teased. "Sorry. I said I believed he was there. Tell me more."

Truth was, I wasn't sure any more. I had sworn I had seen him the night I played Sandy, and in the halls of the school, and then again at the sports hall.

"You can't deny you saw him in school that day."

"I can't say for sure it was him."

"Fine," I snapped, regretting it instantly. "Maths homework already," I said, changing the subject. "I have five questions to finish, how about you?"

"I was thinking, maybe we should hang out there next weekend."

Did she ignore my question, or was she thinking about Simon?

"The skating park?" I asked.

She nodded. I saw the twinkle in her eye. She liked him, which was a good start.

Chapter 21
A Perfect Shade Of Brown

~ Debbie ~

I was nervous, really nervous. Today was the first time I would not have Wendy by my side. She gave me a reassuring smile. We would be okay, she told me. Of course, we would, but it did not make the feeling in my stomach go away. Why had we not thought this through and picked the same choices? Too late now.

Wishing her luck, I watched her walk away. I made my way towards the Home Economics room with my head down as I joined the queue. Shuffling my feet as I waited for the teacher to allow us to enter. I would be fine; I loved cooking, and hoped it would be as much fun without Wendy, even if I did all the work, most of the time.

The teacher stood at the door and ushered us in, I half smiled as I entered the room. The real reason I had picked this subject, was because of my mother. She loved baking and it brought her closer to me. I closed my eyes, just for a second and saw her face, this time the smiling face from the photograph in my room. I willed the image from that day not to enter my head, but it did no good. *Joshua*, I called to him.

"I am here, you will be fine," he said, patting me gently on my arm.

I took a long deep breath and entered the classroom, feeling nervous and scared, but I could do this, Joshua was with me every step of the way. I scanned the faces of the girls in the class. I knew some of them by name, two I knew were Zoe and Chloe, I thought they were cousins, but I could be wrong. One other girl stood out, Rachel. I knew she could cook and envied her, seeing the things she had produced in class. Dare I ask her to be my partner? I moved to an empty table, the others rushed to get the best cookers, but they were still in the same state as last year. They needed replacing. To me it did not matter which one I got. I recalled complaining to my brother last year. He told me they had been that way when he attended, dashing all hopes of them replacing them any time soon. Some of the equipment was older than I was. Maybe when Sally started they might. I laid my bag under the table and settled down on the high stool.

"You look a little lost without Wendy," Rachel said as she approached me.

I looked up and replied. "I guess I am."

"Do you mind if I sit with you?" she asked, tossing her black hair over her shoulder.

"Sure, please do." *Thank you.*

"Thanks, I know you love to cook as much as I do," Rachel began. "I've seen the things you've made, and I know we will make a great team."

I nodded. I knew she was right; working with her would be a pleasure. Of course, I would never tell Wendy.

The teacher silenced us, as she ran through our first task. Hands on cooking, we were to pair up and prepare a vegetable soup. I smiled. I would miss Wendy, even though she left all the cooking to me. Rachel was right we made a great team. I inhaled the aroma of the soup; knowing it would taste good. I poured half into a flask, and offered the remainder to Rachel. She shook her head.

"Are you sure you don't want to take some home?" I asked.

"No thanks, you have it."

It was then I recalled she never took her cooking home, always gave it away. I wondered why. I discovered she just wanted to learn to cook, and told me I could take everything we made home. I nodded and asked again if she was sure. I looked at her; I would never have thought Rachel was as rich as Karen the way she acted. She was nothing like her, who flaunted her wealth. It proved someone with money did not have to be a bitch.

"Yes," she replied. "I am." She stooped down to pick up her bag, and turned to leave.

"Thanks again. See you next lesson," I said, heading out of the classroom. I had missed Wendy, but not as much as I had thought, I would.

Armed with the flask of soup, I marched down the path to meet Wendy.

Reaching the field, I arrived first, keeping an eye out for her. Looking across the field, I watched Mark and Simon pass me, their gang of wannabe girlfriends in tow. They were all giggling as they followed him. I shook my head. They were so obvious.

I felt a tap on my shoulder, making me jump. I shook my head, tore my eyes from Mark, as Wendy stood beside me. She slipped her arm through mine and we walked the short distance to a small clearing on the field. We sat, opened our bags, and removed similar sized boxes and began to eat.

Wendy asked how my first lesson went without her. I told her the truth. I missed her. I told her Rachel was a far better cook than she was, she agreed brushing the crumbs from her uniform. I asked her how her first lesson went. She nodded, and said it went fine.

"She said you can have it all?"

"Yeah,"

"She's nice, not like Karen at all."

"No, she is the opposite of nice."

"She is."

I nodded; we always found something to talk about, from school to family, boys, kissing and of course, Karen. She always managed to get into our conversation.

The bell rang as we packed away our remaining lunch, before making my way towards the main building. The gravel crunched beneath our feet, as the lunch bell continued to ring in the distance.

Tossing my hair back over my shoulder, we entered the main building, making our way across the hall, and out the opposite door. A short cut to the Art rooms. I gently bit my lower lip and followed the others heading to our next lesson. I loved art. The downside was having Karen in our class. We joined the queue, Karen stood beside him. I rolled my eyes and nudged Wendy. She nodded and rolled her eyes too.

~ Mark ~

My first day could not have gone any better. Having Simon at my side made it a whole lot easier. The girls' hanging around us was a bonus. I was not after dating any of them. Today I would enjoy it, but having them hanging off my every word every day, I was not sure, if I wanted that. It made me realise how my cousin felt with his fans following him day and night. Did I feel sorry for him? No.

The only girl in the group I knew by name was Karen. She was attractive, I admit that, and I liked having her showing me around; overall, it was a good start to my first day.

Entering the classroom, I followed Simon to a nearby seat. Art was not my worst subject, or best, but I enjoyed doodling. Taking in the surroundings of the classroom, I noticed things were not much different from the art room back home, I don't know what I expected? I scanned the room, and found the one girl who had captured my heart.

~ Debbie ~

I watched Karen; the poor guy had no chance. She would get him anyway she could. It was always the same. New guy arrives, Karen makes a beeline for him, but of course he has to be hot too. Nerds had no chance. She had an eye for the perfect guy and if she had homed in on Mark, then he must be just that. I could understand why she fancied him; after all, he was off the scale with cuteness. It dawned on me there and then; it was the first time I found another guy cute. Of course, I was still waiting for Joshua. He would come along and sweep me off my feet. *I wished.*

"Quietly please," Mr Jolly bellowed. He shook his head, as he stood before his desk and perched on the edge of it. "Thank you, good afternoon," he said, before taking the register.

Another teacher who explained we would be working towards our GCSE's and then selected something from the pot on his desk, showing us a piece of charcoal.

"You all recognise this art tool?" he asked.

We replied, yes.

"Good. Today we're going to create a picture with this tool. I want depth, shading, and texture. Think about what you're going to use as your inspiration. Don't get too excited," he said as he revealed a large bowl of fruit on the centre table. "You may begin; select your pencil, while I hand out the paper."

The others in the class scrambled to take the best pencils from the pot on the side. There were many new ones among the old. I took out my pencil case. On our shopping trip, we had bought our own. Paper handed to us; we began to draw, lightly at first and then slowly adding texture and darker shading.

The lesson lasted an hour and the fruit sketch began to take shape. I nibbled the end of my pencil, sat back looking at my piece. I looked up and saw Karen still drooling over Mark. I rolled my eyes. *Okay Karen, I get it. You like him, want him, but leave the poor guy alone.* I thought looking at him, taking in the colour of his eyes. It was the first time I saw them, really saw them. They were a perfect brown.

Chapter 22
I'm Not Nuts

~ Debbie ~

Staring at his eyes, reminding myself he was no Joshua. The bell rang; I packed everything away and placed them in my art folder. Two strides and I reached the other side of the room and slotted it back in the cupboard before leaving. Wendy and the others did the same. No one wanted to carry those oversized folders home. I had once, and regretted it. Now I left it in the cupboard.

Our first day back was over.

~ Mark ~

My first day was over, it had gone well. It turned out Simon liked the attention.

Karen fell into the seat behind me.

"Mark, I wondered if you would like to meet up later?"

"That's kind of you, but…"

"We've already made plans," Simon said, interrupting me.

"Another night then," she said, smacking her lips together.

"Um, yeah sure. We can hang out another night."

"I'll hold you to that," she said, placing a kiss on my cheek.

The bus pulled over, she stood, and walked down the aisle, swaying her hips. Turning back, she blew mea kiss. I turned to face Simon, who sat smiling at me.

"I hate to say this, Mark. She's stunning, but she has a mighty sting."

"Does she?"

"Yeah she does."

"Don't say I did not warn you."

"I don't like her, like that, but she is attractive, isn't she."

"Yes and the girl is a sucker for an accent, sorry, just saying. It's not the first time the girls in this school, have swooned over a guy with an accent. There was a brother and sister from Ireland."

"Oh, well thanks, makes me feel wanted." I joked, playfully punching his arm.

Ten minutes later, we walked the short distance to Simon's house. He opened the door and led me inside, down a long dark corridor, into the kitchen, a large open room with yellow walls.

"Don't say it, I know it's bright. My mother's into these mad colours. The hallway's going to be lime green by the weekend, and guess who has to paint it?"

"You?"

Simon nodded. "Of course, you are more than welcome to help me. I hate painting, but since it's just me and mum, it's left to me."

"Where's your dad?" I asked.

Simon shook his head, and opened a cupboard pulling out two mugs. "He shot through when my Mum found out she was expecting me. Anyway it's no big deal." He poured some coke into each mug. "You do like coke don't you?"

"Yeah, of course," I said, sitting down. "We are still going to mine after this, right?"

"We can, but I was thirsty that's all, we can go straight after."

"Sure, or we could hang out here for a bit, but I'd need to ring my grandparents. They might get worried if I am not home soon."

"Oh, we don't have a phone, sorry. We got cut off."

"Oh, is there a phone box?"

"End of the road, but it's been out of order for months."

"I tell you what. I would love to stay, but I think being my first day, I should get back and let them know how it went."

"Of course, should I walk you?"

I shook my head. "I'll be okay. We can meet up later, or I can come back after tea, if you want me to?"

"Sure."

"I mean, if your mum doesn't mind."

"She won't be here, so it will be fine."

"Oh okay, I'll pop back at say half six."

~ Debbie ~

Closing the front door, I made my way to the kitchen, and found it empty. Placing the soup in the fridge, I made my way up to my room, and threw myself on the bed. Closing my eyes, I thought about our first day back, and Mark. I could not help, but think about his eyes. I blushed, feeling as if I had betrayed Joshua. I looked up and silently apologised to him. He would forgive me, he always did. I closed my eyes and found my safe haven.

I look down, finding the familiar dark eyes looking up at me. His smile makes my heart beat faster. The music begins, and I sing. All the time I have my eyes on him. He stands; we continue to gaze into one another's eyes, as he makes his way towards the steps.

I stop singing as he reaches my side. He takes my hand and encases it in his. Joshua pulls me towards him, places his arms around my waist. I lay my head on his shoulder. Feeling the familiar beating of his heart, as I breathe in and out, in time to it. I want to look up, but something stops me. Knowing if I did, I would be lost in his eyes. Then, he would lift my chin and kiss me, but that's what I want, isn't it?

Before I could answer, Steve bellowed up the stairs that tea was ready.

I opened my eyes, looking up at Joshua.

"Debbie, tea," he called again.

"Coming," I replied.

~Mark~

"That's brilliant news. I told you your first day would be fine," my nan said, rolling a layer of pastry on the counter top.

"And Simon sounds like he has become a good friend." My grandfather nodded, peeling apples.

"He has, and the girls seem nice too. One has taken a shine to me, but…"

"…but…" my grandfather said, taking my hand.

"Simon warned me off her."

"Does he like her?"

"Not that I am aware of."

"Leave him alone, Vic," my nan warned, and then turned to me. "You should go get changed. Do you have any homework?"

"Alice, homework, really? Don't you think he should relax tonight? It's been a long day."

"I'm okay. Actually, if it's okay, Simon asked me to go over to his tonight?"

"Of course it is, but you have to be back no later than nine."

"Nine, Alice. He's almost fourteen."

"Nine is fine, I'll be back by then. I'll get changed, do my homework, unless you need help with tea?"

"Nope, all under control." She nodded, patting the pastry. "Making apple pie for afters."

"Sounds good to me. Are we having custard or cream?"

"Whichever one you would like. Or both?"

"I think custard sounds good to me."

Leaving the kitchen, I made my way to my room, and changed out of the uniform into jeans and a t-shirt, I sat on the end of the bed and started on the homework. It took me less than twenty minutes to finish it.

Simon answered the door. I followed him back into the kitchen.

"So, tell me about Karen?" I asked, sitting down at the table.

"Oh, you really want to know about her?"

"Do you like her?"

"God, no," Simon said, pulling up a chair. "Let me explain, she's like a dog with a new toy. She won't let go until she's chewed you up and spat you out."

I frowned.

"I wouldn't lie to you, but if you want to learn for yourself, go ahead."

"What's that meant to mean?"

"We all know she likes you."

"We do?"

"Yes. She won't give up, until you agree to date her."

"She can't be that bad, can she?"

Simon nodded. I rolled my eyes.

"Don't say I didn't warn you."

I looked at the walls, taking in the bright yellow paint.

"Do you really want my help to paint?" I said, changing the subject.

"Do I?" he stated, pouring out the drinks. "If only I could change my mother's mind about the colour, then I would be very happy."

"She does like her bright colours." I lifted the glass and downed half the drink. "What time is your mother due home?"

"Late, she works two jobs. Boring jobs I might add, but my mum wants me to have everything she never had. "Simon refilled his glass. "Plus she's at night school training to be a Nursery Nurse."

"Sounds like she has her hands full."

"She has, that's why I don't mind helping around house, not really. I do draw the line at ironing though."

"Cannot say I blame you there. My mother would never allow me near an iron." *Not that she did any herself,* I thought.

"What does your mother do?" Simon asked.

I held my breath. How could I tell him the truth?

"She travels a lot for her job," I began, telling a half-truth. "My dad too, which is why I'm here at my grandparents."

"Really?"

"Yeah. I wish they'd spend more time with me."

"Sounds like we have a lot in common."

"It does. Now what should we do for the rest of the evening?"

We talked, watched a movie, and that evening when I discovered Simon was also a fan of my parents.

"I'd love to see them in concert," he said.

"Would you?" I said, knowing I could easily get him a ticket.

"You're not a fan?"

"Sort of." I paused. "I like their music. If you really want to, maybe we can save up to go together."

Simons face lit up.

I decided I would ask my parents for two tickets when they played in the UK. Of course, I would lie about how I got them. Not that Simon would care. At least, I hoped.

~ Debbie ~

Night fell. The sky sparkled with stars. One, I liked to think was my mother looking down on me. Would she approve of the choices I made? I liked to think so. I stared out for a few minutes longer, before moving to the task in hand, homework. Opening the book, I decided to tackle one question at a time, until I was done. With another quick glance at the sky, I got to work.

Homework finished, I yawned, and caught my reflection in the mirror. Smiling at myself, I stood, pulled my curtains shut before changing for bed. Seeing Joshua everywhere was slowly driving me mad.

Crawling into bed, I closed my eyes.

Centre stage, the lights shone down on me. I stand ready to perform, checking the audience for him. He is in his usual seat, on the front row. His dark eyes on me; I stare at him, the light flickers on and off, brighter than before, I squint, unable to see. I know he is still there, but as the light dims, all I can see are those dreamy brown eyes. I will him towards me, to hold me in his arms.

I woke dripping in sweat, my skin still tingling from the thought of his touch. I flicked on the lamp and stared up at the poster. The eyes I loved so much stared stared back at me.

Chapter 23
Poor Guy

~ Karen ~

I slept better than I had in days. I stretched, yawning loudly, listening to the wind whistling through my window. I sat up, looking at the time on the clock, the red digits displayed that it was five o'clock. The alarm I had set remained silent. Not that it mattered, I was wide awake. I swung my legs over the side of the bed, and stood rubbing the sleep from my eyes. I tiptoed over to the window and closed it. Shuddering as I crawled back into bed, pulling the duvet up over my head, closing my eyes, thinking about the day ahead.

An hour later, the alarm rang. I hit the off button, sending it flying across the room. It was the third clock in the past year I had broken. It landed on the floor near the door.

Climbing out of bed for the second time that morning, I decided to take a bath. I entered my bathroom and turned the taps on, adding rose petal salts to the running water. The room filled with the scent as the bath filled with bubbles. I slid into the tub, and lay beneath the water, just for a few seconds. I emerged, wiped the water from my eyes and hummed the tune 'I will always love you'.

Twenty-five minutes later, I climbed out of the bath, wrapped a dressing gown around my body.

My uniform lay neatly on the back of the sofa. How I hated to wear the foul outfit. I had tried to get the school to change the rules, asking my parents for help. My father shook his head, having none of it. My mother ignored me, and the question. Why had I even bothered to ask? I should have known the outcome. They never listened to me.

The neatly pressed uniform fitted me snugly. My breasts filled the top half nicely. I slipped my feet inside my shoes, and applied a thin layer of make-up. Ready, I headed downstairs to the kitchen; where the cook had prepared a full English breakfast, which satisfied my hunger pains. The last mouthful eaten, I downed the tea, and made my way out to the bus stop. In a few years' time, I would have my own car, once I passed my test. Already having the car in mind that I wanted.

I boarded the bus, and took a seat with my gang. Placing my bag on my lap, I spotted Wendy and Debbie, laughing, they looked so happy. I reminded myself, new house, and new friends. In my opinion, my money changed her, not me. After a few months of moving into the new house, she changed, and then 'she' came along. I vowed I would never be friends with her again. I tore my eyes away from her, and found Mark sitting with Simon. I pursed my lips, and considered moving closer to him, but decided to stay where I was.

I followed my gang into the form room, and sat in my usual seat; I heard nothing they said, as I watched him. *If I could only get him alone*. His accent drove me crazy.

Our form tutor called out the register, before dismissing us. I stood, waiting for Mark to leave. I had planned to follow him. I just wanted to talk to him. No other guy had resisted me before. This one was a challenge, and I liked that. I wanted him, before anyone else got their claws into him. I had seen the look on Debbie's face when she looked at him. No way was she having him. I walked faster to catch him up, leaving the gang behind, not that they were taking any notice of me, I realised. Not that it mattered. I crept up behind him as I saw the girls approaching him. I scowled at them. They moved away. *Wise choice*, I thought.

"Mark," I began.

"Karen."

"When are you going to take me out?"

"Take you out!"

"Yes, on a date. Just the two of us."

"I can't, I…"

"All you have to do is say yes. You'll enjoy yourself. I can guarantee it."

"The thing is my girlfriend won't like it. I'm sorry Karen, but thanks for the invite."

"Girlfriend," I said, pretending to feel hurt. Even if he did have one, I did not care. "Since when!" I spat.

"I have to go, Karen. See ya later," he said, as my mouth fell open.

I watched him as he hurried away. I needed a plan. I would continue to watch him, discover who the girlfriend was. I had a hunch, and I hoped I was wrong. After all I had never had to ask a guy out twice before, girlfriend or no girlfriend. I was angry, frustrated, and stormed down the corridor, slamming doors shut behind me, with all my strength. I was not about to give up on him. I wanted him even more than before. I searched the halls for him, even when the bell rang I continued to search for him.

I found him, leaning against a wall. His dark brown eyes twinkled as the cool breeze played with his hair. I watched him as he entered the classroom, saw him look at her. I would take him from her, and watch her cry over me winning her man. I just needed to try harder. Besides, compared to her, I was a woman. She was a flat chested kid.

I should have headed to my own lesson, but I could not move. Instead I stood, hidden, watching through the window. *She is the one*, I thought.

~ Mark ~

I stood with the group who rode our bus home; Debbie was among them, Karen, too. I could feel her eyes on me.

"Well done, Mark," Simon whispered.

I could only assume he had meant my lie to Karen. I was not

ready to date her, or take her out, not yet. To her she may have thought I was playing hard to get, but that was not the case. I had not spoken to Debbie, but the thought of her had my skin tingling. I had talked to, had skin-to-skin contact with Karen, and felt nothing. A date may not hurt, but why bother, when I knew it would go nowhere.

"Thanks, I don't think it will stop her."

"It might get her off your back for a while."

"Maybe, I don't know. Having a girlfriend does not bother some girls."

"True, but why didn't you say you had a girlfriend before? Is she back home?" he asked.

Second lie, I could not keep doing this. This was not me. Yet I had to, if I wanted it to be convincing. Maybe I should confide in Simon. Not here, but at his or my grandparents' house.

~ Karen ~

I don't care if it is or isn't her, I will have him. I thought. There was no way Debbie Conway was having my man. I headed up to my room, changed into one of my swimming costumes, and made my way down to the pool I would swim ten lengths, which would make me feel better. I hoped.

~ Debbie ~

The first week of the New Year was coming to an end; I sat in the kitchen, as the cornflakes floated around the bowl as I pushed them around with my spoon. No matter how hard I tried, thoughts of my dream were still on my mind.

Leaving my siblings eating at the table, I said my goodbyes. Crossing the road, I joined the other students already there. Wendy arrived a few minutes later.

The week had passed by so fast that the day itself passed in a blur, I had enjoyed my second lesson of Home Ec. We may not have cooked this lesson, but I found I liked Rachel more and more.

I had eaten the remainder of our lunch, as we sat on the grass, watching the guys play football. As the bell rang, we stood, and made our way to our last lesson of the day, before the weekend arrived, and our first week was over.

I threw my bag over my shoulder, climbed the steps to the mobile, for English with Mrs Row. She handed out the book we would be reading, and working on for the rest of the term, 'Of Mice and Men'.

I flicked open the book and read the opening pages. We read the first three chapters of the book and were set to read more for homework, which made two pieces for the weekend. History and English. I knew Wendy would devour the book in one sitting. As much as I loved reading, I did not fancy spending my weekend reading it.

I had been right, Wendy had read the whole book by Sunday evening, and I decided I should read the book myself, it was a good book, and I enjoyed it. I read the required pages and made notes, so that I did not have to read it again.

Sunday, we headed to the skating park, but the one person Wendy was looking for was not there. "He's not here," I said.

"I know. Hey, we could come back tomorrow night," she suggested.

"On a school night?"

She shrugged.

"Depends how much homework we get."

Monday passed in a blur, once again, the homework was more than we had ever expected and we never made it back to the skating park.

Homework complete, I threw myself on the bed and fell instantly asleep.

Mark had only been in the school a week and Karen was not about to give up on him. It was a good thing I had read the book, as Mrs Row insisted on quizzing us, and I was more than grateful for making notes. I knew the answers, but as the bell rang; we were all relieved and scrambled out of the classroom in need of a break. We raced towards the field and sat on the grass; I had signs of a headache brewing. I looked out across the field, watching Mark; he stood with his rescuer, Simon. I noticed Karen sat on the opposite side, watching him too. The girl had become his shadow, following him everywhere he went. I watched him, guilty once again for thinking about Mark instead of Joshua. I closed my eyes, allowed Joshua's face to swim before me.

The half an hour break flew past.

Double science, I thought, reading the assignment on the board. I sighed as I took down the information, head resting on my arm, as I peered above it to copy down the last few notes.

A creaking noise distracted me from the board; I turned in the direction of the sound. In the doorway stood Mark, I could have sworn there had been a light surrounding him. Blinking, I looked down at my paper, then up again. Mark nodded and took a seat behind us. Simon followed.

"Sorry we're late," Mark said.

How I loved the American accent.

"Hurry up," the teacher said.

I heard them unzip their bags, assuming they were taking out their pencil cases and books. I wanted to turn around, but I did not dare. The other girls did, staring at him from behind, in front and beside him. I heard Mark swallow as he began to scribble notes in his book. *Poor guy, all this attention and it's the start of your second week. Yeah right, like he doesn't love it really.*

Chapter 24
Pretend Girlfriend

~ Mark ~

Another school day ended. I did not have a chance to speak with Simon alone.

Karen continued to follow us as we marched towards the bus; I did not intend to board the bus, not today. I knew the walk would be long, but I needed to clear my head. I had got myself into this situation, and needed a plan to get out of it. Besides I had a feeling Karen did not believe I had a girlfriend. I had to convince her that I did, or come clean.

As we reached the school entrance, two girls in our year slipped their arms through mine and led me towards the bus. I smiled at them, as Karen managed to take their place in one movement. How she did she do that? I had no idea. I attempted to shake her free, but she clung on tighter. Telling her I had a girlfriend seemed to make no difference, maybe she knew the truth. She continued to ask me to take her out; the girl was not going to stop. Nothing stood in her way, she reminded me of some of the girls back home. Girls like that; I wanted nothing to do with. She had looks I would grant her that, and the body of a grown woman. I don't think Karen saw me the day I witnessed her speak to supermarket girl. It was not just because it was her, the words she flung at my supermarket girl, were not nice. I glanced back; I knew Debbie by name now, she walked with her friend, the girl she was always with, Wendy. Simon told me he had liked her for two years, but had never had the courage to ask her out. I knew how he felt. I had no evidence that Debbie was dating the guy who had played Danny. Since the scene in the

Dream World

musical, I had not once seen them together.

Simon had become a good friend in the short time I had been in the UK. He, of course, had warned me about Karen. I had to do something fast, since she had started to follow me everywhere I went, even the boys bathroom. I was not sure I would ever get used to that smell.

Reaching the bus, I managed to remove Karen from my arm.

"We're going to walk," I whispered to Simon.

"You know that's a long walk," he said.

"I do, but we need to talk."

I watched Karen board the bus and climb the steps. I stepped back as the doors shut. She stood, I assumed ready to join us, but the bus pulled away and I waved goodbye. Her face fell. I smiled and turned to Simon.

"Are you going to ask Wendy out?"

"Is that what you wanted to talk about?" he asked.

I shook my head. "No, but wondered if you were planning to."

He shook his head. "Nah, I like her, but I don't think she likes me. Not like that."

"Come on, how you will know that if you don't ask her?"

"Like you fancying Debbie, even though you have a girlfriend."

"About that," I began. I told him the truth. He smiled. I had not expected that.

"So you lied, big deal, I get why you did it. Problem is Karen won't give up."

"I know. That's why I need a plan."

"What kind of plan?"

"That's a good question. All I can think about is either asking one of those girls out, or finding someone who will pretend they have been my girlfriend for ages."

"Ah, yeah since you already said you had one."

"Yeah, that was a little lie. What girl would pretend to be my girlfriend and say they had been for a while?"

"I bet every girl you have met since you started at this school."

He was right, but which girl would want to pretend to be my girlfriend. None of the girls who followed me around would be right for this. Who else could I ask?

~ Karen ~

I could not believe it; they did not get on the bus. I stood watching from the window, almost falling into my seat as it pulled away. I would have gone with them, had I known. He was not getting away that easily, he would be mine. He will agree to one date, and I don't care how long it takes. I will break him.

~ Mark ~

Simon was right. I could ask any girl, but would they agree to lie, to help get Karen get off my back. I had only been here a few weeks, and I had tangled myself in a silly lie, because I did not want to date one girl. I only had myself to blame, but a pretend girlfriend was the plan. It took a lot longer than I had anticipated to walk home. Simon had been right on that, too, but it was worth it. We had discussed many things on the walk back to my grandparents' house. I had noticed a few girls following us as we walked. None of the girls, I would ask to be my girlfriend. I heard them giggling. We walked quickly to where I lived. As I arrived at the house, I swung open the gate, not turning to check if the girls were still following us.

The attention at first was nice, but some days I wished they would leave me alone. It was times like that, I thought about my cousin, and how he loved the attention. It was not for me. I was a one-girl guy.

My nan stepped out of the house, smiling.

"There you are, you're late."

"Sorry, we walked home."

"Did you miss the bus?" she asked.

"No, we just fancied walking."

Dream World

Shaking her head, she allowed us to pass her and with one hand shooed the girls away, who were lingering outside our gate.

"Come on in, boys. Let's get you in where it's safe," my grandfather said.

"Leave the boy alone, dear," my nan said.

I rolled my eyes, my grandfather tutted, and raised his bushy eyebrows. My nan passed behind him and pretended to wipe his bald head. I tried not to laugh, Simon chuckled.

"How'd you boys like a nice ice cream float?" my nan asked.

We both nodded, and headed to the kitchen.

Over the short time I had been here, I had grown to love them more than I already did. They weren't your typical grandparents. My nan still loved to bake, and wrote regularly to her pen pals. One other thing my nan loved to do was talk. On the phone or in person, I had learnt that, the day at the supermarket. My grandfather would take himself outside to his little shed, his retreat. There were no tools in the shed, just an old television resting on a box. He would sit on a deck chair, watch old movies, and smoke his cigar. Even though, he thought my nan didn't know, she did, and liked to tell her friends so. He had no idea she knew.

"He thinks I don't know. Who does he think them in the tin? The fairies?" she told me.

The coke floats stood on the table, just the way we liked them. A huge blob of ice-cream at the bottom, a handful of raisins, and filled to the brim with coke. They tasted fantastic.

"Thank you," we both said.

"We need to think about who will be willing to do this to make the plan work."

"We do."

"I have a feeling this is going to be harder than we thought. Who wants to pretend to date me?"

"Gosh, yes I mean you are perfect, right? Every girl's

dream."

I flicked some ice-cream at him, using my straw.

"Hey!"

"I'm not perfect, far from it."

"Fine, you're not perfect."

I nodded in agreement, and turned my attention to the coke float.

"All we have to do is find a girl who's willing to go along with our plan. One Karen would believe to be your girlfriend."

"Yeah, but who?" I asked. I had one girl in mind. How could I ask her? After all, we had never spoken to one another. Why would she agree to help me?

"I think tomorrow we'll start looking. It's only got to be short term," Simon said. "We could ask Debbie, I mean, since she's not interested in you."

Rub it in why don't you.

"What do you think?"

"I don't know, but Debbie was fantastic as Sandy," I said, recalling how she looked that night she played her.

"She was. You enjoyed her performance?"

"Most of it," I said, realising I had said that out loud.

"What does that mean?"

How could I tell him I was jealous of her kissing Danny? I knew I had no right to be.

Simon left an hour later; I headed to my room and switched on the tape player, my thoughts on her. I could not get her out of my head.

Lying with my arms above my head, I could hear her singing to me. Closing my eyes, I saw her face, her lips. Ever since I saw her on that stage, my dreams had been the same. She played Sandy, and I played Danny, and each time it came to the kiss, I took her in my arms and kissed her passionately.

Chapter 25
One Bite Is All It Took

~ Mark ~

Over the next two weeks, Karen continued to follow me everywhere I went. She even skipped the few lessons she did not have with me. It seemed I could not escape her.

At every opportunity, she would pop out from her hiding spot and ask me out. I tried every excuse, but she ignored them all. She never let anything deter her. She would not give up. I had to do something and soon. So far, we had not managed to ask anyone to help me, and Karen thought I had made up the girlfriend. Little did she know, I had?

Becoming drained by her constant persistence; wanting her to leave me alone. I saw her everywhere I went. Spending time out, became less frequent, as wherever we went, she was there, lurking, making eyes at me. So we stayed in, either at my grandparents' house or at Simon's.

At school, I could not escape her, and found it hard to concentrate on my work, with her staring at me all the time.

Wednesday morning, I pushed open the old gate; it creaked loudly as it swung shut behind me. My grandparents stood in the open door. My grandfather's remaining hair blew gently in the wind. I shook my head, and waved goodbye, pulling my bag up onto my shoulder and made my way along the cracked path, with the grass growing through in a zigzag pattern. My nan once told me 'never stand on the cracks'. To this day, I still avoided them.

I hoped I could avoid Karen. I had a sinking feeling in the pit of my stomach, it would be impossible to. My thoughts turned to the plan I had set in motion, but so far, we had not found the right girl.

I continued avoiding the cracks as I passed a few houses on the opposite side of the street, to where the bus stop was. I looked left, as a blue car sped by forcing me to step back before crossing. Simon stood with his arms crossed. I nodded, and took a deep breath as I laid my bag down on the floor beside my feet.

"I think we need to ask the chosen one today," Simon said, as the bus arrived.

We climbed aboard.

"I agree, but who is this chosen one?" I asked, flopping down into a seat.

"I still don't know who, but the problem is, they may want to be your real girlfriend."

I sighed. He was right. Who would want to pretend to date me to get rid of Karen? He had suggested Debbie once before, and I wondered if she would be the right girl to ask.

"Do you think we should ask Debbie?"

"Actually that might work. Two reasons, Debbie and Karen were once friends. Best friends, I heard. If you date Debbie, Karen won't like it. It could go two ways, get her off your back or it could make her want you more."

"You think it would work?"

"I do. That's sorted, then. We, I mean you, can ask Debbie today."

I gulped. I wanted to ask her out, but not as a fake girlfriend.

~ Karen ~

How dare he try to pull that stunt with me? I am not about to let him try to worm his way out of a date now. I knew he had no girlfriend, I just knew it. *Oh, Mark you will be mine.* I *will make my move today; you will not be able to resist me Mark Hobson.*

Dream World

I licked my lips and sat back in my chair, watching him as the bus travelled the last few yards to the school. Getting on a stop earlier had worked well for me today. He had no idea I was here listening to their every word.

I smiled, as the gang continued to chat around me. I ignored them. They were making plans for the weekend; I knew it would mean I would be paying for it. I liked to, but really, they seemed to expect it. Not one of them offered to pay. Were they really using me?

~ *Mark* ~

The bus drew up beside the school, and everyone stood and clambered down. I saw her then, as I stood on the sidewalk, a smile on her lips. Wendy stood beside her. They walked towards me. Just as she did, Karen pushed past her, knocking her to the ground. I watched open mouthed. Why did she do that? It dawned on me then, she was heading towards me, with a smile on her lips. I turned, and attempted to escape her. I moved quickly towards Debbie, dodging Karen and offered Debbie my hand; she looked up at me, and smiled as she took it. I felt a shot of electricity go through me. She stood and brushed herself down with her free hand.

"Are you okay?" I asked, turning and glaring at Karen, who stood rooted to the spot, hands on her hips. I realised I still had Debbie's hand and let it drop.

"She's fine thank you, Mark. Aren't you, Debbie," Wendy said, nudging her.

"I am," she stuttered.

Had she felt it too? She thanked me and scurried away, leaving me breathless. I should have asked her, I had wanted to, but I could not speak.

"Did you ask her?" Simon said, joining me. I shook my head.

"Mark, you'll have to do it next time, right?"

"Yes," I said, as we headed towards the school, passing Karen. She fell into step beside me and I did my best to shake her off.

"I hear you broke up with your girlfriend!"

My heart began to beat loudly, my mouth dried up. Why had she said that? Did she hear what we had said on the bus? I hoped not. Maybe someone had heard us and told her.

"Where did you hear that?" I stammered.

"Doesn't matter how I heard."

"Oh…" I began. How do I get out of this one?

"Well, I thought we should go see a movie together?"

I sighed; my heart making its own music inside my chest. What to do now, she would never back off now she knew the truth. *Maybe I should take her out, and have the worst date ever,* I thought.

"Okay," I said, hoping this idea would work, and I did not regret it later.

"You…what…did you just say yes. Great, when?"

"Friday night," I replied.

Karen nodded, informing me that would be perfect and raced towards her friends. I assumed to tell them.

"Way to stick to the plan," Simon whispered.

I rolled my eyes. What had I done?

~ Karen ~

I joined the girls, a huge smile on my lips. This was perfect, I had a date with him, and I was going to enjoy every moment of it. I could not wait to rub it in. Debbie would be the next person I would tell, as soon as we reached the form room. I pushed the door open, allowing it to slam on the wall, which made every one of them turn in my direction, just the attention I wanted. I strutted over, my breasts bouncing with every step. I smiled, and reached her table; they looked up, and frowned at me. I smirked.

"Just had to tell you, Debbie, I'm dating Mark now, so keep your paws of my man."

She opened her mouth to speak, but nothing came out, bless her. I stood and joined my gang, flopping down into my seat, a smile on my lips. Friday was not going to arrive soon enough.

~ Debbie ~

Should have known she would get her claws into him. It was only a matter of time. I already knew I had no chance with him, but there had been a tiny flicker of hope when he helped me up off the grass. I had felt the electricity between us, and thought he had too. How wrong was I? Guys like him go for girls like her. Well, he was welcome to her. I watched her join her gang, with a smile on her lips. She was never going to let us forget she was the one to get him first. I turned to Wendy.

"You don't need to say it, but one bite was all it took."

Chapter 26
The Date

~ Mark ~

We made our way to our first lesson. Listening to Simon tell me what a mistake I had made. I already knew that.

"Simon, I know it's a bad idea, I agree, but I was trapped. What else could I say?"

"Maybe, use the word no."

I sighed. Simon was right. I should have said no, but I knew she would hound me, until I said yes. Going on this one date may just get her of my back for good, and to me that had to be a good thing.

We walked inside the classroom to find a seat. I perched on a stool as Simon joined me. I could not look at her, as Mr Jolly told us to continue shading our fruit drawings. I usually watched Debbie during my art lesson, but with Karen staring at me, my cheeks flushed. I dared not look up.

I could not wait until the day was over. Simon heard her tell everyone we were an item.

"I told you, she won't let you go."

What had I gotten myself into? "I don't know; let's just see how Friday goes. If I go."

"You'd stand her up." He shook his head. "Not sure that is a wise thing to do."

"Really!"

"Yeah, just make it a date to remember. "

I rolled my eyes; I had an idea, but was not sure if my plan would work.

Dream World

~ Karen ~

I had waited long enough for tonight to arrive. The girls were as excited about this date as I was. I had chosen my favourite outfit, and now I was ready to get into it. The girls left an hour ago. They wanted to come over, use the pool and help me decide what to wear, not that I needed their advice. I already knew what I was wearing. I could see the envy on all of their faces. Good, Mark was mine and tonight would be even better if Debbie saw us. Not that she would, she rarely went out. What must it be like to be that poor? I tried to remember, but I could not.

~ Mark ~

I wanted the date over with. I dressed in clothes I pulled out of the laundry basket, sniffed them, they had been in there a few days, so knew they would be perfect. I splashed on a generous amount of my grandfather's aftershave, before putting on an old army jacket, which also belonged to him.

I arrived early, and discovered Karen was early, too. I watched her from a distance. I had to admit she looked good, even if she wore a similar outfit to those girls back home. Any guy would love to see her looking like that. The heels made her legs look longer than they were. She stood with her arms crossed, pushing out her breasts.

I waited ten minutes, before strolling towards her. She was pacing, perfect. She spotted me, stopped, and quickly walked towards me. I said nothing and led her inside, paying only for myself. I moved to the counter and ordered my own snacks, waiting for her to do the same. I watched her look at me, knew she wanted to say something about what I wore, but she remained quiet.

A man took our tickets and allowed us to enter; I led her down to the front.

"Wouldn't the back be better?" she asked.

"No," I snapped, seeing her inhale the aftershave, almost choking on it.

"You look nice!" she said.

"Thanks," I said. "Now, can you be quiet? I'm trying to watch the movie." I began to eat my popcorn, not offering her any.

~ *Karen* ~

He left me again. I sat open mouthed as the bus pulled out of the station. My thoughts turned to the date. I could not believe it; he was gorgeous, but not tonight. What happened to him? Had he a twin? That thought sprang to mind. That had to be it. Mark, for some reason, sent him instead. I liked the idea of the twin, but in reality, I knew it was not the truth. I did not understand why he had acted that way? I was used to paying for everything. People expected it. After all, my family was loaded. I could not get the smell out of my nose; it seemed to linger on my clothes and hair. I would need a bath when I got home, a long hot bubble bath. Right now, I craved it. When my friends asked about this date, I would lie. They could never know the truth. It would be bad for my reputation.

The bell on the bus rang, a girl with dark red hair and startling green eyes passed me. Usually I would make some kind of remark, but not tonight. I was fuming. How dare he treat me this way?

He had a nerve; he wouldn't even make eye contact with me. I had dressed to impress. Other guys I dated could not keep their eyes off me. He did not even seem to notice.

The bus arrived at the stop he should have got off at I had pictured us kissing goodbye, before he left me sat alone on the bus, promising he would call me. The bus pulled over at my stop. I stood and made my way off the bus. As soon as my feet hit the ground, the heavens opened and the rain pelted down.

"Typical," I mumbled.

Now I was wet, cold and frustrated. Salty tears fell. The rain disguised them. I put one foot firmly on the road, and crossed to the other side. The concrete beneath my feet made a tapping sound with each step. All the time the rain fell heavier, hair

Dream World

plastered to my face. I stepped onto the opposite path, my heel snapped. *Damn it*, I thought, bending down as a car beeped it's horn and flashed their lights at me. I limped home; misjudging the next step, I almost fell over. In frustration, I removed the shoes and walked the short distance home barefoot.

I cursed under my breath as I reached the driveway, hobbling along the path to the door, through blurry eyes. I fumbled with the key in the lock, finally it slid in.

No one was home. I knew they would be out, having another meal with Jackie and her fiancé. The wedding was all they talked about. I wished it were over already. I knew, even then, they would continue to talk about it.

Reaching my room, I peeled off the jacket, tossed the shoes in the bin and ran a bath. Minutes later, the scent of the bubble bath filled the room. I removed my soaking wet clothes and tossed them into the basket. Switching off the hot tap, I tested the water. Perfect. Allowing my hair to float around me, as my thoughts turned once again to my date. The disaster of a lifetime, and one I would not forget in a hurry.

Closing my eyes, I allowed all thoughts of the date to float away, and thought of only what I really wanted. The one thing no one knew I wanted, and craved more than anything. Something I could never admit. I just wanted to be loved, not by a guy, but by my parents. I needed it, deserved it. What had I done wrong to make them dislike me so much? I did okay at school. Had a group of friends my mother approved of, since she disliked Debbie.

My mother had hated Debbie's mother, and disliked her daughter, too. In fact, my mother disliked the whole family, but inviting them to the engagement party had not been to be kind. Oh no. It was to prove to the Conways how much better we were than them. I heard my mother make snide comments from the first day we became friends.

"Don't be friends with her. If she's anything like her mother, she'll lie to you, betray you and then, when you are not looking she'll turn them all against you."

I never saw it, we were friends and I had liked her. She was kind, but when we moved from the street, my mother had sat me down, and told me, new house, new friends. Now we were wealthy, I could not hang around with her. She made that clear. For a few weeks, I disobeyed my mother. When she discovered the truth, I was grounded for a week. I had never been grounded before. I hated my mother, and pleaded with her to allow me to be friends with Debbie. What she had said about her was not true. I had looked into my mother's eyes and knew it was no good. Jackie stood chuckling in the background.

"Ah. Are you going to cry?" She had said.

At seven, the tears fell as I sat in my big spacious room, all alone. Scared and lost without my friend. I had no choice; I would not speak to her again. Debbie would get over it. At least that was what I told myself.

A week passed, and then two. We never spoke a word. Debbie looked upset, but I moved on, made new friends, and turned my back on her.

A month later, a new girl arrived in school, Wendy. Not only had she taken my best friend, but she moved into my old house. My old life. From that day forward, I hated them both. Which made my mother happy, but I felt betrayed, as Debbie had replaced me with Wendy.

~Mark~

I arrived home, paying the cab driver and walked inside. Tossing the clothes in the laundry basket, I then showered.

Twenty minutes later, I sat wrapped in a towel on the bed.

I then changed, and walked over to Simon's. I would have rung him, but recalled he had no phone.

I knocked on his door, and waited for him to answer. A few minutes later, sitting in his kitchen, a glass of coke in hand. I explained how the date went and the look on her face as I left her on the bus. Simon chuckled.

"She's not going to be a happy girl tomorrow. Are you ready for that?"

"I think so," I said, truth was, I had no idea how she would react. I was hoping she would give up; decide I was not the guy she thought I was. I looked forward to the next day of school; hoping it worked, and Karen would be off my back.

Chapter 27
Dear Diary

~ Karen ~

Changed into a nighty and a dressing gown, I pulled out a pen and my diary from its secret hiding place and began to write,

'Dear Diary,

I don't know what's wrong with me? Do people really hate me? I'm pretty, and popular, but tonight I had the worst date of my life. Can you believe that? Why would he treat me like that? I think 'she' put him up to it. Turning up dressed like a tramp and smelling like something which had died. Did he think I was going to let that put me of? No way. She isn't having him. Tomorrow, I will act as if the date was the best ever, and no one and I mean no one will know any different.

Mark you are mine!!!!

Oh and guess what Diary, Mum and Dad are not here, again. I'm all alone. I can guess where and who they are with... Jackie. Why do they hate me? I just don't understand what I've done wrong. I've done everything my mother ever asked of me.'

I paused and wrote in large letters at the bottom, 'WHAT IS WRONG WITH ME?'

Closing the diary, I sighed heavily, placing it back into its secret location. I lay down and closed my eyes as fresh tears rolled down my cheeks. I fell asleep curled up in a ball.

~ Mark ~

With the date behind me, I decided to stay home. Not feeling in the mood to leave the house. Simon turned up, and we sat in my room, talking about my date with Karen. Hoping it had put her off.

"Shame you didn't ask Debbie!"

I nodded. He was right, if only I had asked her when I helped her up. I should never have agreed to take Karen out. What she did to Debbie, should have made me say no. Now she would never help me out, after taking out the girl who treated her like that. If I was to get her to like me, I had to make it up to her, somehow. I could get her tickets to see my parents. Would that work?

~ Karen ~

I pushed every thought of him out of my head, even though they wanted to know more. I said it was the best date ever, and the kiss was magical. They were happy with that. Stephanie and Annie ransacked my wardrobe searching for clothes to wear for the catwalk. I was bored of these now, but they still loved them. I sat on the end of the bed watching them, as they tossed out the ones they wanted. No one asked my opinion, I was not thinking about them, my mind was elsewhere wondering what they were doing. Something fun I bet. I wanted the weekend to be over, not that I wanted to be in school any more than I wanted to be sat here watching them wearing my clothes.

~ Mark ~

The next morning, I dressed for school, walked across the road and joined Simon at the bus stop.

We sat in our seats and waited for the ride from hell to begin. I held my breath as she boarded, her mouth in a broad smile. My heart sank as she waltzed towards me. She motioned for Simon to move, but he ignored her. She grabbed hold of the rail and was forced to take the seat behind us, a smile still plastered to her face. I sighed and kept my head down. I could feel her breath on the back of my neck, as the bus continued on.

As soon as it pulled over at the school, I flew off the bus, not waiting for Simon. He would catch up. Taking large strides towards the school, I felt someone slide their arm through mine. I knew it was her. I could smell her. God she smelt good. *Stop it*, I told myself, scanning the crowd for Simon. He was a few people behind me, I threw him a help-me look. Not that he could; I had made my bed, as my nan would say. Now I had to deal with her.

She marched us towards our form room. I gritted my teeth as girls stared at me, and saw the disappointment in their eyes. Karen smiled, head held high. There was no way to shake her from my grip. She was not giving up. Now I needed another plan. I let my hand fall loose, and she tightened her grip. Simon followed us, holding the door open for Wendy and Debbie. He waited until they were inside, and joined me at the back of the room.

Karen released my hand, stood before me, while her fingers toyed with the top button of her black coat.

"I had a great time last night!" she announced.

"Me too," I lied, *why did I say that?* I rolled my eyes.

"Good, glad to hear that. I'll see you later," she said, turning on her heel and joining her friends.

"What do I do now?" I asked, watching her leave. "Help me, Simon."

~ *Debbie* ~

Three days later, I stared at the blank monitor during an I.T lesson. I had no idea what to type. I caught a glimpse of Karen out of the corner of my eye, as she sat beside me. I could only assume her being next to me, meant either trouble or she wanted to gloat. I attempted to ignore her, but Karen never gave up. I briefly looked up; she saw it as her opportunity. I held my breath, saw the look of pleasure in her eyes, ready to spill her news, whether I wanted to hear it or not. I rolled my eyes as she began.

"Remember the other day I told you Mark and are together. Well we went out on Friday night and had the best time," she began.

I placed a smile on my lips, *here we go*. "Do you think I care?"

"Of course you do. Everyone does. Everyone wants to date Mark, and I have him!"

"So!" I interrupted, yawning I turned back to face the screen.

Karen continued to tell me all the details of their date. Closing my mind to Karen, I allowed my thoughts to wander as her voice became lost in the background.

I stroll down the road heading home; a car approaches, and stops me. I turn, to discover that the vehicle is a Limo. My mouth is open, as I admire its beauty. The white Limo's windows are blacked out.

The driver opens his door, exits and heads around the Limo to the passenger door. The driver greets me with a nod. I cannot see inside. I lean forward, balancing on one leg. I control my balance. I step forward as the driver places a hand on my shoulder, as flashes of light rain upon the car. Paparazzi. The flashes continue, causing red circles to appear before my eyes. I attempt to focus on the passenger inside, but the circles of light make it impossible. Trying harder, I close my eyes, count to ten, before reopening them. He leans forward and steps out, illuminated by light. I hear my name and spin around.

"Debbie, are you with us?" Mr Bean said, loudly.

I tore my gaze from the blank screen, realising I had slipped into my own world once again. Not that it had been my fault. I needed to escape Karen. I did not need to hear all about their fantastic date. I turned to face my teacher, turning crimson.

"Sorry, Sir, yes I am," I said, turning back to the blank screen.

Karen sniggered.

"Good, now get on, please."

I nodded, eyes fixed on the screen. I did not look at her, or over to Wendy. I knew Wendy would be wearing her I-told-you-daydreaming-would-get-you-in-trouble face.

I placed my hands on the keys and began to work. I focused on nothing else, even the constant giggling coming from Karen was not going to distract me now.

Chapter 28
Rescue Plan

~ Mark ~

We had double science next, two whole hours of Science. I preferred the single lessons, to the double ones. I knew she would be there, watching my every move. Simon sat at the back, and I took the seat beside him. I watched Debbie and Wendy enter the room, followed by Karen. She stormed past them towards us. My stomach flipped. What did she want now?

"Meant to ask, what're we doing tonight?"

"Nothing. I'm busy."

"Doing what?" she asked.

"Working," I said. Another lie.

"Another night, then!" she replied.

"Yeah, right. I'll call you," I said, making a telephone shape with my hand. Why did I just do that? She blew me a kiss. I pretended to catch it, as she turned her back, I then threw it to the floor and stamped on it. I leant forward in my chair and put my head in my hands. Now I would have to take her out again. What was I thinking?

"She thinks we're a couple. How did I get myself into this?"

"I did warn you, mate."

"I know. It's my own fault. I just thought if I took her out, treated her badly she would back off. Instead it made things worse," I said, shaking my head.

"Dump her then! I mean you're not actually going out anyway," Simon replied.

"True. I have no idea how to tell her, or if she would even

listen."

"You're right," Simon said.

Simon nudged me, indicating the two girls by the window. He really liked Wendy, but would Debbie help me?

"No." I shook my head. "We can't ask them."

"Why not?"

"It doesn't feel right, you like Wendy and I..."

"Like Debbie, so what's the problem?"

"She won't help me."

"How do you know, unless you ask her?"

"I can't ask her, while Karen is in the room."

"Mmm, I wonder."

Simon stood, and walked towards the teacher, threw a look back at me, and raised his eyebrows.

Fifteen minutes later, he returned.

A few minutes after Simon returned, a young lady requested Karen to go to the office. Had Simon had a part in that? I wondered, the look on his face, told me he had. This was my chance, my only chance.

I knew he had a hidden agenda, but he was right. Asking Debbie and Wendy may be my last chance. I took a deep breath and made my way over to them, my heart racing as I stopped at their table. They looked up at me. I felt my cheeks flush. I opened my mouth, but could not speak. Simon joined me, and rescued me once again.

"Debbie, Wendy, would one of you lovely ladies be able to help me, well Mark actually," Simon began.

"Since when did you need help, Mark?" Debbie asked.

"Come on Debbie, you have to help; look, you know what Karen's like. She's obsessed with him, and won't leave him alone."

"I do, but he did agree to take her on a date. How can I help him?" She shrugged. "It seems to me you're together now."

She was right; I had agreed to take her out, but we were not a couple. She continued to stare at Simon. Did she fancy him? I

Dream World

hoped not. Wendy nodded at every word he said. I had a feeling she fancied him too. Simon would love that.

"Karen thinks we are," I said, finding my voice. "I don't think she would accept me dumping her, even though she's not my girlfriend. If..." I began.

"...she dumped you," she said, turning to face me. Her green eyes sparkling as she spoke.

"Yes, if she dumped me."

"Why would she dump you?" Wendy asked.

"I need a good reason why she would!"

"And how can we help with that?"

"I don't know. We're lost for ideas. I even planned to ask someone out to get her off my back, but that did not go to plan."

"I see, but I thought you had a girlfriend back home."

I opened my mouth, and shook my head. I had now told the truth on that one. One lie corrected.

"Well," Wendy began. "We could tell her someone else likes her. Knowing Karen, she won't be able to resist another guy's attention. She's done it before."

"Really? You think that could work?"

"Do you have a better plan?" Debbie asked.

We shook our heads.

"That's what I thought. Fine, we'll try and help, but I am not promising anything."

"What's in this for us?" Wendy asked.

"In it for you?" I asked, having not thought that far ahead. I knew what I would like, but I could not ask her that, not my supermarket girl. My Sandy.

"Yeah, you know, we help you out. What do we get in return?" Wendy asked.

"I don't know yet," Simon interrupted. "Maybe we can come up with something, Mark?"

I nodded.

"Okay," Wendy sighed, "If you take too long, I'll make the

decision for you!"

Debbie rolled her eyes.

"Deal," Simon said, before I could answer. I nodded, agreeing.

~ Debbie ~

I had agreed to help Mark dump Karen. Actually, Wendy had. Even though he said, they were not together. I knew Karen, and he was right, she would not allow him to dump her.

I knew why Wendy had accepted to help. She had a plan. I saw the twinkle in her eyes. She already knew what she wanted as a reward, but what we were going to have to do would take some time. We had to think of who would help us, who would make Karen drool. Since she had dated many of the guys already in the school, we had our work cut out.

The two boys moved back to their seats, just in time as the door slammed open and she stormed back in the room. She did not look happy, but then when did she these days. Apart from when she had her hooks into Mark.

He looked even better up close; I dared not look at him. He might see, like every other girl here, I fancied him.

~Mark~

Simon and I made our way to the field. I nudged him, realising she was, as usual following us. We did our best to walk in the opposite direction. *I hope they can help me.* We walked round a corner, and hid as she passed by. We went in the other direction, and chose to hide out in the library, a place she would never go.

I sat down at a table; Simon pulled out a chair and sat opposite me.

"I hope this plan works. I can't hide forever."

"Hate to repeat myself, but I did warn you," Simon said. "On the other hand, it looks like they may be interested in us after all."

"You think?"

"Yeah, Wendy was drooling all over me."

"I did notice."

"So I didn't imagine it?"

"No."

~ Debbie ~

The last bell of the day rang, ending our P.E lesson. We scrambled up to the changing rooms and threw on our clothes. None of us showered. We were desperate to head home. I scrunched my clothes into a ball, tossed them in my bag and walked towards the door. The P.E teacher stood by the door and watched us leave. Usually, she would insist we showered, but today she let it slide. I sighed with relief, none of us showered properly anyway. Every one of us loathed them, and thanked God they were no longer one big shower unit. They had installed single showers for our privacy.

We walked towards the bus stop.

"Thank God, that's over. What a day."

"Yeah, shame we weren't on the same team today."

"I know. She did it on purpose you know."

Wendy nodded. "Come on, we need to think about who will be perfect for Karen."

"I know. We can brainstorm at my house, if you like?"

She nodded.

I needed this, thinking about Mark and the plan, took any thoughts off my mother. I liked thinking about him, but it made me feel guilty, betraying Joshua.

An hour later, Wendy arrived; we sat in my room, discussing Mark and Karen.

"You know, she just had to tell me," I sighed. "It's not like he'd be interested in me, would he?"

"Oh come on, Debbie, of course he would."

"No--"

"Stop it. Look if the guy of your dreams is out there, you'll find him. Trust me."

I smiled; Wendy always knew the right thing to say.

"Who can we ask?" Wendy asked.

"I don't know. She has dated most of the guys in school. We need just one guy she has not dated, but who?"

"I have no idea." Wendy shrugged.

I shook my head, I had no idea either, and not one name came to mind. Wendy suggested I slept over the following night, to plan more and think about it. Maybe she wanted to tell me about her idea for our reward. Although I had an idea what she had in mind.

Chapter 29
Like Mother Like Daughter

~ Debbie ~

Friday night, I stood in the kitchen, alone. Wendy had left half an hour ago, all plans of the sleepover gone. Her brother had taken a tumble down the stairs, and may need stitches.

I placed the popcorn in the microwave, and hit the start button.

Five minutes later, I poured a bag of steaming hot popcorn into a bowl. Taking it into the living room, I set it down on the coffee table. Greg and Sally were already in bed. Steve and Carol had an early night too. My father came in from work, and then went out again. Leaving me to take care of my siblings if they woke, not that I minded, but it seemed my father was spending less and less time at home.

Placing the movie in the machine, I settled back on the sofa with the popcorn on my lap. My eyes felt heavy as the movie began.

The music plays as I sway to the beat, Joshua holds me in his arms. I listen to his heartbeat. He stops, holds my hand and leads me outside to a waiting Limo. A white Limo. I gasp as he opens the door, and allows me to enter. I place one foot inside…

Waking up, rubbing my eyes, I saw my father sat on the opposite chair. He smiled up at me as I sat up.

"I didn't hear you come in?"

"Good film was it, love?" he asked.

"I don't think I saw any of the film."

"It was good, well the last fifty minutes of what I saw anyway."

I chuckled.

"Get yourself off to bed!" he ordered.

I nodded.

"I'll clear this away."

I nodded again as I stood drowsily, and headed to the door, and made my way to my room. I threw myself on the bed and fell instantly asleep.

The duvet became tangled between my feet as I tossed and turned as I slept.

I stand centre stage with the microphone in my hand. I lick my lips; scan the empty seats, hoping he will be taking up one of them. I sing to the empty hall. I saw a silhouette of a person in the distance. I watch as it moves forward. I use my finger to entice him to me. The figure steps forward slowly. I continue to sing and signal the person to come to me. The figure does as instructed.

Reaching the base of the steps, the microphone crashes to the floor, the sound bounces off the walls. I ignore it as I race down the steps towards him. Joshua opens his arms and I dive into them. They encase me. I rest my head on his shoulder, look up see his face, but all I can see is those dazzling brown eyes. It does not matter. He is still my Joshua. I know it is him. It has to be him. I close my eyes and listen to the beating of his heart as he holds me tight.

"Debbie, time to get up, love," my father's voice called.

"Not yet," I whispered. "Just a few more minutes."

"Breakfast is on the table. Don't be too long or it'll get cold."

"I'm up."

I rolled my eyes, pulled the duvet back revealing my bare legs. In one swift movement, I swung my legs over the side of the bed, a loud yawn left my lips as I stretched my arms high above my head.

Dream World

I closed my eyes, inhaling the scent of the freshly cooked bacon. My stomach rumbled as I headed down the stairs.

"Smells good, Dad," I announced as I entered the kitchen.

"Thanks love, but it wasn't all my idea," my father said.

"Carol was up half the night. I thought this would be a good way for her to start the day. Besides I really wanted eggs and bacon."

"Well, I for one am glad you did," I said, taking a seat. "How is Carol? I haven't seen her since the day before yesterday."

"She's fine. Nothing a full night's sleep won't fix. It seems the babies are awake when she wants to sleep. I'm insisting she has a lay in and rest today. Starting with a hearty full English breakfast." Steve placed a plate on a tray along with a steaming mug of tea.

It had been a long time since we had eaten a cooked breakfast, and I would enjoy every bite.

Breakfast eaten, I climbed the stairs the stairs to my room and entered my bathroom and switched on the shower. Waiting for the water to heat up, I pulled out a towel, placing it on the radiator.

Ten minutes later, I wrapped the warm towel around me and went back into my room. I then dried myself and changed into clean clothes. Putting on my trainers, I tied the laces and then walked over to Wendy's.

I took two steps towards the gate, thoughts of my dream drifting in and out of my head. How I wished I had the nerve to sing alone on stage, or with Joshua. Yes, I had played Sandy, but I had not been alone. I had the cast behind me, even during the solo. The one place I could sing alone was in my dream world. Joshua being there eased my nerves.

I looked up at the clear blue sky, noting how brightly the sun shone. I wondered if I should turn back and collect my sunglasses, but decided against it, after all I was only going over the road.

With one foot balanced on the edge of the path, I looked up and down the street, before crossing.

I knocked on Wendy's door; her mother opened it and smiled back at me.

"Morning, love," she said.

"Morning," I replied.

"Come on in."

"Is she up?"

"She is."

I stood at the base of the stairs; as Wendy came through from the kitchen.

"Morning, are you ready?" I asked.

"I am. Do you think we should walk or take our bikes?"

"Meant to tell you mine has a puncture, we'll have to walk. Dad's not had time to fix it yet."

We had two choices on which path to take. One would take us past Karen's. I wanted to take the long route, but Wendy was right, we should take the short one.

We passed her house; outside was a large van. There were men unloading boxes, and Karen's mother was supervising. Wendy and I exchanged looks. I wondered what was in the boxes. I noticed fragile was written on the side, and they seemed to be heavy from the way the men were carrying them.

Karen's mother spotted us and beckoned us over. I tugged on Wendy's arm.

"What you doing?"

Wendy rolled her eyes. "Seeing what Karen's mother wants."

"Why?"

"Come on. You know what will happen; she'll tell our parents we were rude."

"True. She would too."

"Besides if we ignore her and she tells my mother, I'll be grounded. We don't want that. Do we?"

I shook my head, and followed Wendy over to Karen's

mother.

"Hi ladies. My you have grown, Debbie," she said, fluttering her eyes at me.

I nodded.

"How is your father?" she asked. "I have been meaning to send my condolences and all," she began. "Anyway how are you doing?"

"I'm getting there," I answered. After all, it was the truth, and this woman and my mother never got along. I had always known that she thought she was better than we were. Even when she lived opposite. Truth was my mother disliked her, of course, she would never have admitted it.

"That is really good to hear," she said. "Please be careful with those," she shouted to one of the men. "Can't get good help these days. Where was I? Oh yes, I was going to ask you to do me a favour!"

"A favour!" Wendy said.

"Yes, I was wondering if you could let your parents and family know we're having a party to celebrate my daughter's engagement."

"Karen's engaged!" Wendy said, shocked, her mouth wide open.

"Of course not, silly. My daughter, Jackie. You remember Jackie, Debbie?"

I nodded.

"Yes, I do. That's great news."

"It is," Karen's mother said, running her finger down the clipboard she held.

"So, please ask them to come along. There is no need to bring a gift."

"Oh, okay," Wendy said. "I'll tell my parents, as soon as I get home. When is it?" she asked.

"Tonight. Starts at eight o'clock sharp. Sorry, but no 'kids' are invited."

"Not even Karen?" I said before I could stop myself.

"Karen, oh, she hates this kind of party." She frowned. "Anyway, let your parents know, and Carol and Steve, if they feel like coming. Carol's pregnant right?"

I nodded.

"If she feels like she wants to come, then she is more than welcome."

"I will tell them."

"Thanks. Should I call Karen down?" she asked.

We looked at one another.

"It's okay, I'm joking. I know you two are no longer friends. Have fun now." She chuckled as she walked inside the house.

I looked at Wendy's face to read her reaction.

"Who does she think she is?"

"Now, you know where Karen gets it from," I said.

"Yeah, like mother like daughter."

Chapter 30
A Walk In The Park

~ Debbie ~

We turned to leave. Looking up, I noticed Karen standing at the window, watching us. She did not look happy. I had not wanted to speak to her mother either, but Wendy was right, she would tell our parents we were rude.

"Let's get going," I said. "We're being watched."

"Did you see the look on her face?" Wendy asked.

I nodded. "Yeah, if looks could kill, we would be dead."

We carried on walking, and reached the entrance to the park. The path gave us two directions; we decided to take the one which would lead us towards the tennis courts. The park was packed; it looked as though half the school was there.

~ Karen ~

What did my mother say to them? I thought. She hated Debbie and her family, so why call her over. To annoy me? Should I follow them and find out, or dare I ask my mother. Not that she would tell me. I knew that. I decided to get my bike out and go for a ride, not sure if I should phone the girls, but they were not a fan of riding bikes.

Decision made I raced down the stairs, ignoring my mother bossing some men bringing the last of the boxes in. The arrangements for the party were almost complete, getting out of the house appealed even more than before. Another party I was not invited to.

~ *Debbie* ~

With the crowds, we decided to walk around to the play area. It had a set of swings, a slide and a roundabout. The park, too, was full of children and their parents.

"I can't believe how packed it is here today!"

"I know, but it is a warmer day than we expected."

"True. Shall we sit; think about our plans for today?"

"Good idea."

We found a clear spot on the grass and sat down.

"Are you going to tell your parents about the party?"

"I have to," Wendy said.

She was right, we did have to. I knew Karen's mother. She would love to tell our parents we were rude to her. I tugged at the blades of grass beside me. "I can't believe the no kid rule, applies to Karen, too."

"I know. That is odd isn't it? She is Jackie's sister after all."

"I know. Carol and Steve had us there for their party, of course it was not on the scale Jackie's will be."

"True, but really, do they need to spend all that money on some fancy party?"

"Of course they do. They are the Langleys. They have to rub it in."

I continued to fiddle with the blade of grass. I thought about the party, imagined how many guests would be invited, and the entertainment. My mother's face floated before me, telling me, *money meant nothing, family did*. I inhaled, staring at her; I felt tears sting my eyes. She smiled at me and closed her eyes, a white sheet floated over her head. I willed the image away, calling to Joshua. When would I not see that image when I thought of her? He came, took my hand and told me it was okay, and to breathe.

"Are you okay?" Wendy asked.

I turned to face her, nodding. "Yeah, just had a flashback of the…"

"Debbie, it's okay. You're alright."

I did not feel okay, my heart raced, my hands felt sweaty, and I felt close to tears again. Just when I thought I was moving forward, it pulled me right back again, back to that day. Why did she die? Why did she leave me? I tried hard to concentrate on the future, and closed my eyes just for a second.

"Debbie Conway, breathe, just breathe, in, out, in, out, that's it." He takes my hand, and squeezes it. "That's it, look at me." He leans towards me and lays a kiss on my cheek.

"Debs," Wendy tapped me on the leg.

"I'm okay, honest!"

She nods, and points across the field. I knew she was distracting me from my thoughts, and that is what I needed.

"Over there," she said pointing. "Mark and Simon are here!"

"Where?" I asked, searching the field, and the faces of the footballers.

"There, look by the goal."

"Oh, yeah. I see him now." I stared at him, he had nice legs too.

"Shall we stay and watch them for a while?" she asked, of course, she meant Simon, but I was more than happy to watch Mark play football.

~ Mark ~

"Do you see who's watching us?" Simon asked. I turned to look, as he told me not to.

"Sorry."

"Told you they liked us."

I nodded. I hoped he was right. There was no sign of Karen. I had not wanted to come out. Having the feeling she would be lurking behind every tree, or jump out at me. We had been here for two hours, and so far there had been no sign of her.

"Mark, come on, they're ready for the second half."

I nodded, and joined my team ready to play.

~ *Debbie* ~

I drew my knees up to my chin, as we watched the guys play. The sun disappeared and the wind turned cold, sending a shiver through my body. I stood up, pulled my coat around myself, Wendy did the same.

We headed towards town, stopping at the local chip shop and ordered a portion of chips and a fizzy drink.

We headed back to the park, found a quiet spot under a tree, and ate the greasy chips. They tasted great. The guys had now gone, and instead a group of girls from our school were playing rounders.

Chips eaten, we walked home, discussing the party. We arrived at the street where Karen lived, which was already lined with cars. I checked my watch; it was later than we thought. We saw Karen's mother through the window. She still wore the outfit she had been wearing earlier, relieved that the party had not started early. We quickened our pace.

The outside of the house had decorations around the windows, door frames and around the garage too. *If this is just the engagement party, what will the wedding be like?* I knew it would be a far more expensive do than Carol and Steve's. I nudged Wendy as we walked past the house.

"Looks like the party to beat all parties."

"Yep. We'd better hurry home and tell our parents about it," Wendy said. "You never know, they might want to go. It might do your Dad good to get out even if it's only..."

I nodded. "Yeah, he might feel as if he should show his face, Steve, too."

Wendy was right; it would do my father the world of good. We arrived home.

My father agreed to pop over with Steve. They left just before eight. Leaving Carol in charge of the little ones, but she was exhausted. I told her to head off to bed; I would take care of them. She thanked me and went to her room.

Wendy's parents had plans, taking the twins out to the cinema, after David needed a few stitches. Wendy crashed over at mine, watching a movie, until her parents returned.

~ Karen ~

Getting out of the house had been a good idea. I had not found them on my bike ride, not that it really mattered. I spent over an hour riding around. Not worrying about where I went, or who saw me. I felt free, gliding along.

I arrived home, and put the bike away. The house now fully decorated, food and drinks filled the dining room. I was starving. No one would notice if I helped myself, as there was so much food. I grabbed a plastic tub and filled it with goodies, being careful not to get caught.

Ten minutes later, I laid the tub on the table beside my sofa, sat down and tucked in. I heard the first of the guests arrive. The music began. I sat in my room, headphones on listening to my favourite band, eating the remainder of the party food.

~ Debbie ~

A few hours later, my father returned with tales of the party.

"You have never seen anything like it. There were so many people, and I felt so under-dressed. I wish I had worn a suit," he continued. "They had so much food and drink; I think enough for another two parties. She let me bring some home. I've put it in the fridge, you can help yourselves to it," he babbled. I nodded, but would not be eating any of it.

"They had a live band too," Steve said.

"They did," my father agreed. "In the back garden. I can't believe the size of their garden. They have an indoor pool too, which they opened up for people to use. There were chocolate fountains, dips, I could go on," my father said, dreamily.

I nodded. My father had enjoyed his night out, and it had put a smile on his face.

The sun shone through my window early the next morning.

I yawned, rubbed the sleep from my eyes. My thoughts on the dream I'd had, and I closed my eyes, returning to my dream world.

He holds my hand, pulls me closer. The only sound is the beating of our hearts. Then soft music plays in the background. The music changes, a band appears, I stand beside him, microphone in our hands, ready to sing. They introduce me as the lead of 'daydreamers'.

A crowd appears, they scream. I open my mouth to sing, nothing. The crowd falls silent. They begin to boo. Thousands of Karen's boo me.

I must have fallen asleep, as I woke up, switching on the lamp, I shook my head. Not again, this is not *happening. Karen, keep out of my dreams.*

Chapter 31
Aliens

~ Debbie ~

Monday after school, we climb aboard the bus. My thoughts were not on the usual things today, not on my mother, Karen or Joshua. Instead, they were on Carol, and the scan she was having that day. I hoped I could make out the image better than I had on the last scan. We, of course, already knew they were having twins. Yet we had no idea what sex they were. Wendy sat down beside me, putting her bag beneath her feet. We had talked about the scan during the day. We were both excited. She told me she knew Steve would make a good dad, as he was so good with Sally. I had to agree, Carol would be a natural too, I was sure.

We arrived home, and went straight to find Steve and Carol.

"How did it go, Carol?" Wendy asked.

"Good. They're doing fine. "Growing well. We wanted to know the sex of the babies, but neither were in the right position, again."

I looked at Wendy. It looked as if we would have to wait, to find out what they were having. Wendy looked disappointed.

"Don't worry. They're healthy and that is all we can ask," Steve announced as he handed us each a scan to look at.

"They still look like aliens to me," Wendy commented.

"Very funny, sis," Carol said, tossing a cushion at her sister. "Hey!"

"Just because I'm pregnant, Wendy Allan, does not mean I've lost the ability to aim straight." Wendy stuck her tongue out at her, and then looked back down at the image. Steve rolled his eyes. I continued to look at the one in my hand.

"Look, there is the head, legs," Steve explained.

I tilted my head, finally saw the image of twin one.

Handing back the scan pictures, I asked to feel her tummy, she nodded. It felt hard, and something moved beneath my fingertips.

"Did that, did I…I" I stuttered, it was the strangest feeling.

Carol nodded.

I knew the babies were inside her tummy, but being able to feel them was weird, but exciting at the same time. I removed my hand. Staring at her tummy as it moved on its own. Was it a foot or a hand, an elbow or even a knee, I had no idea. It was amazing.

"I want to feel too," Wendy said.

"Put your hand here, Wendy," she said, placing her hand on the side of her tummy. Wendy smiled.

An hour later, alone in my room, I thought about becoming an aunty to twins. I couldn't wait to meet them. I did not mind if they were girls, boys or one of each. For a moment, I thought of my mother, and how she would never get to meet her grandchildren. The thought hit me hard. The tears I had been holding back trickled down my cheeks. I still thought of my mother all the time. The image of the accident would flash in my head, at times I did not expect it. Joshua would always be there, pushing the image away. I still wondered if she would be here, if I had not needed a lift home. I knew she would. I had to move past that. My nan told me it would get easier. She came less often now, too. She had her own life, my father told me.

I lay back on the bed, staring at Joshua.

Since the party at the Langleys, my father had changed. It was one good thing to come out of it. He came home earlier; smiled more often, even spent time with Sally and Greg. I had no idea what caused this change, but I did not care. I heard him calling my name, and rushed to the door.

I met my father at the base of the stairs.

"Hello, love," he said, placing an arm around my shoulder. The contact felt good, and I snuggled into him.

"Hi, Dad, did you have a good day?"

"Not a bad day, you?"

"It was okay. Is that why you called me down?" I asked, puzzled.

"No. I wondered if you wouldn't mind setting the table."

"Sure. What are we having?" I asked.

"Just pie and some potatoes."

"Okay," I said, following him into the kitchen.

Opening the drawer to the knife and forks, and removing enough for the family.

After carrying through the food, I sat down and began to eat. "It's good, Dad. No lumps in the mash either." I lied.

"Just like mum used to make," Steve said.

Silence filled the room. We rarely talked about her, maybe we should. Would that help? Dare I mention that idea? Not right now, no.

"Dad, I'll wash up afterwards," I said, breaking the silence.

"Thanks, love," he said, turning to face me. "You lot are good liars, I think the pie needed a little longer and the mash, well I could have mashed it more."

"Mike, its fine."

My father winked at her. "Thanks, Carol."

Meal eaten, I cleared the table and started the washing up. Carol picked up a tea towel.

"You don't have to help me if you don't want to."

"I don't mind."

"Well thanks," I said, turning the hot water tap on, adding soap and began to wash the dishes.

"Debbie," Carol began.

"Yeah," I said, staring at her reflection in the window.

"If you need to talk, about anything! I'm here for you."

I turned to face her.

"Thanks."

"I do mean anything you'd feel uncomfortable talking to your dad about?"

I nodded, and knew exactly what she meant.

"Thanks, Carol. If I need to talk, I promise I'll come to you."

I turned my attention back to washing the dishes.

Back in my room, staring up at those eyes on the poster, I could not shake the feeling about them. How they looked familiar. I shook the thought from my head and closed my eyes. My mother's face floated before me, smiling. I opened my eyes, picked up her photo frame, and held it close to me. I could not stop the tears from falling, sobbing until my chest hurt. The door opened, my father entered, I watched him through teary eyes. I felt him remove the photo from me and then he held me in his arms. I continued to sob.

"Sorry."

"Never be sorry. We all miss her. She was the love of my life and I miss her every day," he whispered.

I nodded. "Me too."

~ Karen ~

Another day and they are downstairs, discussing the wedding. Yet again, I am not a part of it. Not that I want to be. The food from the party has now all gone. I had enjoyed every last mouthful.

A live band, I could not believe it, they had hired a live band for Jackie's party. If the party was anything to go by, the wedding would be out of this world. I was not looking forward to the wedding. I knew they would ignore me the whole day anyway. Just like they did every day.

Chapter 32
Craig

~ Debbie ~

We stood outside the form room; neither of us had come up with a guy to tempt Karen with. I knew Mark wanted, no, needed us to find one, sooner rather than later.

I knew the real reason we had agreed to help them. Wendy liked Simon. I did feel sorry for whoever we chose.

We headed inside, and took our seats, the chair scraped loudly on the wooden floor. My thoughts were still on putting the plan into action. Most guys fancied Karen, but many avoided her. Each day, I scanned the halls. There were so many couples. I was looking for a single guy, not someone with a girlfriend. Where were the single guys?

"Remind me, why we are doing this again?"

"You know why!" she said.

I nodded. I did, and it proved she had it bad. I would get them together, and my original plan may have gone out the window, but I did have this new one. I would not tell her about it, just play along. Helping Mark meant helping Wendy get the date she wanted with Simon.

"We have to keep looking," Wendy said.

"We do, after double Science, we will have to walk around the school and see who we have missed."

"Agreed."

~ Mark ~

It had been a few days since the girls agreed to help, and

Karen continued to be my shadow. I hoped the girls would find someone to help me out. I could not keep dodging a second date. I had a feeling about what Simon had planned to thank the girls with. A double date. How to ask them was what he was worried about. I had my own idea, tickets to my parents' concert. A thank you, but how to explain how I got them. I would worry about that nearer the time.

~ *Debbie* ~

Break time arrived; we sat on the grass discussing our plan. None were right. Some she had already dated, others were not her type. There were some, who would not even look at her, let alone date her.

"This is harder than I thought," Wendy said.

I had to agree. We were never going to find the right guy.

The last lesson next day, the name of the guy came to me, as I wrote down the Maths equation.

"Got it," I called out, realising I had said it aloud. I looked up to see Mr Savoy raising his eyebrows.

"What do you have, Debbie? Please share it with the class."

"I--" I stuttered.

"We are waiting," he continued.

"I, well I've finished the first set of questions." I lied.

"Good. Move onto page ninety-seven, and complete those questions."

I nodded, *damn it, now I have to do these and the ones in the book.*

The bell rang twenty minutes later. I packed my things away, writing the last sum from the board.

Knowing I would have to complete them, along with page ninety-seven. It was my own fault. I sighed rushing out the door.

"Oh my God, I can't believe I did that," I said.

"It was funny. Anyway what did you get?"
"I know who we should ask."
"You do?"
I nodded.
"Who?"
"Craig. I don't know why we never thought of him."
"Of course, I forgot about him too. Is he still into her?"
"I think he is. I guess he might think he could not compete with Mark?"
"True. Right, all we need to do now is find him."
"We do, but tomorrow. We can spend the day looking for him."

The following day, we wasted no time in searching for Craig. There was no sign of him that morning; so we decided to search again at lunchtime.

Lunchtime we searched the halls, the field and lastly the canteen. Spotting him at one of the tables eating a bag of chips, I slowly walked over to him.

"Craig."

He looked up. "Hi," he said, looking from me to Wendy and back to me.

"Can I sit down?" I asked.

Craig nodded. I sat. Wendy remained standing.

"Craig, do you recall telling me you really liked Karen?"

"Yeah," he said. His fingers poised over the chips.

"I heard a rumour she likes you too!"

"Karen likes Mark," he said.

"Come on, Craig, she likes you. Anyway, I overheard she was over by the old apple tree if you are interested. You could head over there, see for yourself."

"You wouldn't wind me up, would you?"

"Craig, why would I do that?"

"You're not exactly friends."

"No, but I have no reason to lie to you."

Craig stood, and left, smiling. I hoped this would work. Craig was a nice guy, but I knew he had liked her for a long time. What he saw in her, I had no idea, but who was I to judge. I wondered if he hoped the old Karen would return. I did. Watching him leave, I nudged Wendy. We needed to find Karen to make this work.

It did not take long to find her. We raced over to her, as if we had been looking for her everywhere. I hoped she too would believe me. I ignored her friends and stood before her, taking a deep breath.

"Karen, thank God. We've been looking for you everywhere," I said.

"What do you two want?" she snorted.

"Well, I heard a rumour that this guy has it bad for you, I mean really bad."

"All the guys do," Stephanie said.

"Yeah, but this one, well he wants you to meet him at the old apple tree."

"Does he now?"

"What about Mark, Karen?"

"What about him? He doesn't own me." She nodded.

Let's hope this works.

~ *Karen* ~

My day could not get any better. I had wanted Mark to take me on a proper date. The last one I had a feeling he acted that way to push me away. He was wrong, that would not work. Now I had this other guy, wanting me. I wondered who he was. I reached the apple tree, and then I saw him. Craig, the same guy the girls in the toilets were talking about. I had only seen him once since that day they mentioned him. He was nice looking, weird they had called him, but I did not care. I swayed my hips as I reached the tree, plastering a smile on my lips.

Dream World

~ *Debbie* ~

We raced to see the plan in action, and found them together. Now we needed Mark to witness it. Wendy rushed off to go find him, while I remained in place. A few minutes later, she returned.

"He's on his way," she said. "There." Pointing in the direction, he was walking in. We watched him cross the field, and made his way to the apple tree. I watched him, as he witnessed Karen and Craig kiss.

~ *Mark* ~

This had to work. I reached the tree, and saw them together. Using my acting skills I made my way towards them. Craig held her in his arms, hers were around his neck, and they were looking into each other's eyes. I watched them kiss, waiting for them to part. I stood and folded my arms.

"Karen," I began.

She looked at me, and swallowed.

"Are you cheating on me?" I asked.

"I," she stuttered.

"How could you?"

"I'm sorry; Mark, but we only had one date, and to be honest it wasn't what I'd call a date."

I stood, mouth open. She was right it was not a date. That had been the plan.

"Fine. Whatever we had, it's over. You can have her," I said, unfolding my arms and marching away. Turning the corner, I smiled .The plan had worked. Now we needed to repay the girls.

~ *Karen* ~

I watched him leave. I knew I had lost Mark. Not that it mattered. When I kissed Craig, I felt something I had not expected. I pulled his arm around me and placed my lips back on his. Craig was a good kisser. I had no idea if Mark was, since he never kissed me. I knew when I touched Mark's skin; I felt nothing, not even a spark. I never had with any of the guys I dated. Yet when Craig kissed me, touched my skin, I felt my whole body tingle. This shocked me.

"I'm sorry about that. We went on one date, and he thought we were a couple."

"He did?" Craig said.

I nodded. "Yes, now kiss me again," I said, not having to ask him twice. My heart flipped, could he be the one?

I remained in his arms, as the bell continued to ring. I should be changing into my P.E kit, like the rest of the girls, but I did not want to leave. I hated P.E. Craig sat back and looked into my eyes.

"Karen, we should get to class, I..." he began.

"It's okay, we should go. Meet you later. Here take my number." I said, scribbling it down on a piece of paper. I stood, and we walked our separate ways. Did this mean I had my first real boyfriend? I knew what had happened between Mark and myself would be around the school by the end of the next day, but I did not care.

I arrived at the sports hall and entered the changing room. The rumour had spread quicker than I expected.

"What did you do that for?" one girl asked.

"Are you mad, cheating on Mark?" another said.

I shook my head. "For your information, Mark is a jerk."

"A jerk, I thought you said…"

"I lied," I interrupted. "Look, I have a reputation to keep. He's good looking I admit, and kisses like a fish. He's not the same guy you see in school." I paused. "Look I'm with Craig now, deal with it."

"Is he really a bad kisser?" Anna whispered as I changed into my t-shirt.

"Yeah."

"So, how about Craig?"

"Oh yes." I said, dreamily, as I changed into the remainder

of my kit.

I arrived home, my mind on the day's events. I pulled out my diary and scribbled inside it.

'Dear diary,

All this time I had been focused on Mark and all this time Craig was the one. Yes, I made out with him, while I was with Mark, but it worked out well, for me. I cannot believe all this time, he was right there in front of me. Mark may be gorgeous and popular, but after that one date with him, there was no way I could go on a second, no matter what I let him think. A second date was all talk, for show. I have a reputation to protect.

He's a good kisser, not like some guys who are like a washing machine. YUK!

Chapter 33
Stop Living In Your Dream World

~ Debbie ~

We climbed aboard the bus, sat in our usual seats, and all the way home, Wendy's eyes were on Simon, willing him to look our way. I nudged her, she shrugged.

"What they owe us, and they've not even thanked us."

"I know, but it would not be easy to do it in school. Without you know who is listening in."

"True, maybe we should go out for a walk later, to the sports hall!" she suggested.

I knew what she was thinking.

"Okay, why not." I agreed.

We walked to the sports hall, once our homework was done. There were a few others hanging around outside, but Mark and Simon were nowhere to be seen. I sat down on the grass and pulled up a blade, and held it between my hands and blew.

"How do you do that?"

I shook my head. "I don't know, just do this," I said, showing her how I held it. "Then blow."

Wendy tried. "Don't think I'm doing it right," she said, tossing the grass on the ground. "So, now Karen is off his back, we can get our reward. I've given Simon long enough to decide, don't you think?"

"Yes I do. We could always go to his house." I joked.

"Do you know where he lives?"

I shook my head. "No, come on, let's get back, I'm getting cold."

"What we need to do is arrange to meet them tomorrow night or at the weekend."

I smiled. She had it bad.

A few days later I awoke earlier than I had in years. The clock digits flickered in the darkness. Why was I wide awake at five? I perched on the end of my bed, yawning, unsure if I should get up, but it was far too early.

For the last few nights my dream had always been the same. Joshua was there, in the limo. I attempted to see inside, I knew it was him, but I could not see him. Fully awake, I flicked on the lamp, stood, slipped on my dressing gown, tied the belt around my waist and looked up at the poster, those brown eyes staring at me.

I pulled back the curtains, and stared out into the street, it was quiet outside, the sky still dark. *If this is my dream, why can't I see him?* I shook my head. *It's Monday, I wish it was Saturday.* I sighed. *Where had the weekend gone? I had to get up and get ready for school.* I walked into my bathroom and switched on the shower, waiting for the water to reach the right temperature.

I washed myself from top to toe. Stepping out onto the soft rug, and pulling my dressing gown around my wet body. I snuggled up inside it, a towel around my wet hair. I never mastered wrapping it around my head the way my mother used to. By the time, I reached my room the towel would be slipping.

Removing the towel from my head, I flicked on my tape recorder and listened to the tape borrowed from Wendy. The time now read seven-twenty. I made sure the volume stayed low. My clothes laid neatly on my dressing table chair, as I sang softly to myself. I heard Greg crying outside. I reached the door, opened it; he stood there with his favourite teddy bear in his hand. Tears ran down his face. I looked at him.

"What's up, sweetie?" I asked, tying the belt into a knot.

"I wet my bed," he sniffed.

"Oh, Greg, that's okay. We can sort it out. Come on. Don't

worry."

I took hold of his hand and led him back to his room. While he took off his wet clothes, I stripped his bed. The door creaked open, turning my attention to the sound, I saw my father pop his head around the door, nodded and slipped back out.

"See, its okay. Dad isn't cross."

Leaving Greg to have a shower, I snatched the sheets up and tossed them in the wash basket. I washed my hands and headed out of the bathroom. Basket in hand I made my way to the kitchen and placed the sheets in the washing machine.

I poured a bowl of cereal for Greg, as he joined me in the kitchen. Handing him the bowl, I removed the mug of tea and went back up to my room.

Closing the door with my foot, I set the mug down on my desk, staring once again at Joshua. I then dressed for school. *Oh Joshua, what am I going to do about this dilemma?*

Once dressed, I pulled a brush through my hair, pulling it back into a ponytail. I downed the last of the tea before going back down the stairs. Returning to the kitchen, discovering Greg had gone and my father had already left for work. Steve entered the kitchen and sat down beside Sally, as Carol waddled through.

"Morning all, beautiful day isn't it?"

"Morning Carol, yes it is," I replied.

"I thought I would walk with you to take the kids to school. If that's okay?"

"Sweetheart, of course it is. I just don't want you to overdo it. If you feel tired, you head back in a cab. I mean it," Steve said as he took Carol's hand in his.

"Carol, can I feel the baby?" Sally asked.

"Sure," she said, taking her hand, she placed it on her swollen tummy.

A new life in the family was just what we needed.

~ Mark ~

The weekend had passed in a blur. I felt better about the

situation with Karen. I should feel bad about the guy she had her hooks into now. However, he looked happy and she looked happier. I know I was.

Simon and I spent Sunday at the local pool, where we had met.

My parents called later that evening. Two minutes the call lasted. A quick hello and they were gone.

Simon could not wait to get the two girls on their own, to speak to them, to be able to repay them.. I pulled on the last of my uniform, before going to meet him.

~ Debbie ~

Ten minutes later, Steve told Greg and Sally to get their coats. As Carol pulled hers on and joined Steve. I reached for my own and zipped it up, waiting for Wendy to join me at the bus stop.

Thinking about my dream, wondering once again, if I should tell her about it, but could hear exactly what she would say to me. *Stop living in your dream world, he's not real.*

"Morning."

"Morning," I replied.

We arrived at school, and had the privilege of witnessing Karen as she flung her arm around Craig's neck. I shuddered, turning away before I saw them use their tongues.

"Poor guy," I said.

"I know, but Debbie, we did do that."

"Yeah, and he does seem happy."

"We did our bit," she began, as we entered the school grounds. "I've been thinking."

I nodded, "Have you?"

"Yes."

"Don't tell me, you want Simon to take you out on a date as your reward?"

Her mouth fell open. Yes, I knew her so well.

"How did you…"

I smiled, as Mark and Simon fell into step beside us. She

closed her mouth and her eyes widened.

"Boys," I said, facing them.

"Thank you," Mark said. "I cannot thank you enough, for what you did."

"It was our pleasure, but you know you owe us, right?"

"We know we do, don't we Simon."

Simon nodded. I could see his cheeks flush. I stared at Mark. "I think we should decide on the reward, after all you have had a few days to decide on it, don't you think?" Wendy said.

"Well, we, yes. I guess, we have." He nodded.

"Good, we will let you know what we decide."

Wendy's eyes remained on Simon, as I dragged her into the classroom, to the back and sat down.

"Wendy," I said, as she once again shrugged.

"What!" she said. "They had their chance, now, we need to make our plans on where they are going to take us."

I had no idea; I had never been on a date? After all, I was still waiting for Joshua to sweep me off my feet.

"Earth to Debbie!"

I shook my head, "Sorry, I was thinking."

"Look, your dream guy won't mind. Besides, you're going for me more than anything, right?"

I tilted my head.

"It's not like you really like Mark is it?"

Did I like Mark? Yes, I did, but not like that. Not the way I was in love with Joshua.

Chapter 34
Mean Girls

~ Karen ~

A whole week had passed since the breakup with Mark, not that we were really dating. Some people thought I was mad, for being with Craig. I had only gone to see who this person was, because she said there was a guy. There was no way I was having her make a fool of me, but if there was no guy, I would have the last laugh.

It could of course have been a prank, but Debbie was not like that. I shook my head, stopping myself from remembering the girl I knew. I had moved on and I would not look back. My mother would not stand for it. My friends would not either. I had a reputation to uphold. I was, after all, Karen Langley.

Did they think I was stupid? I knew Debbie was the reason I had lost Mark, setting me up with Craig. Truth was she did me a favour, as I had never felt this way about any boy. Everyone who did not like the fact I was with him, would have to deal with it. I knew why she did it too, her attempt to get Mark, and if the way they were acting together earlier was anything to go by, it worked.

~ Debbie ~

The following Monday morning, we sat in the form room; I crossed my arms and stared out the window. The blackbird was back. I recalled the daydream I had the last time, and checked beneath the tree, there was no one there today. I leaned back in the chair and stared at the empty blackboard.

The door opens, the inside is black. I lean forward, attempt to see inside. I lean closer, and lose my balance.

Crash. I landed on the floor and turned red, and quickly clambered back into my seat, hoping no one had seen me. Wendy held her hand over her mouth. I clamped my mouth shut. Rubbed my leg and rolled my eyes. I really needed to stop daydreaming, I was going to hurt myself, or get into trouble, but I could not help it. I sighed as the teacher entered. Karen and her gang scrambled to their seats. She grinned at me. Had she seen? Surely, if she had she would have said something wouldn't she?

I had hoped her dating Craig might change her, put her in a better mood. I was wrong. Our form tutor reeled off the names. I paid attention and said I was here, before heading to our first lesson of the day, Maths.

We entered the corridor, when I heard her voice call out my name.

"Hey, Debbie."

I rolled my eyes and stepped forward. One of the girls from her gang stepped before me, blocking me.

"You know that looked like fun," she said.

"Yeah, you should do it again. I think we all saw your dirty knickers," Anna called out.

My cheeks flushed red again, these girls were just plain rude. If I had worn a skirt, then they would have seen my clean underwear. I let it slide. They were just being mean.

"Come on, Debbie you should have put that performance in the musical. The guys would love to see you flash them your knickers," Karen shouted.

"Her mother's knickers," Tracey hollered.

I gritted my teeth, they had gone too far this time, I saw red. I wanted them to hurt; I stepped forward, ready to do what? I did not know, but Wendy grabbed me by the arm and gently pulled me back.

"Debbie, don't do this," she whispered. "Walk away, you're-
-"

Dream World

"That's it run away," Karen interrupted.

Mr Turk stepped out of his classroom and stood with his hands on his hips looking from me to them.

"Get to class now, move it. Karen, Debbie come and see me, at the end of school."

"Yes Sir," we both replied.

Everyone hurried away. I clenched my fist. She had really done it this time. I was angry. I hated her. I made my way down the corridor in the opposite direction to Karen.

"Debbie, take no notice of her. She's an evil bitch."

"I know, but she went too far that time."

"She did, but you're better than her, remember that," Wendy said.

An hour later, first lesson over, we parted, heading to our separate lessons. I made friends with a few of the other girls in my class, but no one that would replace Wendy. I joined the queue and waited for our to let us in, my thoughts still elsewhere.

The remainder of the day flew by. I turned to Wendy.

"I have to go see Mr Turk, I won't be long."

Wendy nodded. "Okay, I'll wait for you."

I stood outside his classroom, knocked on his door, and waited until a voice called,

"Come in."

I entered.

"Ah, Debbie. Take a seat."

I sat on the nearest one; there was no sign of Karen. Mr Turk continued to mark his books. I sat quietly, waiting for him to speak. The small hand on the clock ticked noisily, taunting me. I knew the bus would leave on time. If I waited any longer, I would end up missing it. I waited, and waited. Then finally, he lifted his head.

"Where's Karen?" he asked.

"I have no idea, Sir."

I looked towards the door. Still no sign of her.

"Right, I'll deal with her later. About today, I am going to give you a warning. Next time it will be detention."

"But Sir, I--" I began.

"You're dismissed."

I wanted to protest, but knew it could end with a detention or worse, standing parades and a detention. I stood, left the classroom and dashed for the bus.

Arriving too late, I saw it pull away. *Great, now what do I do? I've never missed the bus before.*

I shook my head. The thought of walking crossed my mind or catching the local bus, but I had no cash on me. Walking seemed my only option, even if it did not appeal. I hated the thought of walking alone.

"You missed the bus too?"

I turned to find Mark stood beside me. I could not help, but stare at his eyes. Eyes so much like those on my poster. I shook the thought from my head.

"So, why did you miss the bus?" he asked.

"I had to see Mr Turk."

"I see."

"What about you?"

"Simon and I were heading to the bus, as usual when I remembered Mr Jolly had asked me to go and see him. I told Simon not to wait. I did not expect to be so long." He paused. "He had one of those art folders for me."

"He did?"

"Yes, but he had misplaced it, took him five minutes to find it."

"Well they are a must have, better than your work getting ruined."

He nodded.

"I was thinking of walking home."

"We could walk together," he said.

"We could, I did not like the idea of walking home on my own."

My heart raced, I was not sure I could be alone with him. I might like him more than I already did. *Stop it*, I told myself.

"Or, we could catch another bus. Is there one?"

I nodded. "Yes, but I don't have any money on me."

"I'll pay."

"I..."

"I insist."

Ten minutes later, standing at the bus stop, we waited for it to arrive.

The bus pulled over at his usual stop, he stood, and smiled at me.

"See you tomorrow?"

I nodded. "Yes, and thanks again."

"My pleasure."

I watched him leave, and then turned my attention to the other passengers sat on the bus. Some were college students, others parents and their children. Until Mark left me, I had not noticed them.

The bus pulled over at my stop. I stood on the path; opened the gate as I heard footsteps behind me.

"Debbie, there you are. Oh my God, I am so sorry. I wouldn't have got on the bus if I had known you'd miss it."

"Don't worry, Wendy, Mark paid me to get on the bus."

"Mark!"

"Yes, he missed it, too."

"Did you ask him if Simon liked me?"

I shook my head.

"Sorry. I guess I just didn't think about it. I was more worried about how I was getting home."

"Debbie, I'm so sorry. I won't get on the bus unless you are on there, too."

"It's okay, honest."

Wendy hugged me, I had not minded in the end; after all I had ended up spending time with Mark. He was a nice guy. I had heard the rumour of his date with Karen. I did not believe it. He smelt nice to me. I closed the gate; Steve met me at the door.

"Wendy said you missed the bus, I was--"

"Steve, I did, but a boy from school called Mark paid for me to get a bus home, and I'm okay. Home in one piece."

"Mark?"

"Yeah."

"As long as you're okay?"

"I am."

"No worries. Main thing is you're home and you're safe and sound."

I took the stairs, two at a time to my room. Almost knocking my younger brother over as I bounded onto the landing.

"Sorry, mate, you okay?"

"Yeah, I'm good. You missed the bus?"

"I know, silly me, huh!"

Greg nodded, and made his way down the stairs as I went into my room.

I stared at the poster above my bed; there was something about those eyes.

~ Mark ~

I arrived home, my grandparents rushed to the door to greet me.

"There you are, did you walk home again?"

"I just missed the bus. Anyway, I got the next one home, sorry to have worried you."

My nan offered to make me a coke float. I accepted the offer and made my way to my room. I changed and lay on my bed. I really liked the girl, but how could I tell her?

I wondered what they would come up with as their reward. I had an idea myself, but Wendy had been right, we had long enough time to tell them. Maybe I would make it up to them as well. I knew Simon wanted to take them out. It had been a year since I had taken a girl out. She wanted one thing. She had dated me to get closer to him. I wanted a girl to like me for me. I hoped Debbie would be the one. Time would tell. Even though I knew she liked Joshua, recalling the t-shirt she had worn.

Chapter 35
A Double Date

~ Debbie ~

Wendy wasted no time in telling the two boys her plan for the date. It could, of course have been any date. We were new to it, and I had no idea what her plans were until Thursday lunchtime. She insisted they sat with us. Although my lunch box sat open, I did not touch it. Simon continued to stare at her the whole time she spoke. I had been right about those two; they were going to make a perfect couple. I had a feeling Mark did not want to go on this date with me, the way he sat and squirmed in his seat.

I did my best to ignore him, and listened to Wendy continue on with her plans. Usually she would have run them past me, but I think she made them up as she went along.

"Okay, that's a date," Simon said, nodding. "We'll meet you in town, around six-thirty, is that okay with you two?" he asked.

I nodded. I hoped my father would agree to the boys taking us out, but then again, I was not going alone. Wendy's smile spread further across her face, if that was possible.

"Well, we better go, we're meeting the guys to play football, see you later."

We both stood, and watched them leave. I closed my lunch box, still not in the mood to eat what was inside it. The boys hurried away. Wendy seemed happy with herself. I looked forward to the date, but more for her than myself. Even though it was Mark we had helped, it seemed she was going to be getting more out of it.

Mark and those eyes were all I could think about.

"Mark who?" Joshua asks.

"No one," I tell him.

Saturday afternoon, Wendy arrived at my house. Nervous was an understatement. I thought she was going to be sick. This reminded me of the opening night of Grease, and the look on Mary's face. The one night I had played Sandy, he had been there in the front row, staring up at me, I was positive it was him. Certain, he had been watching me. Now, I knew I imagined him. He was not real. He was in my head. Unless of course he had a double, someone who looked just like him. I pushed the thought from my head and turned to face Wendy, who had used my shower and was now wearing her dressing gown, and a towel wrapped around her head.

"So, our first date. A double date, are you excited?" she babbled.

I was excited for her. I liked Mark, but he was not the guy I wanted to date, not the guy who sent shivers down my spine, not the guy whose lips I wanted pressed against mine. Instead, I nodded and headed to the shower.

"Be right back, and Wendy, don't disappear into your dreams of Simon, will you while I'm gone."

She picked up one of my pillows and tossed it at me.

"Hey," I yelled throwing it back and missing.

She shook her head. "Hurry up and get showered, we need to get ready, I don't want to be late."

"You do know it's only three, right?"

We had dressed up for this date, Wendy's idea not mine. I had wanted to wear a pair of jeans, but she insisted we made an effort I had finally agreed to the dress. I wore one of hers, since I did not own many. We had helped each other by fixing our hair before leaving the house, with our made up faces. I recalled the wolf whistles made by my father, Steve and the look on Greg's face. I had hugged them all before leaving to catch the bus, with Wendy chattering about how this had worked out perfectly.

The boys were on time, and without a second thought hooked their arms through ours leading us towards the cinema. The queue was long, but that did not bother us. I was far too impressed by what the boys were wearing and that smell. I found myself inhaling. Mark smelt good. Maybe I had been worried after the rumour of the date with Karen. Whoever and whatever he had done on their date, he was not about to repeat on ours. Yet this was not a proper date, it was a thank you.

He acted like a gentleman, opening doors, insisting on paying and led us to the back where we watched the movie.

~ *Mark* ~

The night had gone well, the movie ended.

I stood and allowed the girls to leave the seats, and Simon followed them, catching up to Wendy. He was not about to let her walk off alone. He slipped his hand into hers and she accepted it. I smiled. They made a cute couple. I walked beside Debbie, my hand loose by my side. I could not bring myself to hold her hand, the fear she might push it away.

We walked towards the nearest restaurant that served pizza. We planned to do everything Wendy wanted. Simon offered money to pay for the evening, but this was on me. I would not let him pay, after all, they had done this to help me out, and this was my treat.

The four of us found a table near the front, and ordered an extra-large pizza with five different toppings. We tucked in, and once every last piece was eaten, we shared a large bowl of ice-cream.

I enjoyed the evening. The girls were happy, I was too. Simon was the happiest I had ever seen him. He had the girl of his dreams; I just wish I had mine, my supermarket girl. She walked beside me as we came to the river, the moon shone on the water, as we stood together. Close enough I could feel the electricity between us. I wanted to tell her how I felt, that I liked her, and I wanted her to be my girlfriend, but those words stuck in my throat. I remained quiet, allowed her to talk if she wanted to.

I liked her and knew she liked me, and not because of who my cousin was. I knew she was a fan of the show, but that did not matter. She liked me, Mark Hobson. Not Joshua Lawson's cousin.

~ Karen ~

Another night of wedding plans, but I had wanted to go out. I had plans to meet Craig, but here I was being measured for the bridesmaids dress. I did not even want to be one. They never even asked me if I did.

I stood on the stool as some woman told me to lift my arms, lower my arms, do this, do that. I sighed, wishing this was over already.

"Mum, she won't keep still?" Jackie whined.

"Karen, do as you are asked," my mother said, and poured herself another glass of bubbly. I was sure they had almost drunk my father's entire case of champagne. Not that they seemed to care, as he would order more.

My mother picked up the designs for the dress, and together they looked at them, nodding to one another. Of course, they did not show me what they looked like. I should have guessed that would be the case. The woman continued to measure me, and told me to lift my arms for the tenth time. The sound of the doorbell had me stepping down, but the stern look on my mother's face had me rooted to the spot. Instead, Jackie stood and marched from the room.

She returned with the biggest grin on her face. She whispered in our mother's ear and she then peeked out of the window. Who was at the door? I wondered. Suddenly realising it had to be one person, which would make them react like that. I did not care, I liked him, and I was going to date him no matter what they thought.

I had to ask who was at the door, to be sure. My sister smirked.

"Does our Karen, have a little boyfriend, oh isn't that sweet." She puckered her lips and made kissing noises at me.

I stamped my foot, pushed the woman out of my way and stormed towards the front door. Hearing them call after me. I ignored them, as I opened the door and walked out. I slammed it shut, finding him gone. I raced to the end of the drive and called out his name. I liked him, liked him a lot. He stopped walking and turned to face me. I raced towards him and threw myself in his arms, where I belonged.

~ Debbie ~

The night came to an end, and I had enjoyed it more than I thought I would. Simon and Wendy by the end of the evening were a couple. I smiled. The plan in the end had worked. Yes, it had not been the original plan, but still she was happy.

They walked us home, all the way to the top of our road, and Simon stopped. I assumed he did not want to kiss her outside her house. I could not blame him. The moment his lips crushed down on my best friends, I turned and faced the other way. Mark looked just as uncomfortable.

"Thanks for a really nice evening," I said, knowing it sounded lame.

"You're welcome, we should do it again, and by the looks of it, we may be spending more time together."

He may just be right. It looked as though we were not going to separate those two any time soon. They still had their lips locked, and I was not about to stand here and watch. I moved onwards, towards my house. Mark followed and walked me to my gate. He leaned towards me and kissed me on the cheek. I held my breath, as his lips touched my skin. Why had my skin reacted that way, I liked him, but I did not like him that way, did I?

I thanked him again, and rushed inside the house, confused by the reaction. I raced to my room, and right now, I needed my mother more than ever. I kicked off my shoes, and dove on the bed, turning to look at the picture of her. I picked it up as tears flowed down my cheeks. I held it close to me.

"Why are you not here," I whimpered, closing my eyes.

My mother's face floated before me, the image clear, and then it changed in an instant, to the scene of the accident. The white sheet, the sound of my screams as they cover her and the flashing lights, the noise. I will Joshua to come to me, take my pain away. Yet I deserve it, I had betrayed him. I liked another boy, not him. I had liked the kiss. I had liked the feeling of his touch.

I continued to call Joshua, but he did not reply. Tears fell one after the other, until sleep took me. A hand slipped over me, and I felt his breath on my neck, comforting me. I felt safe in his arms.

The Dream World Series

Daydreamers
Book 2

S.J. Hitchcock

Prologue
One Day At A Time

~Debbie~

Has it only been nine months since I witnessed the death of my mother? It did not seem possible. Thinking about her, causes my heart to ache, and tears threaten to fall. I wish she allowed me to walk home, or catch the bus. If she had, she would be here now, safe, and alive.

The guilt will be with me forever. If I close my eyes, I see the blue van, my mother's face, and hear my screams. This is when Joshua comes to my rescue, I depend upon him to hold me and make me feel safe. Wrapped in his arms, a wall appears to protect me from the memory which haunts me.

My dream world is my safe place, and since my best friend started dating Simon, I drift there for other reasons too. Witnessing them suck face is enough to drive me into Joshua's arms. I'm not jealous of Wendy, I am happy for her. I just never expected her to forget I am there.

It is rare Wendy and I spend any girly time alone any more, usually there are four of us. Wendy, Simon, Mark and myself. People assume I am dating Mark, they're wrong. We are just friends.

Something in my dreams is different, and no how much I try, I cannot see his face clearly. I decide these dreams are mine, and if I want to see him, then I will.

Carol's bump grows every day. We cannot wait for the twins to be born. Wendy and I have our thoughts on the sex of the babies. Secretly, I hope it is one of each. Wendy insists they will both be boys, odds are in there favour. As both sets of twins in her family are.

The highlight of my year has to be playing the lead role Sandy, in Grease. Playing her has given me confidence, but it was only for one night. Could I play the lead for longer? Auditioning for a part in the play may just be the distraction I need. My first birthday without my mother is fast approaching, making me fifteen.

Turning sixteen scares me even more, without her by my side.

Chapter 1
To Be A Teenager Again

~ Debbie ~

School was over, all I wanted to do was get on that bus, and get home. One other thing I wanted more than anything, was to not witness them snogging on the journey home. I knew it would not happen, but I could wish. How they managed to last that long amazed me, not coming up for air. I had only kissed one boy. Danny had been gentle, but I wanted to kiss Mark just like Danny had kissed me when I played Sandy. If I closed my eyes, I could imagine it. I felt guilty for thinking that. I had always wanted Joshua to be the one. I was confused, how could I want them both. I had to choose. Yes Mark was real, but Joshua owned my heart.

Sitting at the back of the bus, facing the window, I did my best to block them out. Mark sat silent beside me. I was too afraid to move, in case I accidently touched him. I kept my hands firmly on my lap, looking past their reflection, concentrating on the outside the window.

Arriving home, I made my way to my room to finish my homework, before Wendy was due over. I flicked the book open to the page with the sums on, and stared at them. They were harder than I recalled, and I found myself staring into space, thinking about Joshua and what it would really be like to have him kiss me. I had that look on my face; I could hear Wendy telling me to snap out of it. I shook my head and got to work on the sums.

I heard my father call, "Dinners on the table."

Dream World

Then a few seconds later there was a knock on my door, and he popped his head around it.

I turned and replied, "I'll be right there."

"Don't be too long, or your tea will get cold."

I pushed my chair under the desk and followed my dad down to the kitchen. I liked having him home at this time of the day, and hoping it would be a regular thing.

The following morning, after another night of tossing and turning, I heard Greg calling my name. I closed my eyes, attempting to ignore him, pulling my pillow over my head, but I could still hear him. Unable to ignore him any longer, I threw back my duvet, and placed my feet firmly on the floor.

Pulling on my dressing gown, I made my way to his room, muttering,

"I'm up. I'm up."

Marching down the hallway, I felt instantly guilty as I entered his room and found him lying on the floor, clutching his stomach, crying. I looked at his bed, at his rumpled sheets. The scent of vomit hit my nostrils.

"Oh, Greg, sweetheart, let's get you into the bathroom." I wanted to leave his room before the stench made me vomit too. Taking his hand I led him out and down to the family bathroom. Entering he was sick again; it hit the floor, and splashed up my legs, reaching the hem of my dressing gown. I took a deep breath and guided him to the toilet. *Nice one, Greg, I'll have to shower before school,* I thought as I removed it, and rinsed my legs.

"Stay here, Greg, please don't move; and keep your head over the toilet," I instructed.

Greg nodded. I made my way down the stairs to my dad's room and knocked on his door. I waited a few seconds, before entering, and found it empty. Shaking my head, I walked back into the hall and took the stairs one at a time. Carol stood at the top.

"Were you looking for your Dad?"

I nodded.

"He left for work about twenty minutes ago," Carol began, "and Steve's gone to get some milk." She paused. "Sorry you had to deal with Greg, I can't deal with vomit, at least not today."

"It's okay." I shrugged.

I looked at her belly, thinking how close her due date was getting. I knew taking care of a child with a sickness bug was not something she should be doing. I smiled and returned to the bathroom to check on Greg. Entering just as he was sick once again.

I helped him change into clean pyjamas and settled him on the sofa downstairs, placing a bucket below his head, and a warm blanket over him.

"Will you be okay, while I take a shower?" I asked.

He nodded.

I decided to change his bed, before showering. Not sure if I should wash the sheets or throw them away. I asked Carol what she thought I should do with them. We both agreed throwing them away was the best option. I then asked her to let my father know that Greg was sick and I planned to stay home to take care of him.

Sheets safely inside a plastic bag and tossed in the bin outside. I checked on Greg, he was still asleep, I then made my way to the kitchen, and flicked the kettle on.

I added a teabag to my mug as Steve returned with the milk. I explained to him that Greg was ill and I planned to stay home and take care of him.

While I had been taking care of Greg, I had forgotten about Sally. Steve found her in the playroom. She had dressed herself. Her trousers were inside out and her top back to front, but she insisted she did not want to change them. Steve left with her a few minutes later.

As the door clicked shut, I re-checked on Greg, he was still asleep. Placing the mug of tea on the table, I sat and watched him. It was times like this when I missed my mum. If Greg had fallen ill a year ago, he would have called out for her, not me. Sometimes he forgot. He was not alone, some days I did too.

I needed her as much as Greg did. I needed Joshua to hold me, to make me feel better, but sometimes he did not come when I called. Sighing, I climbed the stairs and entered my room and took a sip of the tea.

I stepped into the shower, allowing the water to run over me as tears began to fall. I was not crying because I had to stay home. I was crying because I wished my mother was here to take care of Greg, and me.

Half an hour later, I checked on Greg, he was still sleeping. I tip-toed past and entered the kitchen, finding Carol sitting at the table.

"Is he okay in there?"

I nodded. "He's still asleep."

"I'm going for a walk in a bit, is there anything you need or want while I'm out?"

I shook my head and made a start on the evening meal.

Food prepared, I sat on the chair opposite Greg.

The television was on, but I did not watch it, there was nothing on that interested me. Daytime television was so boring. I pressed the off button and closed my eyes, my thoughts were on my last dream, and how I needed Joshua to hold me. No sooner had I closed my eyes, did Greg groan, and I was brought back to the present with a thud.

It had been the longest day. Greg was still on the sofa, drifting in and out of sleep. As soon as my father arrived home, he took over. I went to my room, and curled up in a ball and fell asleep. My dad called me down for tea an hour later.

Tea eaten, Carol insisted on clearing up. I offered to help, but she told me no.

I had wanted to help, I did not mind, but she shooed me out of the kitchen. I chose not to argue, and made my way to my room.

The poster above my bed called to me, I closed my eyes and imagined Joshua on a beach. The sand, the waves, I could see it all.

I walk along the beach, feet sinking into the warm soft sand. I scan the crowds, step forward and continue my search for him. It is then I realise, I'm surrounded by a swarm of women. They all look like models, every last one of them. I look down at my immature figure compared to theirs. How can I compete with them? If Karen was here she would fit in no problem. Ignoring my thoughts, I sink my toes further into the sand, and watch the women with awe. They step back and reveal a guy standing behind them.

I stare at him, eyes wide. He walks towards me, his hair blows gently in the breeze. He steps closer, and closer, until I can only make out the outline of him. I am sure it is Joshua. I take a step backwards, suddenly I am falling.

Two days later, Greg was better, free of the bug, and able to go back to school. I had taken three days off and could not wait to return to school. I never thought I would think that, but I did, plus I missed spending time with Wendy. She had popped over with work from school while I was off the first day. She did not stay long, as she did not want the bug. I did not blame her. I was lucky I did not come down with it.

I was ready to head back to school and be a teenager again.

Chapter 2
Girl's Night Out

~ Debbie ~

Friday morning, I showered, before getting ready for school. I dressed and made my way down to the kitchen to fix myself some breakfast. Two slices of toast. I ate one slice, and took the second with me. I hurried out of the house, before I was asked to stay home; I had missed school, and could not wait to see Wendy. She stood at the bus stop, hands deep in her pockets, leaning on the bus stop post. She did not see me approach. I stood beside her, and gently nudged her.

"Debbie," she said turning to face me.

I smiled. "Who were you expecting, Simon?" the moment the words were out of my mouth I regretted it, and apologised.

"I thought I was going to have another day without you."

"Sorry," I replied, and looped my arm through hers as we watched for the bus.

"It's okay, you're back now."

"You know I would rather have been at school with you."

"I have to admit as much as I like children, I don't think I could deal with them being sick." She screwed up her face and scrunched her nose.

"Wendy, trust me, if you had to, you would have."

"I don't know."

"Can I just remind you, you chose childcare, babies are sick all the time." I tilted my head and raised my eyebrows at her. She knew I was right.

"True."

I nodded again.

"Anyway, I think we should go out tonight and celebrate your freedom," she suggested as we boarded the bus.

"Sounds like a plan." *A night out was just what I needed.*

Simon fell into step beside us, slipping his hand into Wendy's. Mark walked beside me, silent. I didn't speak either.

We stood outside our History classroom, waiting for Mr Turk to let us in. It was not my favourite subject. As we stepped inside the room, he bellowed that we were not to sit where we wanted. *What did I miss?*

"Until you act like young adults, I will treat you like the children you are." He paused and pointed at Karen. "You are to sit here at the front."

"But..." she begun to protest.

I was unable to hide the smile on my face.

"No buts, now you, sit here!" He pointed to a table at the front.

Register taken, he started the lesson, and I did my best to pay attention.

Today the lesson dragged, I wished the bell would hurry up and ring.

Ten minutes later, it did. We sat silent waiting for him to tell us we could leave.

We walked to the field and sat on the freshly cut grass. I took out a biscuit and snapped it in half, stuffing the smaller piece in my mouth.

"Any ideas what we could do later?"

"No, do you have any?"

"Well, we could go to the disco they're having at the youth club?"

"Maybe," I agreed. "Any other thoughts, before we decide?"

"We could go to the cinema?"

I nodded. A movie was a great idea. There was one I wanted to see and who better to go with than my best friend.

Dream World

Wendy had taken the window seat, forcing me to sit in the middle. I looked down the aisle, and grunted. I hated sitting here. Wendy talked about our plans for later, as the bus pulled away. I had hoped it would be just us. Then the bus stopped abruptly and I flew forward, landing on the cold metal floor on my hands and knees. I heard sniggering behind me; they laughed, but didn't offer to help me up. I grunted again and slumped back into my seat red faced, crossing my arms across my chest.

The driver apologised, but it was too late, I was already humiliated.

Ten minutes later, I climbed down the steps; my face still red.

"Why me?"

Wendy shrugged and said it could've been worse. How? I asked her.

"You could have landed on Mark."

She was right. Would that have been worse?

"Of course, it would have?" Joshua informs me.

I slammed the front door, and made my way up to my bedroom. I rarely used the family bathroom, unless I wanted to soak in the tub. Right now I needed to relax beneath some bubbles.

Eyes closed, I called out to Joshua, and slipped into my dream world.

"I'm here," he says, holding out his hand.

I extend mine, and he takes it, pulling me towards him. I am in his arms, his lips are all I can see, and think about. I want him to kiss me, but before he can, I hear knocking and then my name being called. Joshua fades away.

I opened my eyes, and stared at the door, trying to guess who was on the other side.

"Are you going to be long? Wendy has called four times already."

"What time is it, Steve?"

"Five. When you get out, I suggest you ring her."

"Okay, thanks." Surely, I had not been in the bath that long?

I pulled out the plug, and watched the water as it swirled and gurgled as it raced towards the plughole. I stood wrapped in a towel watching the last of the water disappear. I then made my way back to my room, leaving damp footprints on the hallway carpet.

Dried and wrapped in my dressing gown, I phoned Wendy.

"About time."

"Sorry, I didn't realise I had been in the bath so long. I guess you're ready to come over." Knowing she would want to borrow something of mine, as I often did with hers.

"I'll be right there; you can tell me if my outfit looks okay."

"Okay, see you in a minute."

I waitcd at the base of the stairs for her.

"Debbie, are you eating before you head out?" my dad asked entering the hall.

"Depends on what we're having?"

"Macaroni and cheese."

"Will there be enough for Wendy too?"

"Sure."

In my room, we sat and ate, before I chose what to wear. The food tasted amazing, we had not had it in ages, and it was one of my all-time favourite meals. Dad had made it just like my mum used to. I closed my eyes and saw her face. I willed Joshua to hold me. He told me everything was going to be okay. I hoped he was right.

Food eaten, I picked out a few outfits and laid them on my bed.

Wendy stood before the mirror, asking if the top went with her skirt and boots. Before I could reply she asked to borrow one of my tops. I handed her the one I knew she wanted and told her to keep it.

"Better?"

She nodded.

"Good. Will I do?"

"Yes, now come on, let's go."

I leant against the post, watching for the bus. Wendy offered me some gum, I accepted.

"I can't wait until we are old enough to drive."

"Me too, just think how many times we've waited for busses, that are either late, or just don't turn up."

"Or that are full," I added.

"Exactly."

We arrived in town, and walked to the cinema, joining the queue. The few people who stood in front of us moved forward as they allowed us in. We paid, brought snacks and entered the theatre where our movie would be playing.

We sat as the lights dimmed and the movie began.

I wondered what coming here with a date would be like. I had expected the boys to have joined us, but glad they didn't. We chose the middle row. On a date we would have chosen the back. I could not help but look up there, just the once. When I looked back at the screen, Joshua's face was staring at me, talking to me. My mouth was open, but I didn't care.

"That was great, we should do this again."

I nodded, staring at the screen, his face no longer there, and the end credits of the movie were playing.

Had I even watched it?

We walked down the aisle following the others out.

"Ice-cream?"

I nodded.

In the ice-cream parlour there were a few empty tables; we picked one near the front and ordered two chocolate sundaes.

"I had a feeling the guys were going to join us tonight."

Her face dropped. I had not meant it to sound like it did, but really there was no other way to say it.

"I thought you were happy for me!" she dug her spoon in the

ice-cream, not looking at me.

"I am. It's not that I don't like him, I do."

"So what's the problem? Tell me, we are meant to be best friends."

"We are. I just miss it being the two of us now and again."

"Like tonight?"

I nodded. "Yes, like tonight."

"Okay," she licked her spoon before scooping up more. "Promise me, you will always tell me the truth, even if it hurts me, okay?"

I nodded again, as I ate my own, which was melting and dripping over the side of the dish.

We finished and made our way out. We had plenty of time before we had to be home.

"What should we do now?" I asked.

"No idea." She shook her head. "What do you think?"

"I don't know. Maybe we should just head home?"

"Home!"

"Oh come on, Debbie, your Dad said you had to be home no later than eleven."

"I know, but where could we go?"

"The disco is still going on, fancy popping in there?"

"Why not." She was right, the night was not over; we had plenty of time left.

About the Author

Sarah Hitchcock was born in Norfolk, in a small town called Kings Lynn. She always was a keen reader, and one day decided to attempt to write her own, and never looked back. Today she has many novels in various stages of editing and re-writing and ideas for many new ones.

After finishing high school and then training to work with children, Sarah started her first job. She currently works as a pre-school teacher.

Sarah has four children, and three dogs, and a partner who has to put up with her rambling on about all her WIP's.She recalls spending hours thinking about her characters and their storylines. To this day, she often falls asleep thinking about where she can take new and old characters.

Other Books

The Dream World Series: Dream World: Book 1
The Dream World Series: Daydreamers : Book 2
(*coming soon*)

Glossary

GCSE – General Certificate of Secondary Education
Home Ec. – Home Economics – Food and Nutrition
I.T – Information Technology
Form tutor – teacher who takes the morning registration.
P.E - Physical Education
P.E kit – Gym kit
Niggle – to criticize/annoyed
Bluetac – a re-usable putty – often used to hold up posters.
Favourite - Favorite
Supermarket – Grocery store
Trainers – Sneakers
Trolley – Grocery cart
Corridor – Hallway
Pants/knickers – Underwear
Jumper – Jacket
Garden – Yard
Bathroom – Restroom
Boot – Hood/Trunk
Film – Movie
Holiday – Vacation
Post – Mail
Caretaker - Janitor
Taxi – Cab
Potato crisps - Potato chips
Chips – French fries
ill – sick
Hoover – Vacuum cleaner
Pavement – Sidewalk
Jug – Pitcher
Tea-towel – Dish-towel
Pushchair – Stroller
Cooker – Stove

Railway – Railroad
Lift – Elevator
Dummy – Pacifier
Underground railway – Subway
Nappy - Diaper
Rubber – Eraser
Waistcoat – Vest
Tap – Faucet
Sello tape – Scotch tape
Pyjamas – Pajamas
Apologised – Apologized

Printed in Great Britain
by Amazon